Mishipeshu
The Legend of Grand Island

By

Matthew F. Winn

Other Books by Matthew F. Winn

The Sandman
Bring Me a Dream
Circle of Friends
Every Picture Tells a Story
Stealing Rembrandt
Chasing Shadows in the Dark
The Legacy
Shadowman
The Watcher (YA) (ebook only)
Bokeh

Coming soon

Jack Kerouac Can Kiss My Ass
King of Hearts
Driven
You Are Not Supposed to be Here
Merrow

Cover photography by the author
See more photographic works at www.splashofsunset.com
Published by Artist's Point Press

For

Kayann

Grand Island, Michigan – 1870's

Chapter One

Patrick McPhereson gulped the last of his warm beer as a myriad of meaningless conversations drifted about the crowded tavern. Every single one of the drunken ramblings assaulted his ears with each syllable uttered. On the rare occasion he forced himself to venture off the island, his island, for the clamor of town it reminded him of why he preferred to live his life in near solitude perched atop a three-hundred-foot cliff overlooking Lake Superior. Nearly a lifetime ago, he had learned human beings were horrendous creatures and were best avoided at all costs. He would not have even hired the Swede as his assistant had it not been for his wife's nagging and the state's insistence.

He tugged at his navy-blue suspenders to adjust his woolen trousers and bobbed a nod in the direction of the barkeep who took his cue and pulled him another pint of dark beer which he then set on the lacquered bar in front of his taciturn patron. McPhereson sipped at the black ale knowing it would prove to be one too many once he was back out onto the lake blanketed under the ebony of night.

"I am telling you, it was the fifth body today," a young man with wild eyes said as he tried to convince his drinking companions of some great conspiracy plaguing the land.

"That's impossible, there has been no news of any wrecks in the area," an older mariner replied, pulling at a loose thread on his rusty sweater. A ring of smoke smelling of brandy hung above his head like a halo. He tapped out his pipe on the wooden tabletop and refilled it with loose leaf tobacco from a pouch he then stuffed back into the pocket of his mariner's jacket hanging on the back of a worn tavern chair.

"Maybe there was a wreck further north, up near Thunder Bay perhaps," another man with coal for eyes and wild flowing hair to match added to the conversation.

"No, any wreckage coming from the north would have never washed past the peninsula at Copper Harbor to make it this far south," yet another ancient mariner chimed in with his two cents.

"And from what I hear, the men were torn apart like sharks had gotten after them. Lucious told me one of them were even missing their head," the young lad clamored on.

The table of men laughed at the expense of the boy's tall tales. Freshwater sharks indeed.

Patrick slammed down the last of his pint, donned his threadbare keeper's cap and started for the door. As he passed the table of gossiping mariners he stopped, put his meaty hands palms down on the roughhewn wood.

"You damned fools, don't you know, Superior never gives up her dead." The door of the pub slapped shut behind him.

"Yeah, well maybe this time she did," the youngest of the three called after him, his voice creaking on his words.

"Hey, McPhereson," the man in the rusty sweater called after him. "How is that Swede working out for ya?"

The men all laughed until the eldest one stopped long enough to say, "I hear the light's been dark pretty near a week past now. Maybe them bodies are floating up because it be your island sinking them ships." The gathering of men all burst into another round of raucous laughter.

The youngest of the bunch crossed the line with his next remark. "Maybe the Swede is too busy with your squaw to notice the light needs tending."

The bar fell silent, and the older men glared at the young mariner who immediately regretted his words. McPhereson stepped back through the door and glowered at the table of fishermen who all quickly distanced themselves from the lad.

"Patrick, he didn't mean nothing by it. The boy is young and stupid," Arn Longfellow said, taking a long, nervous pull from his pipe while giving McPhereson an obsequious glance.

The lighthouse keeper stood over the table of men, his massive shadow casting a chill over the impetuous young man. His fists were balled at his sides and his red beard seemed to be aflame with anger. His usually sullen eyes were dark with fury, and it took every bit of self-control he had not to whip the youngster near to death.

"Please, Patrick, give me this one. I'll school the boy," Arn pleaded.

Patrick jammed a sausage sized finger into the boy's face, grunted something unintelligible, and spun around on his heels with spittle clinging to the corners of his mouth. He slammed the door behind him and disappeared into the foggy evening.

"Boy, if you weren't my wife's son," Arn said.

"Pa," the boy started. Arn balled up a fist and the lad wisely held his tongue.

Patrick cursed himself for indulging in a last pint as he wrestled the last of the winter's provisions for the lighthouse onto the boat. He also cursed the Coast Guard for not delivering his supplies as usual, but in their defense, they were busy with the bodies washing ashore at Sand Point. Were there really five of them as the boy said? Something was not right about that.

Patrick said a quick prayer for the dead mariners and loaded another crate into the thirty-footer. Hopefully, the lake already had her fill and could not stomach even one more wayward son.

As he stowed the supplies he could not help being bothered by the men's remarks. Was the light truly dark? Had the Swede been derelict in his duties? He did not like the young man, but he didn't think he would be so lax in his duties as to allow the lamp to burn out. Their cajoling instilled in him a sense of urgency to get back to the island, that and he had been away from his Bonni for far too long.

4

The young man's words dissipated like the fog. Patrick's wife would surely beat the Swede to death were he to try something libidinous with her.

The crew of the *Diana* finished loading her up with supplies and her deck hands tossed off the mooring lines. Standing on the empty pier he scowled as he watched the *Diana* pull out of Munising Harbor and tack toward the western side of the island. She was a smaller vessel than most cargo ships on the lake, only seventy-foot-long, but she cut the water with grace and precision. She was employed to shuttle supplies and guests to the newly developed hunting consortium on the western side of Grand Island. She employed a larger crew than most with eight men not counting the captain. She was a true beauty, double masted with nary a scuff on her brilliant white hull.

Patrick's home, the lighthouse on Grand Island, sat a mere one-half mile off the Michigan mainland and was nearly fifty square miles in size. And while the main harbor for the island was a straight shot from the Munising docks McPhereson would have to round the panhandle, through the channel and up the eastern coast of the island as there were no roads leading from the southern end of the island, north to the lighthouse. He would be required to trek the mile and a half upgrade to the lighthouse to fetch his mule and wagon to move the supplies. Unless of course his ever-thoughtful Bonni anticipated his arrival and staked Gus and the wagon down at the landing for him.

McPhereson was not thrilled to have this new consortium on *his* island, but they purchased the land fair and square and managed to keep to themselves thus far.

From the gossip he was able to gather while in town he learned they were group of wealthy mine owners from Calumet who pooled their money and created a high-priced hunting experience geared toward rich folks with nothing better to do. He was told they stocked their compound with Cervidae not found in the wilds of Michigan for elite hunting expeditions. However, that did not explain the crates of raw meat he saw the deck hands loading when he arrived at the docks earlier in the afternoon.

With the *Diana* out to sea the bustle of the docks fell to a low murmur coming from two old fishermen at the far end the pier. Ripples of waves slapped against the side of his boat with a deceiving gentleness. They could easily turn into waves that could sink him within a matter of minutes this time of year. It was time to leave this heathen's den until spring.

He shoved off into the foggy night in his life saving station boat with the tavern conversation still nagging at his brain. Rowing the boat was more of a two-man job, four or more when it was laden with supplies or rescued sailors, but Patrick enjoyed the exercise and the solitude, so he often made for the mainland solo. It was not possible to row the boat like a normal rowboat by himself until he outfitted it with a longer set of reinforced oars with wider blades and reinforced oarlocks. He kept another set of oars on hand just in case as they had a propensity to snap in heavy seas. It was arduous work, but he was still beefy for a man in his late fifties, and it granted him a certain sense of satisfaction from the accomplishment. It also allowed him to imbibe a pint or three on occasion without having to suffer the jabber of company. It was nearing autumn which was a mere knock away from winter's door in this part of the world. This was the third trip this week, so he was nearing the point of exhaustion.

The past several days had been hot, unseasonably hot and the sky clear so once night began to fall the temperature cooled off considerably. This gave rise to dense fog surrounding the island. It was a new moon, so the night proved to be as black as squid ink, especially with the fog rolling in from the lake. Again, Patrick cursed himself for two hours wasted in the pub, making the four-hour journey bad enough in the daylight, but on a foggy night it would be brutal. At least he would have the light to guide him home.

With the warm glow of Munising fading in the distance off his stern Patrick veered the boat toward the eastern side of the island passing through the small channel at Sand Point. He hugged the eastern shore to avoid the sandbar that reached out into the channel every summer but disappeared in the winter. One of life's conundrums he would never know the answer to. One of the coast guard seamen was busying himself with what appeared to Patrick to be a very large lake trout. Odd, bodies washing up on the shore and the seaman took the time to go fishing? Maybe his tired, old eyes were playing tricks on him.

A faint scream drifted out across the channel and echoed back at him from the sandstone cliffs. "Damned fool doesn't even know how to use a filet knife," he said and went back to rowing the boat methodically down the coastline. A second scream reverberated off the cliffs and a chill ran up Patrick's spine. There was no way to tell where the screams were coming from, but they were faint and distant. He rested the oars and after several minutes of silence he laughed it off as nothing more than a curious barn owl who made their way onto the island and was toying with him.

Patrick cut the boat to the port side and headed into the shelter of Trout Bay on the eastern coast of the island. A chill wind blew across the bow of the boat, so he pulled the collar of his Navy peacoat up and tilted his cap down. He was more than slightly distressed by the thickness of the fog rolling in off the lake. A seemingly impenetrable wall spread out in front of him all the way across the bay to the cliffs on the other side. Again, he lifted the oars and studied the landscape as he coasted through the water. There was something wrong, very wrong.

"That good for nothing, Swede, he let the damned lamp go dark," Patrick cursed the darkness and dropped the oars into the water with a resounding splash rudely interrupting the stillness of the night.

He laid hard into the oars knowing he had at least another hour of rowing before making Northeast Point and another half an hour to the beach at Echo Lake Creek. That would mean any ships in the area trying to navigate into Munising harbor would not have a beacon for the better part of two hours. He cursed his wife for talking him into hiring the lad, he was much too young and carefree to handle the responsibility. And what in the hell was Bonni up to anyway that she would not notice the light had gone out? Then he began to worry, maybe she got the fever. Maybe both had fallen ill.

In a near panic Patrick chopped at the black water until his arms were burning and then he dug in even harder. The wind shifted and was blowing straight out of the north making the effort to row that much more difficult. With the cliffs to his left and deep water to his right he had no other option than to keep rowing straight ahead as hard as he possibly could.

The fog had grown so thick that he could barely even see the bow of his boat let alone the rocky cliffs or the treacherous boulders that lurked just below the water's surface. This forced him out into deeper waters where he did not want to be as this also put him directly into the face of the wind.

A loud, inhuman scream split the night snatching Patrick's attention away from trying to navigate through the fog. The clamor invading the night was the sound of wood against rock. That lazy Swede had gone and done it now. Never in all his years had Patrick allowed a ship to come anywhere near these cliffs. In just one short month the Swede had done him in. There would be hell to pay for this one there was no doubt in his mind about that.

He stopped rowing and laid down as flat as he could, allowing him to be able to peer from beneath the blanket of fog. There was a flash of light off in the distance, a lantern maybe. But it was too far off his starboard side to be a ship floundering against the rocky coast. Slowly he rowed out toward the source of the light, but it disappeared before he could reach it. Patrick gave two long, hard pulls on the oars before lifting them out of the water and dropping them back into the boat.

He stood up in the lifeboat as it glided gracefully through the water. He turned an ear to the lake side and did not hear anything, so he turned back toward the shore, or at least what he thought was the shore. The fog was even thicker and to his chagrin he realized he was turned around with no sense of direction. And to make matters worse, the night was playing tricks on him. Shadows danced all around him and he swore there was something moving in the water around his boat.

Patrick stood still in the boat trying to locate the source of the wind. It was coming from the north so once he found the direction of the wind, he would have his bearings again. It was a good plan, but the wind seemed to have suddenly died down. He was getting ready to sit back down when he heard a muffled slapping against the water. At first, he thought it was a few lakers feeding on night bugs but then he recognized the sound, it was the hull of a boat slapping the water as it drifted aimlessly in the night.

He looked up in time to see another lifeboat coming at him broadside from out of the fog. He braced as the bow of the wayward boat slammed into his, threatening to capsize him. When the two boats collided, they sprayed enough icy cold lake water into his face to blur his vision. He grabbed a cloth from the deck of the boat and wiped his face. Patrick's blood ran cold when under the glow of lantern light, he saw that it was not water that sprayed him, but blood. His face was covered with cold, sticky blood.

Several minutes passed before he was able to gather his composure enough to pull the other boat toward him. Stenciled along the side of the vessel was the name *Bonni*. He swallowed hard and waited several moments before he found the nerve to peer over the side into the boat. He recoiled in horror but also felt a sense of relief. Instead of his wife Bonni whom he dreaded to find, there was a man, more specifically, half a man lying in the bottom of the boat. The man was face down, but Patrick was certain of who it was. The corpse bore the same tattoo of a wolf on its forearm as did the Swede.

Patrick trembled as he reached into the other boat and rolled the man over. He gasped and fell backward into his own boat. Quickly he scrambled back up to his knees and vomited violently over the side. The Swede no longer had a face to speak of. What remained of the man resembled ground meat.

He fought back his nausea and waved the lantern over the putrid gray corpse of the dead man. Patrick was by no means a medical man, but he witnessed his share of gruesome injuries, all of which paled in comparison to the Swede's grievances. His legs were not just torn away; they were missing. The hull of the boat was filled with buckets of the Swede's blood that undulated from stem to stern as the boat rocked in the slow rolling waves. Patrick could think of nothing on earth that could have caused the man's injuries.

The foundering ship's scream split the night once more, snatching Patrick's attention away from the Swede. By the sound he knew it would not be long before she slipped beneath the black depths. He lashed the other rowboat to his stern as quickly as he could and started off toward the sound. Once he rounded Northeast Point, he could see a glow burning through the fog which thankfully was starting to blow back out into open water. He spied the fantail of a schooner listing hard to the starboard. It was the *Diana*.

~   ~   ~

Bawazigaywin, or Bonni as Patrick called her because it was the name of a beloved antecedent of his and he couldn't pronounce her real name well enough to keep it from sounding vulgar, stood at the edge of the forest wishing her husband was back from Munising. The young Swede was missing, the lamp was dark and there were men milling about somewhere within the shadows of the trees looking to do her harm. She should have stayed away from the consortium as Patrick warned her, but she knew those men were up to something, something terrible, something evil.

While she was out getting buckets of lamp oil from the oil shed, going about business as usual, was when she first noticed the light had gone dark. It was then she realized that not only had the men followed her back through the forest, but some of them had somehow beaten her back to the lighthouse. Bonni was hurrying back to the tower to relight the lamp when the Swede came tumbling out of the front door with three, large men coming after him. She might have gone to help the man had there only been two of them, but three would only mean she would suffer the same fate as the assistant keeper. No, her most favorable option was to scout from her position safely tucked within the shadows until an opportunity to help the lad presented itself.

With every blow the Swede endured the more her guilt piled into an insurmountable heap. They were after her, after what she pilfered from them, not the poor lad who was now collateral damage. She was the one who snuck into their camp and snooped around. One of the men hit the Swede, Siger was his name she recalled. The blow was so hard that the young man went completely limp. Then they lashed the Swede to their wagon and disappeared into the night back toward the consortium's compound. She waited until she could no longer hear the wagon wheels clacking against the hard pack before emerging from the shadows.

Bonni danced through the shadows of the outbuildings until she was tucked into the shrubbery at the rear of the lighthouse. From there she made her way inside after determining there were none of the consortium men lingering around. Against her better judgment she knew she could not just hide, she must find a way to help the Swede before they killed him, but she needed to relight the lamp first. Quickly she made her way through the house to the tower anteroom and started up the wrought iron spiral staircase nearly one hundred steps to the top. Before she even got to the lantern room, she knew the lamp was still lit from the heat radiating through the steel floor.

Confused as to how the lamp could be lit but not emitting any light through the tower's lens Bonni cautiously opened the hatch to the lantern room and peered inside. It was empty so she turned and pulled herself up into the hot chamber through the portal in the floor. She was inspecting the lamp when a subtle sound, just the hint of a squeaky hinge, alerted her that someone had entered the house.

Hurriedly, Bonni peeled back a loose section of the plating in the cupola and slipped the stolen documents inside. She pressed her foot hard against the plating until she heard it pop back into place enough to appear normal. She knew Patrick would never make it back to the island in time to save her, but maybe, just maybe he could put an end to the sheer madness being perpetrated on the island.

"I know you're up there Mrs. McPhereson. Let's not make this difficult, my boss just wants to have a few words with you."

Bonni glanced around the tiny room before quickly deducing there was no viable place for her to hide. She crept three paces across the room and over to the hatch leading out to the widow's walk. The person below her was creeping up the stairs and she found herself cursing Patrick for not fixing the latch on the hatchway. She was trapped in the lantern room and would be just as trapped out on the catwalk one hundred feet above the earth. She almost answered the man, thinking for a brief moment that maybe he did just want to talk, but she stopped short, knowing in her heart that was hogwash.

For a brief instant she contemplated dumping flaming oil down the enclosed staircase, but she knew the man would not be able to escape the tower before being burned alive and she didn't have the heart to inflict that level of cruelty on another living creature even if her life depended on it. Once outside onto the widow's walk the night air was cool and she was stunned by what was obscuring the light's lantern glow. It just couldn't be possible.

She was distracted just enough for the man to have snuck up the stairs and out onto the catwalk behind her. She sensed his presence at the last second and side stepped his attack. As he passed to the side of her, she threw out a kick to the back of his knees which sent him sprawling across the metal deck and under the safety railing. He grappled with the slick painted surface of the catwalk in a futile effort to remain on the solid platform. Bonni never even had a chance to help the man before he plummeted over the edge to his death.

Once the initial shock passed, she gathered her thoughts and started down the long spiral staircase, trembling with each step. Her morality forced her to go to the man and see if by some chance he survived. Maybe there was something she could do for him. At the very least she might be able to pray over him before he left this world.

Bonni gagged at the sight of the man's broken body. Most, if not all of his ribs were broken, and the bones punched through his clothing in jagged spikes dripping with blood and obliterated tissue. His blood was forced through his mouth and nose coating his face in bright red foam. She said a prayer, closed the man's starburst eyes and rose to her feet to leave. She must rescue the Swede. She never saw the blow coming.

Chapter Two

Patrick eased his rowboat up to the fantail of the *Diana* which was riding high on a rock and listing to the starboard side. Water hissed ominously as it rushed over the rock and into the hull of the ship. The wounded vessel gurgled and belched in distress.

"Hoy," he cupped his hands around his mouth and called out to the darkness. The night was eerily quiet with no sound other than the groaning of the ship as it settled while the water did its best to claim a new prize. To his chagrin he received no response to his call and heard no signs of life on board the vessel.

As he eased around to the port side, he held his lantern out at arm's length. Patrick trembled as he leaned over and used his left hand to guide himself down the side of the boat as close to the bow as he could manage. His hand slipped, and he dipped a shoulder into the ship which caused his boat to push away, nearly dumping him into the lake, and dousing his lantern in the process.

The next several minutes were spent trying to relight the lantern with shaky hands and a nagging scream in his brain telling him to leave whilst he still had the chance. Once the lantern was relit, he held it out near the ship and nearly dropped it again when he saw his smeared handprint along the side of the ship. He looked down at his hand to see it was covered in blood. Her hull, once a pristine white just hours before, was now coated with bloody streaks from bow to stern. Patrick fought the urge to leave the ship and head for shore. He sensed there was something dreadfully amiss. There was far too much blood for there not to be any remains, be they man or beast, strewn about the deck or floating in the water around the wreckage.

The ship groaned and slipped off the rock, sliding another foot deeper into the water. With great trepidation Patrick crept along the ship's side using a gaff instead of his hand to propel himself. When he approached amidships, he heard a faint moan coming from above him. It was such an unfamiliar sound that he was not sure if it was human or animal. Even with his arm outstretched the lantern's glow could not illuminate much more than a small area right in front of him. He lashed the lantern handle to the gaff and held the contraption as high above his head as he could.

Emotion washed over Patrick and tears burst from his eyes as he looked up to see a man skewered onto the broken yardarm, his legs and most of his torso were missing. Entrails dangled down toward the deck like a grotesque jellyfish. How the man was even alive was something he could not fathom. He clamped his eyes shut

17

hoping to erase the image of the man's pleading eyes staring down at him. The only consolation was Patrick knew the man was already as good as dead and there was nothing in his power he could do to help him.

The damage to the ship did not appear as though they hit the rocks with enough force to catapult a man up into the yardarm, let alone rip him in two. It was then he saw another crimson stain splashed down the side of the *Diana,* thick, gooey strands of blood leeched through the scuppers stretching down in macabre red fingers grasping at the water below.

"Hoy, anybody up there?" he called out again, startled that his own voice was foreign to him.

Once he made his way down the length of the ship, he saw the vessel had split in two and the bow was completely under water. He held out the lantern and called out several times with no answer. He argued with himself whether or not he should climb onto the ship to search for any survivors. If it were to break loose and sink it would suck him down into the depths with it, so he did not dare proceed any further. Patrick was about to pull away from the wreckage when a muffled sound found his ear.

"Who is up there? Are you injured?"

The boat was listing both toward the stern and to the starboard side. He did not relish what would amount to walking the plank, but he also could not, in good conscience leave an injured man behind to sink with the ship. He lashed the bowline of his rowboat to a cleat on the gunwale and swung the lantern from side to side until he found a path of least resistance to the captain's cabin where he was certain the sounds were coming from.

A halyard dangled free from the broken yard arm low enough that one long stride and the extension of his gaff he was able to grab it to help pull himself up the angled deck. His boots slipped on the slick, blood-soaked deck making the chore nearly impossible which was further hindered by the lack of light. Not one single lantern onboard was aglow, and he could not carry his lantern and pull himself up at the same time. He hung his lantern from the side of the ship as high up as he could and continued with his ascent.

He made it about ten feet up the deck when something moved out of the corner of his eye. He turned his head ever so slightly and nearly let go of the rope when he spotted a furry beast along the starboard rail.

"McPhereson, you're a crazy old bastard, it's just a baggywrinkle torn loose from the rigging," he said with a chuckle meant to calm his nerves and tossed the bundle of fabric aside.

Adrenaline coursing through his veins had run its course and he was now operating on fumes. He grabbed a piece of fallen sail to help pull himself upward, but it tore loose and sent him sliding down the deck. Dazed he looked over at the remnant of canvas and realized it wasn't a sail at all, but a man's arm ripped from the socket. Before he could register what it was he was seeing the man's torso slid down the deck and slammed into him knocking him back to the point where his journey began. Disgusted, he grabbed the lantern and made his way back down the deck to his boat. There were no survivors, and he wasn't about to risk killing himself to retrieve bodies from the wreckage in the middle of the night.

"Please, don't leave me," a weak voice called from the shadows above.

Patrick shined the lantern up but couldn't see anyone. Whomever was up in the wheelhouse must have been hiding behind the mangled corpse. He put the lantern in the boat and braced himself.

"I cannot make it back up there to you. You will have to come down to me."

"But I'm scared," the voice squeaked.

"I know you are, just slide down here and I will catch you," Patrick said, looking up at the shadows where the voice emanated from.

A large school of lakers splashed somewhere out in dark waters stealing his attention. He heard a gasp from above and without warning a body came sliding down the deck at him. He barely recovered enough to catch the lad who, by the looks of him, was not yet into his teens. His white blouse was in tatters and saturated with blood.

"Are you hurt?"

The boy just shook his head.

"Are there any others on board?"

Again, he just shook his head.

"Where did they all go?" Patrick asked.

The boy pointed out into the black of night with tears streaming down his face. As Patrick swung the lamp in a wide arc it illuminated what was left of the Swede in the other boat causing the lad to recoil. He covered the man's body the best he could and turned the boy so he faced the opposite direction. He shoved off away from the *Diana* and out into open water.

"We need to get out of the way before she sinks. Are you able to row?"

The boy nodded, scooted next to Patrick, and grabbed an oar. They started chopping at the water and Patrick was surprised to find he had to work in order to keep up with the lad's tempo. It was clear the boy wanted to get away from the ship as quickly as possible. Once they were out and away from the ship, they angled for the beach which was less than half a mile away.

The fog completely dissipated revealing two things, the light in the tower was indeed dark and there were two, maybe three glowing lamps on the horizon. There were more ships heading straight toward the island undoubtedly thinking they were clear of the land and were on an unobstructed course for Munising Bay.

Suddenly there grew a cacophonous sound from the water. Lakers. A huge school of lake trout were making a beeline straight at them. The fish hit the side of the boat so hard they nearly spilled Patrick and the boy over into the frigid water. Many of the fish in the tail of the school were so exhausted they were swimming in death spirals on the surface.

Only two things Patrick knew of that would make the fish react this way, a feeding frenzy of which he saw no baitfish when he held the lantern to the water or there was a predator even larger than they were in the lake. The boy saw this and screamed. He dug his oar into the water as hard as he could. McPhereson gave him the benefit of the doubt and dug his oar in as well with every hair remaining on his balding pate standing straight up on end.

~   ~   ~

Muffled voices echoed through the darkness easing her out of her induced slumber. Bonni opened her eyes, but she was blindfolded so she couldn't see where she was. She reached to take the cloth off her face and found her hands were bound to something as well. A chair maybe? No, as her consciousness slowly came back to her, she realized she was lying prone, on her back. Her head was pounding so badly she struggled to stave off the need to vomit. She fought against the hammering in her brain and strained to listen in on the conversation.

"What you are proposing is complete madness," a man's voice said.

It pained her to strain her ears to listen, but she sensed they were talking about her so Bonni knew she must endure the agony. The more information she could cull from their conversation the better off she would be in the long run. It was obvious they thought she was still unconscious, and she wanted things to remain that way.

"You have not struggled with your morality thus far, why now?" Edgar Wientraub commented with a smug, but forceful grin.

"Because we have never applied this procedure to a human being," Oleg Tiaarnen argued.

"Eh, her kind are not much more than animals in my opinion."

"Fortunately, I do not share your ideals of racial superiority. She is a human being no matter what your convoluted reasoning may be. This is where I draw the line."

"Somehow, I had a feeling you would say that. It is advantageous that I am much smarter than you give me credit for, doctor. I have watched you perform these procedures so often that I feel confident I can perform them myself, so I believe I am no longer in need of your services," Edgar said.

The room echoed with the sounds of a brief struggle and what she could only imagine was a man being strangled to death. A gunshot split the darkness and she gasped instinctively, tipping her hand.

"Ah, Mrs. McPhereson, I am so glad you could join us," Edgar said as he pulled her blindfold away from her eyes. "I have big plans for you. Big plans indeed."

The raucous sound of people running across a wooden floor interrupted the brief silence. Muffled shouts echoed from outside the building. A guttural growl reverberated against the walls followed by the sounds of fighting from somewhere else in the building. Men screamed in agony from all four points of the compass and then all fell silent.

"What a pity. It appears as though we have run out of time to share pleasantries. Let's get started shall we," the man said, pulling the blindfold back down over Bonni's eyes.

In his hubris he didn't realize the woman managed to get her arm free from one of her bindings. In a blinding move Bonni struck the man in the nose with a closed fist and while incapacitated she grabbed him by the wrist, jerked him toward her and slammed his arm down on the corner of the wooden table, breaking both bones in his forearm.

The man howled in pain and dropped to the ground. Bonni quickly untied her other arm, got to her feet and before the man could recover, she planted a solid kick to his good shoulder. Once more he screamed out in pain. But shockingly he smiled up at her and laughed.

"It seems our guest of honor has arrived."

Bonni felt a shadow blocking the doorway even before turning around to see what entered the room. A foul odor of dead fish and rotting meat invaded the small space. She slowly turned around to see standing before her the most hideous creature she ever laid eyes on, ghastlier than anything she could have ever imagined in her wildest dreams.

Before her in the doorway standing on two short, reptilian legs, was a large snake-like creature. It was almost comical in appearance, but Bonni was not in the least bit amused. Without warning the beast rose to nearly six-feet-tall and flared its enormous head. At first, she went cold with fear thinking it was a large king cobra, but the coloring was wrong. She then remembered the hognose snake in her garden that had given the Swede one hell of a scare. But this was no ordinary puff adder. No, this abomination had been bred with something, with many different things.

Long armlike appendages dangled at the creature's sides like tentacles yet seemed to also be rigid as if to have bones. At the end of each appendage were two hooked fingers that flexed as the beast undulated in the shadows.

Slowly it moved forward until Bonni ran out of room to retreat. It gave a long, loud hiss while spreading its head and neck wide. It stared her down with crystalline blue eyes while flicking its angry red tongue. The beast flared its head even more to reveal the entire head and neck was rimmed with needle-like teeth. The outer rim of its head and neck began to glow, bathing the beast in a beautiful iridescent shade of blue. Bonni found herself fascinated by this repugnant yet stunning creature. Before she could react, the creature struck. It latched onto her and enveloped Bonni in a fleshy cocoon. Pin pricks of pain invaded her flesh, and just before she lost consciousness, she prayed death would come mercifully quick.

Chapter Three

Not wanting to be on the water any longer than absolutely necessary, Patrick angled the two lifeboats on a bearing straight for the shore. Something just wasn't right about the way the fish were behaving and whatever happened aboard the *Diana* was something more than a shipwreck, and beyond anything he cared to brave. He spent the majority of his life on this lake and never in all those years had he witnessed this type of behavior from fish.

"What is your name, lad?" he asked between pulls on the oar.

"Olaf," he responded with a voice still trembling with fear.

"Ah, another Swede. What were you doing on that ship? You are much too young to be a crew member."

"My uncle is the captain. I was to spend the summer with him learning the sailing trade." Tears

26

streamed down his cheeks in rivers and his chest heaved with every word.

"What in the hell happened on that ship?" Patrick asked.

The boy shook his head and trembled. He pulled up his oar as if to listen to the water. Patrick could see the shore and wanted to make way as fast as possible, but he followed the boy's lead. A peculiar sound drifted across the water toward them, it was a noise he was not familiar with, in fact, it was as foreign to him as a duck's meow. As the sound grew closer, he held the lantern out over the water. Coming at them was the largest school of whitefish Patrick had ever seen. That large of a school was odd in and of itself, but whitefish usually schooled in deeper waters this time of year and should have never been this close to shore.

He was leaning over the boat, mesmerized by the swirling mass of silver fish when he spied something among them. Something translucent was heading straight up at their boat from the depths. He recoiled into the bottom of the boat to escape the attack, but young Olaf was not so lucky. A beast leapt from the depths, grasped the teen in its clutches and returned to whence it came before Patrick was even able to clearly make out what committed the dastardly deed.

"Lord almighty, what in the hell was that?" Patrick screamed and reached for the boy's oar, digging into the water with every ounce of his remaining energy. He knew the lad was gone by the streak of blood staining the side benches and spilling into the black water. He was gone and there was no rescuing him.

Patrick spilled out of the boat as soon as the water was shallow enough to touch the sandy lake bottom. He abandoned both the supplies and the Swede's corpse and clamored up the cold sand. He sat with his rump in the sand for several minutes trying to catch his breath and comprehend what had just happened. The lake was black and still, but he sensed there was something out there watching him, stalking him.

"Patrick McPhereson, you did not see a shark," he said aloud to himself. One sided conversation was commonplace for those working in isolated duties such as lighthouse keepers and he was quite adept at it.

He argued with himself over what he saw but it was a losing argument. Truth be told, it happened so fast, he didn't see much of anything. As he calmed down, he was able to start the long hike up to the lighthouse. He knew he should be running but he just didn't have the energy. And that was no damned shark, it grabbed the lad with appendages similar to hands. Maybe talons. But a bird would have come from the sky, not from the depths. Maybe it was a reflection on the water he had seen.

Every shadow and every twig branch snapping underfoot nearly sent him into a panic. In his haste he inadvertently left the lantern in the boat leaving himself at the mercy of the dark forest. He stopped to rest for a moment to catch his breath when it dawned on him that the only noise in the forest was that which he was causing himself. Nothing moved. Not one bird sang, not one bat squeaked, the only thing alive in that forest was himself.

He shoved his thoughts away and hurried down the trail. Within a few minutes he spied the glow of the lantern from the porch of the lighthouse. He ignored the house proper for the moment and went straight for the shed near the cliff's edge. He retrieved his spyglass from inside the door and gazed out into the night. The night was too dark and the ships still too far out to make them out, but he could see the whiteness of the seafoam kicked up by their bows splitting the water. Both ships were on a dead run straight for the island.

Patrick glanced up at the darkened tower and stifled the urge to curse the Swede, this one was not his fault. He grabbed a bucket of oil from the fuel shed and the lantern from the porch before heading up the spiral staircase nearly one hundred feet to the lantern room. He was still ten feet from the top when he realized there was heat radiating from within the lantern room which perplexed him as it meant the lamp must still be lit.

Cautiously he lifted the hatch and peered up into the spherical room. He felt relieved to find it was devoid of life. He set the lantern and the oil up onto the platform before dragging himself up into the small chamber. His heart was still racing so he took a moment to compose himself. As he suspected, the lamp was indeed lit. He turned and looked at the glass and chuckled a nervous snigger to himself. The glass was covered with luminescent blue moths of a color he never laid eyes on before. Insects covering the windows happened from time to time, the usual culprits being mayflies in late spring. Though he would have to admit, in all his years he never witnessed them thick enough to completely block out the light. He grabbed a whisk broom hanging on a hook inside the lantern room there for just such instances and went out onto the widow's walk to clear the panels of glass encircling the cupola.

Patrick was able to swipe away one swath of the insects, but they fluttered away for only a brief moment. Within seconds the insects regrouped and refilled the vacated spot before he could even sweep away another patch. He watched in amazement as these simple creatures worked in unison with one another. Anticipating his next move, they interlocked their legs creating one solid blanket of moths. Another swipe of the broom netted him negative results.

McPhereson was incensed. How the hell could a bunch of insects get the better of him? He went back into the lantern room and grabbed the lantern. He opened the gate on the front of the lantern and held the flames up to a section of the moth wall. A piercing scream split the night so loud it forced him off the widow's walk and back into the lighthouse tower. Fifty or so of the charred creatures dropped onto the catwalk writhing in agony. The remaining moths spread out to cover the gap and darken the light once more.

Having endured enough of these shenanigans Patrick grabbed the lantern and the broom and went back out onto the widow's walk. The moths began to make an eerie chattering sound as if they were communicating with one another. He reached the lantern out to them once again and before he could even get the flames near them, they all lifted up and away from him in one single interwoven sheet of scaled covered wings. It was a rhythmic movement akin to the rise and fall of a lung sucking in a full breath of air before slowly releasing it.

The creatures were a beautiful translucent blue, and he really didn't want to do them any harm, but they were leaving him no other choice, the lamp simply could not remain dark. He tried to remove them gently once more and again they simply moved out of his way and then returned to place. Frustrated, he went back into the lantern room, drew a cup of oil from the bucket and went back out on the catwalk. He doused the insects with oil, lit the whisk broom with the lantern and threw it into the stirring mass of moths. Immediately the insects erupted into a huge ball of fire. The moths that managed to escape the flames still clung to the glass while the rest of the swarm turned their attention on Patrick.

He swatted at them with his arms, more out of annoyance at first. But then one of the creatures lit on the back of his hand and not only bit him but actually tore a piece of flesh from his appendage. Another, then another took precisely the same avenue of attack. Then they viciously started going for his face and any other place where his tender flesh was exposed. Terrified, Patrick covered his eyes and ran into the lantern room, had it not been broken he would have dogged the door behind him. He forced negative thoughts of the poor Swede out of his head. It had been the lad's task to repair the door, which for obvious reasons he was unable to finish the job.

The acrid smell of charred moths stung his nose as he tried to catch his breath and make some sort of sense out of the current situation. Flesh eating moths, how preposterous, but plausible. Moths that thought and acted as a singular unit, impossible. And yet that is exactly what happened.

The shadows in the lantern room flickered and danced, directing Patrick's attention to the windows. The remaining moths formed an alliance and were swaying in and out from the glass like a palm frond fan. They undulated in a rhythm that seemed to grow in intensity with each swelling pass. All at once the moths slammed into the glass, cracking one of the panes from corner to corner, and as hard as it was to fathom, the insects were coming after him.

Quite certain their intentions were less than congenial Patrick grabbed the entire bucket of fuel oil and splashed it onto the interior glass of the lantern room. The moths swooped out once more and he timed it so when they hit the glass, he tossed the whisk broom torch into the room, dropped down onto the platform below and dogged the lantern room door closed.

The creatures let out such a scream it forced him to drop to his knees and cover his ears. What hellishness had that accursed hunting consortium bring to the island? He navigated his way down the stairs and out of the lighthouse tower. He was relieved to see that the beacon was shining through the darkness allowing the inbound ships safe passage around the island.

Before slipping on a clean shirt, Patrick checked his wounds. There were bite marks reminiscent of teeth on the back of his hand instead of an insect sting one would expect from moths. This was like something out of Shelly's Frankenstein. Even though it was too hot for it, he threw on his peacoat and slipped a raincoat on over that for protection.

"Let's see the little buggers bite through this," he said and headed for the stable to fetch Gus.

Right away he knew something was off, the mule did not whinny or snort as he usually did when Patrick approached the stables in an effort to wrangle a treat of molasses oats. Slowly he cracked the door just enough to peek inside. What he saw sent him reeling. Gus was over on his side and was being devoured by a ravenous beast unlike anything he had ever laid eyes on. His compatriot was still alive and looked over at him with pleading eyes. What sort of creature sups on the living without showing mercy? Even the most vicious of jungle cats suffocates its prey before consuming them.

The banqueting beast resembled the moths in color but did not have wings. It had short, stubby arms of translucent blue in their stead. The face was humanesque but was not that of a human. Rows of needle-sharp teeth ringed its oval mouth like a cross between a lamprey eel and a shark. He swore the thing looked up and him and smiled before slamming its face back down into the shredded flesh of the dying mule.

Suddenly the absurdity of the situation forced his mind to career from thought to thought, one of which was of his wife. Wracked with guilt Patrick eased the stable door closed and headed back up to the house expecting to be set upon by the fantastical beast at any moment.

"Bonni," he called out in a low whisper as he searched from room to room. The living quarters were relatively small so within five minutes he checked every room of the house and there was no sign of his wife anywhere.

33

Gratefully there were no signs of a struggle nor was there any blood anywhere in the house. Wherever his wife was hiding he prayed she was still alive. Remembering the ships headed his way he grabbed the signaling lantern and ran out to the cliff's edge hoping to signal them as they passed by.

Patrick brought the first ship into focus with his spyglass. They were two hundred yards and closing fast not making one single evasive maneuver to avoid crashing into the island. He stretched the glass to its limits and scanned the deck, there seemed to be no one on board and certainly no one at the helm. The ship looked to be the Robert E. Murry, but she had been bound for Thunder Bay three days prior. Something serious must have happened on board to cause her to turn around.

The Murry's captain was Heb Wallace, as competent a captain as any on the lake. Patrick signaled the ship that she was on a collision course but there was no response. She was just a little over one hundred yards out and he could make out dripping wet red splotches all over the deck as he witnessed on the *Diana*. It was then he saw three wakes churning up the waters behind the boat and they were closing fast.

There was movement on the deck, it was Heb. Patrick watched helpless as the man drug himself up to the wheel with only one arm. The left arm was completely gone from the socket leaving a mangled stub of torn flesh. He saw that the captain, instead of steering out and clear of the island was lashing the wheel to maintain the collision course into the three-hundred-foot cliff side.

The Murry closed within fifty yards and Patrick could see the panic in Wallace's face. But he could also see the man's determination. The three trailing wakes disappeared, leading Patrick to believe there was flotsam trailing behind the ship, possibly timbers were caught up in the rudder which was why the ship was not diverting course.

McPhereson was befuddled, a storm appeared to be following the ship. In fact, if it weren't such a preposterous notion, he would swear the maelstrom was attacking the ship as lightning was striking the vessel like cannonballs.

Patrick signaled the Robert E. Murry again out of desperation. There was not enough time for the ship to avoid the rocks at this point. The captain managed to return a one-word response.

"Run."

Chapter Four

"It is imperative we get off this island at once," Dimitri said with near panic in his intonation. "Did you see what that monstrosity did to the Swede from the lighthouse and then to the other men."

"Relax, we are not going anywhere, the Diana will be here within the hour. She is loaded with rifles and more men. When she arrives, we can put an end to all of this," Robert commented, drawing deep on his cigar and jetting a hazy gray plume toward the ceiling of the converted storeroom.

Robert Langley was a large man, a strong man, and an extremely very dangerous man to argue with so Dimitri kept his comments to himself for the time being. Robert currently enjoyed the pleasure of serving as the head of the consortium, mainly because he was the only ranking member still alive. True, they encountered some unforeseeable setbacks, but he was bound and determined to see this thing through, mainly because it would make him even richer than he already was.

"Dimitri, please, have a seat and let us discuss this like rational men," he said with a wave of his arm and a look on his face that meant that as an order, not a request.

"Robert, with all due respect, there is nothing to discuss. When the Diana gets here, I want to get off this island. Hell, I want off this island right now."

A woman's laughter from the other room interrupted their conversation.

"Is there something you wish to say Mrs. McPhereson?"

"Your plan will not work. I will not leave here, especially not with these things inside of me."

"I am afraid that decision is out of your hands. Dimitri and I will be leaving this place just as soon as the Diana arrives and we finish what we came here to do," Robert said and took a long, measured draw from his cigar.

"You and that Russian foolishly think you are going to get off this island, but I can promise you, if by some chance you do make it out of here, it will not be while still breathing."

"I will play along with your little game, just what makes you so certain of that?"

"Because Mishipeshu will not allow it."

"Who is Mishipeshu?" Dimitri asked, shooting a nervous glance at his boss.

"Not who, what," Robert started. "It's just another native superstition created to control weak minded people," Robert said. "I suggest you save your strength Mrs. McPhereson, you are going to need it."

"All I need is to remain alive long enough to watch Mishipeshu tear you limb from limb."

With that Robert got up, strode across the room, and slammed the door between the two rooms.

"Robert, I want to leave this place, now."

"Unfortunately, that will not be possible. When the Diana gets here, there will be far too much work to do and I will need all hands-on deck, including yours."

"You cannot be serious? Work to do. You saw what that thing did to Henry and Matthieu. What work could we possibly have to do that is so important we should risk our lives?"

"After breakfast we will start building a cage from the materials the Diana has on board."

"The Diana was supposed to be here last night. And what on earth do you have in mind that requires a cage?" Dimitri asked, afraid of what the man's answer would be.

"We need to capture that thing, and when we do, we will need a cage to put it in," Langley said.

"Why on earth would we want to capture it? We need to kill it if that's even possible," Dimitri said.

"Kill it? I don't want to kill it you fool, I want to breed it," Langley said and stubbed his cigar out on the worn tabletop.

Chapter Five

The Robert E. Murry died with a dreadful sound. Timbers shrieked as they splintered against the unforgiving cliff face when the ship slammed into it at full speed. Heb Wallace was catapulted through the air, slammed into the sandstone wall and fell lifeless into the water below. The sandstone cliff would be forever stained with his memory.

The Murry only employed a crew of six men but there was enough blood in the water to make it look as though she had a crew of twenty. Not one single soul floundered in the water below leaving Patrick to suspect they were all long dead before hitting the rocks. All but the one-armed Wallace of course. But where did the bodies go?

Without warning a horrific sound arose from the wreckage. Patrick trained the spyglass down onto the water and was aghast at what he saw. The water boiled with the fervor of a feeding frenzy. Something he only heard about from tales woven by sailors who sailed the

Amazon. But piranha could never survive in these icy waters, could they?

He then turned his spyglass to the remaining two ships who seemed to be following the Murry's lead. In fact, they seemed to be steering straight for the wreckage and not away from the beacon as would be expected. Once they were within signaling distance, he tried to contact them. Not wanting to see them suffer the same fate as the Murry he filled a bucket with five gallons of fuel oil and started to descend the zigzag staircase that traversed the cliff face. The ship destroyed the lower platform and with it the first fifty feet of scaffolding so he would not be able to reach the bottom as he hoped. He removed his shirt, rolled it up tight and tied it with his belt. He used the shirt to wick up some of the fuel oil and he tossed the remaining liquid down onto the wreckage. He lit the shirt on fire, waited until it was burning good and hot before he dropped it down.

The wreckage of the Robert E. Murry exploded into a blinding ball of fire that leapt up at Patrick and threatened to cook him alive. Luckily, the flame ball stopped climbing and the initial flare-up subsided. The surface of the water raged, and an inhuman shriek split the night. The audible assault was so piercing it robbed him of his equilibrium and forced him to his knees. Almost as soon as it began the noise dissipated and the seas grew calm.

Patrick got back to his feet and looked out over the lake. It was all for naught. Instead of steering clear the other two ships corrected their course and headed straight for the flaming wreckage. There was nothing more he could do, and he did not wish to witness the wreckage of two more vessels, so he began his ascent up the stairs. Had everyone gone completely insane?

Once more a pang of guilt ate away at him for not continuing his search for his beloved Bonni, but she was a strong lass quite capable of looking after herself. Hopefully, she escaped the island before all this madness began. Although Patrick never fancied firearms, he grabbed his Colt Navy from the tool shed. He checked to make sure it was loaded and put on fresh percussion caps. It was time to pay a visit to the consortium as he was certain this madness was all their doing.

The consortium hunting cabins were on the southeastern end of Echo Lake which was a good four miles from the lighthouse with little to no trail through the dense, heavy woods. A hike Patrick was not relishing in the least and especially not in the dark on no sleep with only God knew what lurking about in the forest. He loaded a rucksack with water, smoked whitefish, and his Colt with more ammunition and powder before heading out. He grabbed a machete from a hook in the tool shed just in case he found the need to blaze a trail.

As he was skirting the stables, he almost forgot about the pitiful creature inside. The building was dark so he could not see inside through the cracks, and he didn't dare venture inside lest he become part of the meal. He prayed to the good Lord above that Bonni was not in there with the ill-fated mule.

Patrick's wife was a large woman, not fat mind you, just large and she was nearly as strong as he was. Not to mention, she was twenty years his junior so if anyone were to survive this ordeal it would be her. He found himself missing her chestnut eyes, delicate skin, and warm embrace. The smell of wood smoke mixed with the delicate aroma of Trailing Arbutus his wife would rub on her neck and wrists while tending to the lighthouse was haunting him.

He held his compass in one hand and the lantern in the other though he was not convinced the light was a promising idea. While it may allow him a narrow band of vision it also allowed anyone, or anything to spot him from a long distance. He continued south on the narrow winding path stopping every couple of minutes to listen to his surroundings and cover the lantern's glow. The utter silence enveloping the woodland was unnerving. It was unnatural.

Patrick looked over toward the east side of the island and saw a little patch of bruised eggplant sky. It would be at least another hour before the sun was up, which would be just about the time he would be arriving at the consortium's encampment. He trudged on through the forest with a singular purpose, to find his wife. The combination of silence and darkness was chewing away at Patrick, but he forged on despite his apprehensions. With each new step came another new scenario playing out in his overactive imagination. Within an hours' time he made it to the north shore of Echo Lake and from there travel was much faster once he was able to get out of the dense woodland and follow the sandy shoreline south.

He swung the lantern out over the surface of the lake every so often and caught not one single glimpse of life. No tadpoles, no frogs, no minnows, not even any spiders lurking in their webs, nor one single Jesus bug showing off its water-walking skills for the world. Now that he thought about it, there were no mosquitos or black flies either, which was even more telling than the lack of wildlife. Had those perplexing moths devoured every morsal of life on the island? But how could moths, even wicked little beasts such as those manage to devour fish?

The day was breaking, just enough for him to see the shimmering black surface of Echo Lake without the aid of his lantern. He heard something break the surface somewhere out toward the center and watched as centrical ripples danced toward the shore. He breathed a sigh of relief, there was something alive in the lake after all. His relief was short-lived once he realized that whatever exited the lake's depths did not return. There was no slapping tail or loud splash from the fish's body hitting the water upon re-entry.

His entire body trembled with fear as he crouched low to the ground. He could not shake the feeling that he was being watched. He shrugged the sensation off as the consortium having posted sentries. It was entirely possible one of the men had thrown a rock into the lake either out of boredom or had seen Patrick and wanted to toy with him.

The sun painted the island in a golden glow and Patrick was able to see much further ahead of himself which helped to lessen his apprehensions. He smelled smoke from a campfire or wood stove, so he moved toward the acrid, yet pleasant aroma. He scanned the trees along the shore until he caught the slightest tendril reaching up through the boughs. Once he found his bearings, he stayed low and made his way toward the smoke.

There were two men sleeping outside on the ground near their tent. Why were they not inside the tent? He didn't recall the night being a particularly hot one, in fact, it was a cool evening with just a hint of autumn in the air. It made no sense for them to be outside of their shelter. He crept closer until he was close enough to see their faces and didn't recognize either of them. What he did see stopped Patrick dead in his tracks. The ashen color of their skin and their wide-open eyes told him these men were not sleeping and were in fact dead.

Once he drew near enough to see them in their entirety, he saw there was not much left of them at all. Both men were torn apart, split in two from the midsection. Small wisps of steam rose from their brutalized corpses in the cool morning air signaling that not much time had passed since their deaths, which set his nerves on their very last edge. There was a thick black ribbon of ooze trailing down the sand where the remainder of their bodies were dragged down into the water. It was a good thing he hadn't eaten dinner nor breakfast or he surely would have rid himself of it.

He only visited the compound two or three times and while familiar with the layout of the camp he could not remember what purpose each of the buildings served. He crept toward the longest of the buildings hoping it was the bunkhouse. There was a smokestack jutting out of the far end of the building, so he assumed it was the building designated for cooking. Maybe they were having breakfast and that was the reason why no one was milling around

44

outside. He knew that was just wishful thinking as there was only a whisper of smoke exiting the stovepipe, a clear indicator the fire was down to its last few embers.

Patrick stopped long enough to pull the Colt from his rucksack and slip it into his waistband. He also moved the lantern to his left hand and drew the machete. Not wanting to be encumbered, he left the rucksack behind a log by the smoldering campfire and crept up to the building. He eased up and peered in through the dingy window. There were two men sitting at the table with plates of food in front of them. The plates looked untouched and several days old. He moved around to the next window to get a better angle.

He recognized one of the men but not the other. The man facing him was Charles Ingrahm, the wildlife manager he met when the consortium first moved to the island. The men looked oddly at peace as if merely sleeping but Patrick knew better by the dark pool spreading out from under the table.

Around to the other side of the bunkhouse he found two more men in their bunks, staring blankly at the ceiling, their lives collecting in a pool on the floor below. He needed to find Bonni and get the both of them the hell off the island.

Patrick was feeling lightheaded, so he went back to where he left his rucksack, but it was gone. The rucksack itself was not gone, the contents were gone and the sack itself was shredded. Twenty-five yards down the beach he found the powder, shot and caps but all his food was gone. It was not the fact that someone or something was watching him that bothered him the most, it was the strange tracks left in the sand. They were unlike any creature he had ever encountered, but also human-like in appearance.

Chapter Six

Patrick fought against his hunger, thirst, and fatigue as he continued searching the deserted compound. He would have abandoned the lantern but many of the buildings were dark inside, darker than he wanted to subject himself to. He fought the urge to call out to Bonni, if she would hear him so would any creatures, man, or beast, lurking about.

He managed to locate the camp's armory and found it empty save for a couple of fishing rigs, bits and pieces of broken firearms and a bow with no arrows. There was a wooden rack with slots designed to hold at least ten rifles, but there were none stored, and the broken debris was merely one or two rifles at best. On the floor lay a couple rifle stocks, one barrel and a trigger mechanism. He found no powder or balls lying about with the fragments of firearms, nothing he could fashion into explosives. Either the rifles were stolen or there never were any to begin with. He left the small armory and shut the door behind him.

The next building in line was a rectangular building butted right up against the shore of the inland lake. As he neared the end of the structure, he saw another dark smudge in the sand with humanoid tracks leading into the water. Whoever this person had been, there was not a single trace left other than a fine black powder interspersed with the sand.

His hand quivered as he reached for the door handle and found it unlatched. He was still acutely aware of how quiet the day was. There was not one single bird singing a glorious song, not one frog declaring he was king of the pond, absolute dead silence. He prayed the hinges on the door were recently oiled as a squeaky hinge would be heard throughout the forest under the given circumstances.

Patrick crept into the room as if he were a burglar trying to steal the crown jewels. He dialed down the wick on the lantern to minimize the light output before squeezing in through the door to allow as little sunlight in as possible. Once inside he retreated for a shadowed corner to evaluate the situation. The room was dead quiet and remained so for a solid two minutes. Satisfied he was safe for the moment he turned up the lantern and made his way through an alcove into a large rectangular room.

The room was void of furniture save for two long wooden tables. There was a long counter that wrapped from the short end of the room and spanned the length of the room to the other end. Atop the counter was a scattering of glass jars and bottles, some with a bluish-green fluid, some with what appeared to be water, others contained a fine, black dust and the rest were empty.

There was an odd smell permeating the air of the room. Fruity and pleasant on one note but decay on another.

Patrick eased step by step toward the back wall where there was an odd display eliciting his attention. He saw something similar being shown around in town several years back. There was a crazy old coot who kept showing off a collection of butterflies pinned to a piece of birch bark stretched flat. Called himself a lepidopterist, whatever the hell that was. He always talked about going on an expedition to some island Patrick had never heard of. Even though it was interesting after a pint or two, he never really showed much interest other than simple curiosity.

In front of him was a much more sophisticated version. There were a dozen different specimens were pinned to the board and a pencil outline was drawn of them. Although very much different from one another, they were all remarkably similar as well. Given the fact the actual specimens had all disintegrated into a fine black powder like what he saw on the beach Patrick was left to review the drawings and notes beneath each pinned sampling.

Patrick rummaged around in the drawers and found glass vials with glass stoppers filled with liquid and what appeared to be insects. He realized they were preserved specimens of the same creatures once pinned to the board. He arranged them according to the drawings, progressing from left to right. One of the vials contained a moth identical to those that attacked him on the widow's walk, and he shuddered. He was no scientist, but this looked grim, very grim indeed.

According to the drawings and notes, each of the creatures pinned to the board seemed to be in a series of progressions, changes from the previous, an evolution if you will. The first pinned to the board was miniscule, much too small for Patrick to discern any details. He did not bother inspecting the first three specimens in the vials but the fourth was clearly a larva of sorts and the one after that was a larger version that resembled a caterpillar. This one was suspended face up with a double set of fangs top and bottom exposed.

The translucent blue moth was the next in the series which made sense of the natural order of things as he knew them. Again, this one was arranged in the vial with its gaping maw against the glass facing the viewer. Patrick rubbed raw spots on his arms and neck where chunks of his flesh was pilfered by creatures just like this one. Its wings were a shimmering translucent blue even in death. Its body was only slightly smaller than his pinky and the head about the size of his thumbnail. It was large as moths go, but not the largest he had ever seen. About the size of a Luna moth, he reckoned.

The next in the series was another larva stage, only much bigger than the first. Patrick's eyes were drawn to the right. The transformation of this larva to the next stage was shocking and the next progression even more shocking than the previous. There was something almost amphibian about this progression of the creature if they were even the same creature at all. The only familiarity about them was their odd translucent blue coloring and each stage of the creature bore a more vicious set of teeth than its predecessor. There was something on the second table covered by a stained sheet. It was disturbing to note that even though covered he could tell that the thing was as big as a small child. Patrick was about to pull the sheet back when he heard a moan from the shadows behind him.

Patrick spun on his heels, swinging the lantern with his left hand while brandishing the machete in his right. "Is there someone in here?"

The person, or what he hoped was a person, moaned again. He followed the sound with both the lantern and machete extended at arms lengths.

"You must be the keeper," a disembodied voice said.

Patrick shone the light in the direction of the voice and illuminated the man's face. He did not recognize him.

"How would you know me, when I have never laid eyes on you?" Patrick asked.

"Hard to miss a large man with an even larger flaming red beard. My benefactors told me all about you before they met their fate of course."

"Who the hell are you? And what in the world happened here, on my island?" he bellowed.

"My name is Zachary Rutherford, from London. Pleased to meet your acquaintance. I'd extend a hand, but I believe both of my arms have been broken," Edgar said, hoping the man bought his sham accent.

"A Brit? What are you doing in these parts, and specifically on my island?"

"First, let me correct you, this is not your island, only a small portion of it apportioned to the lighthouse and grounds, the rest belongs to us."

"A man in your position should not be so easy to quibble. So, you are one of the consortia?"

"In a manner of speaking, yes. I am not an owner, nor a partner, but I do work for them. Or at least I did before all of this," he said and bowed his head.

Patrick sighed and found some blankets to help make the man at least a little more comfortable. He up-righted a chair and pulled it up next to the man.

"And just what is all of this? What killed all those men in the camp?" he said, scanning the lantern around the shadow filled room.

"Honestly, I wish I could tell you, but I don't know exactly. It is some sort of organism, but I have never seen anything like it."

"Some sort of organism?" Patrick questioned.

"Organism is another word for living thing," the man said.

"I know what an organism is. If you weren't already injured, I'd rap you on the noggin. And in fact, any more sarcasm and I might still do just that. And by the way, I was one of the first classes to graduate from the University of Michigan."

"My heartfelt apologies for my crass behavior, sir."

"Where did this organism come from? Did you bring it here to the island?"

"No, no one brought it here. It seems old lady Superior does indeed give up her dead."

"Please feel free to elaborate, before I get any more agitated than I already am," Patrick said, resisting the urge to give the broken man a severe thrashing.

"This thing," he started with a nod of his head at the table with the covered specimen. "It just floated up one day this past spring. It was encased in a large chunk of bluish-green ice. The same color as the larvae, and moths," he explained.

Patrick got up from his seat and started for the table. He wasn't sure if he would have the nerve to uncover it, but he had to at least take a gander.

"No, don't do that, it might still be infectious."

"Infectious? You mean to say it was carrying a disease? That's what caused all of this death?"

"Infectious might not be the proper term."

"Then just what is the proper terminology?"

"It was harboring an unknown form of parasite. Hell, it is some form of parasite. When we thawed it out and began to examine it, something unexpected happened," he said.

Patrick noticed the man's stomach seemed bloated. It appeared to be moving as well. He chalked that up to the shadows dancing around from the lantern's flickering flame.

"What happened, exactly?"

"I started to take a tissue sample to analyze it when the cadaver spewed forth a liquid the same color as their flesh. It splashed on two of the men and within hours they were deathly ill. I tried to treat them but not knowing what was happening to them my efforts were futile."

"Treat them? So, you're the camp physician?"

"Of sorts, but I am more of a scientist than a doctor."

"Pardon my ignorance for one moment, why would a hunting camp need a scientist?"

"That is privileged information I'm not at liberty to disclose," Zachary said, his voice laced with sarcasm and disdain.

"Zachary, or whoever in the hell you really are, you have obviously mistaken me for a man of tolerance and patience. While I can see you are gravely injured, and normally I would never harm a wounded man, under these circumstances I am about to take that piece of lumber over there and rap you on the head for each uninformative response you provide," Patrick said with a measure of anger in his voice as he rose to his feet.

"Listen, you can go get that piece of wood and beat me to death, and that I would welcome because I am already a dead man," he said. "Look at my stomach, can you see it move?"

"Yes. What is your point?"

"They are already inside of me, growing, changing and soon they will be inside of you too," he laughed.

Patrick ignored the man and went back to inspecting the various stages of the specimens on the table. He still couldn't gather the nerve to uncover the largest of them on the table. Zachary was prattling on, and on which was giving him a throbbing headache. Something he said caught Patrick's attention.

"What was that you said about a woman?"

"I said I couldn't believe a woman bested me, but she was pretty near as big as any man, even you, I supposed," he said and wheezed out a weak laugh.

"Big woman? Was she a native?"

"I never gave it much thought, but yes, I imagine she might have been."

"What happened to her? Where is she?"

The man continued to ramble on about nothing and was making no sense whatsoever. Patrick spun on his heels to tell the man to shut up and answer his questions but was immediately frozen with horror. The man's eyes were an angry red and pulsating as if they were going to explode. Long, spindly tendrils reached down, out through the man's nostrils and danced around like antennae investigating the air. Patrick screamed and drew his revolver. Without another moment's hesitation he put a bullet between the man's eyes.

The man's corpse began to flail about and emitted an unruly noise. He threw a blanket over the body and dragged the cadaver out through the door and onto the dirt. Patrick doused it with oil from the lantern and set the body ablaze. A horrendous smell invaded the air, not from the smoke of the fire or even burning human flesh but emanating from the vile creatures harbored inside of the dead man as they cooked. He went back inside, barred the door shut and opened a window; he was not finished investigating this place yet.

He was rummaging through the mélange of beakers and vials when a muffled sound from the back of the building caught his attention.

"Patrick?" He heard his name being called.

His blood turned to ice, but once he heard his name being called once more and this time he was not frightened, it was clearly Bonni's voice. He searched the parts of the building he had failed to search earlier and found a locked door. Using the old piece of lumber, he battered the lock until it broke free. Bonni was inside the locked room, which turned out to be an icehouse, so it was freezing cold inside. Patrick fought back tears the moment he saw her. No longer did she radiate youthful beauty, her smile was gone, and her cinnamon skin was almost alabaster white.

"Bonni, my love, let me get you out of here," he said, cradling her up into his arms.

"No, Patrick, you must leave me in here. Save yourself."

"What in tarnation are you talking about? I have to get you out of here, you are near froze to death."

"No, Patrick, look," she said, pulling open her blouse to expose her protruding stomach.

"My God, woman, why didn't you tell me you were with child?" he asked, looking at the belly of a woman about two months overdue.

"I am not, my love. They are growing inside of me. It is why I am in here. According to a conversation I overheard between a couple of the consortium men the cold slows down the organism's progression."

"You freezing yourself to death is not the solution. We need to get you to the mainland, to a doctor."

She shook her head vehemently. "No, we cannot leave the island and we cannot allow others to come here. These beings, whatever they are, will spread like a plague. We cannot let this plague loose. You need to kill me and burn my body," she said, reaching up for his face with her delicate fingers.

"No! I cannot and I will not," he protested.

"Patrick, you must."

"No, I will get you a doctor."

"There is no time. I can feel it is nearing."

"You can feel what is nearing?"

"The hatch."

Chapter Seven

Refusing to believe there were no other options Patrick began ransacking the small outpost searching for any information about these creatures that might help him discover a way to put an end to Bonni's plight. These men were obviously studying these parasites, maybe even cultivating them, for what purpose he could only imagine. Whatever this was, it was an evil pestilence that had to be stopped.

He found several notebooks hidden in the bunkhouse. Whoever hid them knew this had gone sour and was trying to relieve themselves of culpability.

"It seems these men in this consortium were trying to play God," Patrick said to Bonni as he pulled up a chair next to her. "You are shivering, let me get you some blankets."

"No, that would warm me up and make things worse. I heard them talking while I was on the table, one of the men said that I was to be kept cold until they were ready," Bonni said, her deep chestnut eyes no longer full of warmth and luster.

"What did he mean by they?"

"I'm afraid he didn't tell me that, but from all the screaming I have heard, I don't think it is a good thing," she said, trying her best to smile back at her husband. She was more afraid for him than she was for herself.

"What are we to do?" he asked with tears streaming down his face.

"We pray."

"You know I was never much on that stuff."

"I know. But you need it now more than ever before, Patrick."

After an exceedingly long pause he asked, "What did they do to you?"

"It's much too late to concern yourself with that. You need to concern yourself with how to undo what has been done and I'm afraid that is something you cannot do."

"There has to be something in these notes," he said, flinging pieces of parchment about the room.

The notes were drawings and mostly written in Latin which he, even with a formal education, did not read fluently. What he could understand frightened him to the core. *Gravidus,* he did understand to mean pregnant. It was one of the words that struck a humorous vein in him. But it was scratched out and instead the word *incubo* was scribbled. He understood the word to mean incubate, though he wasn't certain. So, did this mean his Bonni was being used as an incubator? For what purpose? What was she gestating, certainly not blue moths?

On one of the pages there was what he recognized as Cyrillic writing that he couldn't understand. These were

Russians? What were Russians doing in this part of the world? And why were they on his island? There was one word in English, Triton, that he was not familiar with and an Anishinaabe word as well, Mishipeshu. He had heard the name once or twice before and knew it to be a native legend, a mythological beast who lived in the lakes according to native lore. But surely, they did not truly exist.

Guilt chewed away at Patrick like a ravenous dog. He wanted to hold Bonni, to make everything better, but he knew he couldn't, he feared nothing was going to make this better. He went through the notes several times over but most of them were worthless because of the language barrier. Much of it was in Latin, some of it Russian and several other languages he did not understand, one of which he was certain was Germanic in nature.

Hunger and fatigue were winning the battle, leaving Patrick with little to no energy and a limited ability to think. He needed to decide on a plan because doing nothing was not going to be an option. But he needed to know exactly what it was they were up against.

"Bonni, this word here is familiar, do you recognize it? Mishipeshu," he said, holding the piece of parchment where she could see it.

"It is an Ojibwe word. It is the name given to the water panther who protects the people of the lakes, more specifically, it protects the copper. I told the man what he was doing was wrong and that Mishipeshu would come to punish him."

"Mishipeshu is just a legend."

"Maybe, maybe not. I am more inclined to believe in legends after seeing what I have seen here tonight."

"What were these men up to?" he asked more of himself than his dying wife.

"There is a shack down by the lake, which is where I first saw them, and they saw me. They were going in and out of that shack, but I never saw what they were up to," she said. "And they followed a trail north many times hauling a wagon."

"I need to go see what they were up to. I'll see if I can find some food while I'm at it," he said.

"Do not bother, I do not think I could eat anything anyway," she said.

Patrick took a long look into her eyes and his heart ached. It was painfully obvious she had completely given up. But he had not, not quite yet.

The sun was completely up, and he found he felt more at ease in the dark of night. He crept through the compound down toward the lake until he spied the shack Bonni referred to. It was not very big, about as large as a boathouse, but he didn't see any signs of a boat, oars, or the like. Once he came around to the lake side of the building, he saw the door was ripped from its hinges and there were massive splotches of dried blood on the face of the building as well as the sand in front, though he saw no trace of human remains. He looked around for a fish cleaning station to explain away the blood stains but found nothing that even remotely resembled such a thing and there were none of the tell-tale piles of fish scales shimmering in the sunlight.

The shack was empty save for a few tools he didn't recognize that looked worn from hard use. There were some torn nets and heavy fishing tackle along with marker buoys but nothing that made any sense to him in relation to what was going on.

Patrick turned and looked out over the calm lake with a heavy sigh. The sun was over the trees now and it was going to be a gorgeous day, if you didn't count the man-eating moths and bizarre monsters lurking about.

The sun glinted off a metallic object and caught his eye from further down the lake shore. Patrick gathered his nerve and left the limited safety of the shack and made his way down the beach. Once he was within a few yards he saw a couple of brass rings with shreds of white fabric connected to the metal hardware. He inspected the article and saw the fabric was a heavy canvas and was ripped away from something larger, a sleeve maybe. Further down the beach and closer to the water's edge he saw another piece of brass, but much larger than the first.

There was a large, dark stain in the sand around the larger piece which turned out to be a large brass globe. This piece too had a scrap of shredded white canvas fabric attached, and the blood on this piece was still moist. A chill rippled through him as he fought the urge to run. The brass globe was too heavy for him to lift on his own, so he rolled it over to get a look at the other side.

Patrick cried out, fell to his backside, and scrambled away from the debris. Whatever, whoever was inside the globe was still partially there. Their head anyway. After several minutes he was able to crawl back on his hands and knees and look inside the glass-covered cage of what he now realized was a diver's helmet. Even with his face forever frozen in terror he recognized the man as one of the mariners he saw on the *Diana* on more than one occasion. He had been a good-looking lad once, but now his ashen face was locked in a perpetual scream.

He saw diving suits like this one a few times before during salvage operations. A man would put the suit on and be dropped into the lake over a shipwreck. A pump on board the ship would supply him with air through hoses in the suit. The salvage worker would then affix chains to the wreckage to be lifted or dragged to shore or simply salvage anything of value if the ship were too severely damaged to be repaired. But there was no wreckage around the island to salvage anything from so what were these men after?

It suddenly dawned on him that whatever ripped this man into pieces dragged the larger portion into the lake and he was currently standing within a foot of the water. He felt the searing heat of hungry eyes studying him from beneath the depths. He drew the Colt and tried to steady his hand as he cautiously backed away from the water's edge.

A low, guttural growl emanated from behind Patrick setting his hackles on end. He swung around and aimed his revolver at a snarling wolf standing less than ten feet from him. The beast was as black as the night itself with glowing yellow eyes and an ominous snarl filled with flesh tearing teeth. He almost fired a shot but realized the wolf was not even paying any attention to him, it was growling at the water beyond his shoulder. This unnerved him more than if the beast would have been ready to attack. Something in the water disturbed the creature more than he did.

The wolf's hind end was high in the air while his front end was tight to the ground and his hackles were at full attention. Silvery strands of saliva dangled from its canines and the animal's eyes hinted of fear. It scanned to the right ever so slightly to glance at Patrick but then its attention went right back to the water. He took that as a sign the wolf was looking for an ally not an adversary. He turned the pistol toward the water and eased himself closer to the animal.

"What's in there boy?" Patrick said, his voice trembling.

A shadow moved back and forth beneath the water twenty feet from the shore. Whatever was in there, for all intents and purposes, it was pacing. The silhouette beneath the water fluidly changed from fifteen feet long and slender to a fat blob. Patrick thought snake, but there was no snake in these parts that large, let alone one that could survive beneath the water. Did those bastards bring an anaconda to his island? But that wouldn't explain the torn flesh of its victims.

Surface tension on the water broke into a slow torrent of ripples leading outward from the center. His instincts warned him that he was still too close to the water. He started to ease back, and the wolf followed his lead. Not wanting to face whatever was hanging just below the water's surface Patrick fired two rounds into the shadow which quickly disappeared out of sight. He let out a triumphant sigh when the wolf relaxed its defensive posture. An oily slick of translucent blue spread across the top of the water indicating he hit whatever lurked beneath the surface.

Patrick made his way back to the bunkhouse where he left Bonni and was saddened the wolf decided to part company after a few minutes of travelling together. The brush moved every once in a while, alerting him to the fact the beast was shadowing him, it just chose to stay out of sight.

Rummaging around in each of the buildings he managed to find some hard tea biscuits and a canteen of water.

"Bonni, my love, I found some biscuits and some water," he said, offering them to her.

"Thank you, Patrick," she said, breaking off a piece of biscuit and taking a mouthful of water to soften it. "What did you find?"

"I found that we need to get off this island, and fast. There is some kind of creature in the lake."

"No, Patrick. I cannot leave. Whatever is growing inside of me must die on this island. Besides, I do not have very long on this earth. You must kill me, and then you must burn my body to destroy whatever this is inside of me."

"No, there has to be another way. I will not kill you and I sure as hell will not set you ablaze."

"There is no other way. It was how they destroyed the larval stages of these things. They burned them."

Bonni continued to press the issue and Patrick continued to ignore her while he scanned through the notes and sketches. He stopped at one of the pages, something about it looked familiar. Using a larger map that was pinned to the wall he determined that the place in the drawing was some sort of bunker located on the northeast end of the property between the lake and the lighthouse.

"Here are the biscuits and the water, I'll be back as soon as I can," he said, bending to give Bonni a kiss on her forehead. He tried to ignore that her belly looked like something inside of her was clawing to get out. He filled the lantern with oil he found in one of the cupboards, lit it and headed out, not sure what he was looking for or what he might find.

Patrick stayed on a path high above the lake, stopping every few hundred feet to check the map. He never ran across this bunker during his daily jaunts through the forest, so he reckoned it must be well hidden. After several hundred yards he was pleased to see he picked up a travelling companion.

"I am delighted you decided to join me, I sure could use the company," he said. The wolf seemed to return the greeting with a head bob and a canine's smile.

The mismatched pair plodded through the thick trees with no luck finding what Patrick was searching for. He was checking the map again for the tenth time when the wolf meandered out into the trees, stopped, and gave a slight whimper. It took several reenactments of this behavior before it dawned on Patrick that the animal was trying to get him to follow. They wound their way through even thicker and more dense woods until the wolf stopped at a small clearing.

The two of them looked at each other for several minutes until the wolf began pawing at the ground. Patrick helped him until he came upon a solid, metallic object beneath the deadfall and dirt covering. He spent another fifteen minutes digging at the earth until he was finally able to free the hatch. Another fifteen minutes was spent breaking the locking mechanism free with a large rock.

"After you," Patrick said to the wolf whom he named Varg which was Swedish for wolf, one of the only words he knew in the language and only because it was part of the Swede's tattoo. It seemed only fitting since he never even bothered to learn the Swede's name and the lad was quite proud of the tattoo.

He held open the door to the underground bunker. The wolf whined and backed away several steps. After several attempts to coerce Varg to follow him, the wolf simply refused to capitulate by plopping its belly hard to the ground. Patrick looked around for a long, sturdy branch and lashed the lantern to the end of it. He held the makeshift pole out in front of himself and crept down the stairs one at a time while Varg waited patiently outside the manmade cavern.

The stairs leading down zigzagged from the right to the left, eight steps per section and four sections in total. He estimated that each step was approximately a foot apart from one another suggesting he dropped down nearly forty feet below the surface. He could hear the wolf padding down behind him, but the creature was much more wary and hung back two entire sections of the staircase.

Once off the stairs the first room opened into a cavernous square chamber. In the dim lantern glow, he spotted several sconces affixed to the walls. He opened the cap on the first sconce, dipped his finger into the oil reservoir and it came out wet. He found a lighting candle in a small tray built into the sconce and used it to light the lamp. He went around and lit the remaining four lamps, illuminating a non-descript square room with flat, unadorned walls. He had heard mention of this brick like building material but never observed concrete up close. Patrick thumped at the wall a few times to gauge the thickness and was impressed at the sturdiness of the structure.

There was not much in the room other than the sconces and a few medical supplies. There was a long table but no chairs. There were gouges in the wood at the top and bottom and the top looked stained. He noticed some scratches on the floor. A shadow on the far wall alerted him there was a passageway.

He turned the wick up on his lantern and eased it into the narrow corridor. Varg finally decided it was safe and joined him in the large room but did not want anything to do with the narrow passage. The hallway was less than six feet long allowing him to easily see into the next room before entering. This room was similar to the first but looked more like living quarters. There were two sets of bunk beds against the north and the west wall. There was a small wood burning stove located on the east wall with a large pile of lumber and a pantry filled with water, dry goods, salted fish, smoked meats, and other assorted staples. This would do nicely indeed.

Another corridor led to a room with three more of the diving suits he found on the beach and a hand operated device he determined to be an air pump. He lit one of the sconces in this room which revealed a large tarp covering the floor.

"Varg, come in here and give me a hand if you wouldn't mind," he called out in jest. Varg simply sat at the far end of the corridor and whined.

Patrick struggled to get the tarp pulled away. Whatever was under the tarp was extremely heavy. Once he uncovered the materials, he saw why they were so heavy. It was copper, the purest he had ever laid eyes on, smelted into ingots. There was some gold as well and bags of stones. These bastards had been mining under the island. He figured he was going to have plenty of time to explore this bunker more once he and his wife were safely inside, so he put everything back the way he found it.

Varg was visibly pleased when Patrick came out of the last chamber and headed for the stairs and eventually out of the cavernous place. As they were leaving, he noticed that the steel door sported several sliding bars used to lock the bunker from inside once a person, or people and a wolf were safely away from whatever danger lurked on the surface. Maybe his little family would be able to weather this storm after all.

Chapter Eight

As luck would have it, Patrick located the utility cart Bonni mentioned not far from the bunker and started back for the compound with it in tow. Varg's sheer stubbornness convinced him to take a higher route away from the water on the return trip. Even away from the water he could feel the eyes of something lurking beneath the surface following their every move.

"It looks like you plan to be in it for the long-haul buddy," Patrick said, patting the wolf on the head and scratching him behind his dark ears. "Hope you like beans and hard tack."

Varg panted and drooled.

"Bonni, my love. I have found us a place to hunker down until this evil passes," he said, bursting into the bunkhouse out of breath. It was starting to get dark, and he didn't want to make the trip back to the bunker under the blackness of night.

There was rustling from further into the building and Bonni came shuffling out of the ice room. She was haggard and hunched over, looking decades older than her true age.

"Is that a wolf?" she said, rearing back away from the animal.

"Believe it or not, he is a friend and quite harmless. We need to hurry before it gets dark."

"Why, what's wrong?"

"There is something out there, something monstrous. I need to gather all these notes, charts, and drawings so when this ordeal is behind us, we can show the authorities what has transpired here."

"Patrick, that is why I love you so, you are always such the optimist," she said with a measure of sadness in her eyes.

He helped her out of the building, onto the utility cart, and made her as comfortable as he possibly could. Deep in his heart he knew she was right, he was being overly optimistic, but be damned, he was not about to leave this world without a fight.

"Varg, you keep her safe while I finish up in here," he said to his new companion who seemed to understand exactly what he said and took a defensive posture over Bonni.

Patrick gathered all the information related to the consortium and what they had been up to on the island that he could find. He convinced himself to take the array of larvae and moths pinned to the piece of board even though they were just dust and hand drawings at this point. Only after he gathered everything outside and packed it onto the utility trailer with Bonni did he go back into the building to see just what was under the tarp. He barely made it through the doorway when Varg started to growl. He hurried back outside to find the animal down in an attack posture, his black fur bristling with energy.

"Patrick, I think your friend believes we should be going now," Bonni said.

He pushed the cart down the trail a hundred feet before he stopped and ran back to the building. He doused the inside with lantern oil, set a piece of paper on fire and tossed it inside. Whatever was under that tarp would not survive an inferno. With the building ablaze the trio made their way down the path.

There was an object in the trail ahead of them, so Patrick stopped pushing the cart. Warily he crept up the path to get a better look at whatever was lying there. It was a carcass of something dead, but there was the same translucent blue hue to the hairless skin as with the moths. He swallowed hard and walked up to the object once he realized it was not breathing or even moving.

He poked at it with a long stick without any result, so he moved in for a closer look. He realized it was not a corpse of something dead rather, it was molted skin. Like a snake that had shed. He stretched the aquamarine-colored skin out until it was flat. Whatever this thing had been, or was, proved to be a menagerie of creatures. In some respects, it looked snake or eel-like, other parts looked like a fish, but it was the arms and legs that disturbed him the most. They resembled human appendages.

"Whatever this creature is, it has grown and shed its skin." Patrick said, running with the cart as fast as his old legs would take them.

72

While pausing for a moment to catch his breath Patrick saw three shadows, a man, a woman, and a child moving quickly through the forest on the other side of the lake. Moving fast as if they were being chased. He thought he recognized the man as one of the consortium laborers. For a brief second both men turned and made eye contact with one another. Against his better judgement Patrick waved the man and his family over to them. There was more than enough room for the man and his family in the bunker. An ominous shadow appeared behind the trio, and they darted off into the shadows leaving Patrick to continue on their own quest for safety.

Patrick was winded from running with the cart once more. Varg padded alongside him glancing up as if the beast wished he could help. The sun was completely gone now, and the only light was from the bruised horizon. The lantern he left burning by the entrance still glowed in beckoning. He wanted to stop and listen, to see if they were being stalked or followed but he didn't dare.

A bowel loosening screech split the night causing Varg to whine and pick up the pace, but he relaxed a bit after a second reverberation, when it revealed whatever was making the noise was a fair distance away and behind them closer to the lake. Even though winded, Patrick kept driving forward. Bonni was being bounced around like a rag doll but kept her criticism to herself. Another scream echoed, this time much closer than the last.

"What in the hell does that thing want?" Patrick asked between breaths.

"Me, I am afraid Mishipeshu wants me," Bonni replied.

"Mishipeshu did all this?"

She shook her head. "No, Mishipeshu is trying to stop this from happening."

Patrick set the cart down and took ten seconds to catch his breath before opening the door to the bunker. Varg padded down in front and disappeared for minute only to reappear as if he made sure the coast was clear. He cradled Bonni in his arms and worked his way down to the second platform before setting her down. He ran back up the stairs and brought the cart down to the first landing before returning to bar the door shut.

It took the better part of fifteen minutes to get Bonni settled onto one of the mattresses he pulled from the bunk beds and laid on the floor.

"This is going to be a one-way trip," he said to the wolf. "Follow me upstairs and I'll let you out. At least you will have a fighting chance up there."

The wolf sat down and looked at him with a measure of sadness.

"How can I make you understand? We are not leaving this place, ever," he said. He tried to pull the animal along, but Varg was having none of it.

Patrick pulled a generous piece of jerked meat from a sack on the pantry shelf and held it out to the wolf. Varg sniffed at it which caused him to drool but when Patrick started up the stairs with it, the animal laid down and whined. They went through this ritual several times before he finally gave in and tossed the wolf the jerky. He turned to start back down when he heard something moving above him. He put his ear as close to the metal door as he could and held his breath. There was definitely someone or something up there trying to open the door.

"Captain? Dimitri? Edgar? Anybody? You have to let me in, it's after me," a man's voice called out.

Before Patrick could even begin to think about responding to him, the man let loose a blood curdling scream then all went quiet. Nearly thirty seconds of stone, cold silence passed before there was a loud thump against the metal barrier. He said a quick prayer for the dead man and quietly made his way back down to the main chamber. He shared the piece of jerky with Varg who chewed on it for a few brief moments and dropped it out of his mouth onto the floor.

"No appetite? I can certainly understand that. And I understand why you opted to stay down here with us. At least down here I think we might have a chance at survival, however slim that may be," Patrick said.

With each passing day Bonni's condition worsened. Both Patrick and Varg ate just enough to stay alive but that was about it. Day after day Patrick sat with his back against the wall, one hand holding Bonni's and the other penning page after page, chronicling the last few weeks on the island. His wife deteriorated day by day and he knew it wouldn't be long before this charade would end. Varg only left their company long enough to patrol the perimeter of the bunker and then he would return to lay at Bonni's feet on the bed. It had been quiet outside for nearly twenty-four hours, so Patrick was contemplating scouting the area outside.

"Patrick," Bonni called out weakly. "You need to leave, now."

Patrick went to his ailing wife's side, knelt beside her, and took her hand in his. He kissed her lightly on the forehead and did his best to ignore the thrashing beneath her blouse.

"I will not leave you," he said with tears flowing down his face.

"You must or you will surely perish."

"Then I perish. I will not leave you to suffer this fate alone."

At that moment, the wolf strode over and sat down beside Patrick. He lifted a paw upon the bed to rest on Bonni's leg. She picked up her Bible and began to read from the New Testament.

"Come to me, all you who are weary and burdened, and I will give you rest. Take my yoke upon you and learn from me, for I am gentle and humble in heart, and you will find rest for your souls. For my yoke is easy and my burden is light," she read.

She read the passage several times, and with each reading the creatures within her belly squirmed and wriggled with more voracity. Setting the Bible aside Bonni began to chant a native song her mother would sing to her when she was just a little girl about hummingbirds, summer flowers and sunshine. She gripped Patrick's hand and they both cried.

The somber mood was shattered when Bonni shrieked in pain and her midsection burst open, spewing a plume of translucent blue fluid over the three of them. Patrick tried to protect the wolf with his body, but Varg howled in pain as its flesh was attacked by the ravenous parasites. Patrick fell to the floor where he writhed in agony but still held the animal close to his chest in death's embrace as they thrashed about in the throes of death. Bonni lay completely still in the bed as she was already dead.

Chapter Ten

Aarne Halla held his daughter's tiny face in his large, dirt encrusted miner's hands while fighting back his tears. The forest resounded with the screams of dying men while his wife Hanna took her last breath at his feet.

"Kukka, my little flower, do not look at her. Do not remember your mother like this," he said, averting his child's eyes away from the mutilated corpse of her mother. "I need you to listen to me very carefully and do exactly what I say."

"But Papa," the little girl started to protest.

"No debates this time, Kukka," her father said as he stroked her fine, golden hair. "You must run. Run as fast as you can and do not look back. Not for anything, do you understand?"

"No, Papa, I won't leave you."

"Child, you must," he said with a measure of panic in his voice. He could hear the creature moving through the forest toward them.

The hair on Aarne's arm began to stand straight up on end and he knew the beast was close. A rucksack with three copper ingots sat at his feet next to his dead wife. A deep, hollow growl rippled through the forest and his stomach fluttered. He was too scared to turn around to find out which of the beasts was stalking him and his family. The ones those damned scientists concocted or the creature from the forest he had yet to see but knew it was there all the same. The creature who seemed to have a desire for the copper they pulled from the bottom of the lake.

Aarne spun slowly around a full three hundred and sixty degrees looking through the trees while listening for the creature's growl. At the moment, regret was his only companion. How he wished he could turn back the clock to his time in the mines at Calumet. That work seemed like child's play compared to this place.

He didn't steal the copper and he sure as hell didn't want it, but he took it thinking he may be able to strike a bargain with it to gain passage off the island. Aarne felt a surge of electrical energy to the north of him and was certain the beast was close. It was time to make a deal with the devil.

"Kukka, listen to your father. The Andersens must have made it to their boat by now and are coming around the west side of the island. They were going to pick us all up, but your mother and I will not be making that trip.

"Papa, I will not leave you," the six, nearly seven-year-old cried in defiance.

"I have already told you, this is not up for debate. Do you remember the cave we found on the beach while looking for shells?"

She nodded her head and sniffled.

"Good. Now, it's over in that direction," her father pointed his arm to the west. "You run as fast as you can, when you get to the beach you find that cave and you stay hidden there until you see the Andersen's boat. Once you see their boat you run down to the water and wave your arms until they see you. You tell them that your mama and your papa are not coming, and they are to get away from the island as fast as they can," he choked through his tightening throat.

"Papa?" Kukka squeaked out. She suddenly understood why her father was so frightened. She also knew why she must obey him.

In front of them the largest cat she had ever seen walked out of the trees and into the small clearing. Kukka was fascinated by the shimmering beast but terrified as well. It glistened beneath the tiny shafts of sunlight beaming through the trees, and lightning bolts sparked along its shimmering body. It snarled at them baring its long fangs causing the creature's nose to wrinkle. Whiskers as thick as her arm swept back from the cat's face as it sniffed at the air. Kukka giggled, the cat was wiggling its rear just like her tabby at home. But her elation quickly turned to horror when she recalled what her tabby did after wiggling its furry behind.

"Kukka, honey, you need to run now," her father said while taking the three ingots of copper from the rucksack and setting them on the ground. "There's some food and water in the bag in case it takes the Andersens a little while longer than expected to get away. You take the sack and run, run to the west," he said as Mishipeshu took several steps toward them.

The beast let loose a terrifying scream that caused Kukka to take to the wind. She ran like she had never run before.

"That's it Kukka, run, run as fast as you can," Aarne called out without even looking at her. He feared that if he looked at his daughter running away then he would go after her. He knew that if he were to do that then the creature would surely follow.

Aarne felt a pinch, and then a tingling in the hand holding a copper ingot. He glanced down to see his hand radiated a peculiar shade of blue, so he held it up closer to his face to see there were tiny little worms wriggling about on his skin, many of which were in the process of burrowing into his flesh.

Mishipeshu sniffed at the air and was saddened to learn this human was tainted which meant he must perish. The creature watched the little girl running through the forest but chose to let her go, the child was not tainted so she would not die this day.

"If this is what you are after, take it," Aarne said, tossing the copper ingots to where the beast stood snarling. "Please don't hurt my little girl," he said with tears flowing down his face.

Suddenly Aarne was knocked to his knees by an internal pain unlike anything he had ever felt before in his life. He glanced down to see his stomach had grown to grotesque proportions and was writhing about as if something were trying to get out. He glanced up at the big cat with confusion in his eyes to see a certain sadness in the beast's expression and he realized his fate was already cast in stone.

Mishipeshu let loose a mournful screech, secured its hind feet, and leapt through the air. Aarne Halla never even had a chance to react. The beast mercifully tore his throat open and severed his spinal cord in one quick motion leaving behind a pile of fine black soot. She picked up the three copper ingots and slid them into a pouch under her scales. She sniffed the air once more, turned toward the west and headed for the beach.

~   ~   ~

Kukka's short little legs pumped as hard and fast as she could manage until she finally collapsed from exhaustion. She heard the big cat's cry and even though she was just a little girl she was smart enough to realize what it meant. She was all alone in a world she barely knew.

The forest was eerily quiet once she caught her breath enough she was no longer gasping and wheezing. She fought the urge to go back to her father with every fiber of her being. She must be strong now, for Papa. Between sobs and breaths, she caught the faintest sound of water and knew she was heading in the right direction.

Fighting against her fatigue she dragged the rucksack along the root strewn deer path toward the sound of the water. She knew animals used the path to go back and forth to get a drink from the lake, so she was in no danger of getting lost. The sun was starting to go down and the forest was getting darker, which actually made it easier for her to find her bearings. She knew the open sky would lead her to the water, but she also knew she needed to be careful she didn't walk off a cliff.

Aarne Halla always wanted a son but was blessed with only the one daughter. From before she was even able to walk her father taught her to be strong and self-sufficient. She was out fishing him by the age of five and killed her first deer with a bow and arrow when she was only six. She never knew it had been her father who had placed the kill shot. There was one thing for certain though, Kukka was a survivor.

By the time she reached the beach the sun had set beyond the horizon and the bruised sky was quickly fading to black under the moonless night. She easily found the cave which offered her a good vantage point of the lake so she would be able to see the Andersen's when they came around Gull Point, but would they be able to see her in this darkness?

Kukka rummaged around in the rucksack her father gave her and set the contents on the sand beside her once she determined what they were according to feel as it was much too dark for her to see much of anything. She took a long drink from the canteen of water and nibbled on one of the butter sandwiches he packed for her. The bread was dry, so she took another drink of water from the canteen and replaced the cork.

With a sense of urgency, she dug through the rucksack looking for the fire-starting kit she knew her father would have packed. The poor child was nearly frozen from the dropping temperature but also from a growing sense of fear. If her father forgot to pack the fire-starting kit, then she would surely freeze to death without heat.

The child felt relieved once her hand touched upon a small tin in the bottom of the rucksack. There were only five matches in the tin with five oil-soaked cotton balls and five long strips of cloth. She went outside of the cave down to the beach and dropped down on all fours. Using her hands to feel around in front of her she found several smaller pieces of driftwood and two large pieces as well. Using one of the smaller sticks she wrapped one oil-soaked cotton ball around the stick using one of the long strips of cloth. Her little fingers were ice cold, so she stuffed them under her armpits to warm them up enough to be able to strike the match against the striker in the tin.

First, she scraped at one of the larger pieces of driftwood with the small pocketknife her father put in the sack for her. She scraped away the wet outer wood until she was able to scrape some dry fibers into a small pile of kindling. She then broke a few of the smaller pieces into sticks and placed them on the pile of kindling. Kukka then carefully struck the match knowing that it would drip molten sulfur on her if she was not mindful of where the head of the match was pointed. The cave, which was more of a small grotto than a cavern, exploded with white light causing her to slam her eyes shut for several seconds. She touched the flame to the cotton ball before it died out and set her kindling stick ablaze. She put the burning ember onto her pile of kindling and within minutes the cave was bathed in the warm glow of a campfire.

The fire was going strong enough that she felt confident she could leave it alone and went back out onto the beach to scrounge up more wood. Making several trips she managed to amass a nice pile of firewood and began to feel less like she was going to freeze to death in the night. But now she was facing an even more immediate problem. She needed to move the fire to the beach somehow or the Andersen's would never see her.

Kukka made her way back out onto the beach and scrounged around until she found a flat piece of driftwood. Using this piece as a tool she dug a small pit and used the excess sand as a windbreak. The process was slow and tedious, her efforts severely hampered by the cold and lack of even the slightest sliver of moonlight. Eventually she managed to dig a deep enough fire pit and returned to the grotto with another armload of driftwood using the glow from her fire as a beacon.

Knowing she would not be using the rucksack again she cut open one of the seams and loaded it up with driftwood and her remaining kindling. She was going to have to maintain two fires, one in the cave for warmth and a signal light on the beach so she planned accordingly and only used enough wood in the rucksack to get the fire started. She knew that once the fire was lit, she would be able to see the beach much better and thus would be able to find more firewood.

After arranging the wood inside the rucksack, she hefted it to make sure it was not too heavy for her to carry. Once satisfied she would be able to move the fire to the beach without burning herself, she scooped out some coals with one of the flat pieces of wood and dumped them into the sack onto the dry wood and kindling. She quickly carried the smoldering bundle outside and placed it into the hole she dug near the water. Within minutes it produced enough flame for her to add more kindling and then finally larger chunks of wood.

Kukka felt much more comfortable once there was a blazing fire on the beach and a modest fire in her cave. The Andersen's would surely be able to see her fire once they rounded Gull Point and headed south. Suddenly she felt ill at ease. What if they didn't head south at all? What if they simply headed west toward the safety of Marquette? She got a sick feeling in her gullet and went back to the cave to get her canteen.

~   ~   ~

Sven Andersen loaded his wife and their six-month-old baby girl onto the small fifteen-foot sailboat before wading back to shore to retrieve the five copper ingots he liberated from the compound. This entire venture had gone sour, and he lost an entire year's wages, a loss he was not willing to accept.

Olga Andersen sat on a small bench seat and leaned against the gunwale of the boat. She had not uttered a word since witnessing the carnage at the campsite. He was both grateful and somewhat envious of her semi-catatonic state. She was much easier to handle than she would be had she been hysterical.

As soon as they were into open water and away from the rocks Sven set sail and steered a course to the west. Guilt tugged him toward the south, but he refused to relent to the useless emotion. Sure, he promised Aarne he would pick up the man and his family but there was no way in hell he was going to risk beaching the boat with monsters roaming the island. Besides, Aarne and his family were probably dead by now anyway.

Once away from the shadow of the cliffs an orange glow hung on the horizon to the east. The compound was ablaze which meant there was no reason for him to head for the southern end of the island. If he headed west, they would surely reach Marquette before daybreak. Once there they could alert the authorities.

Sven was adjusting the sails when an inhuman scream split the darkness. He glanced down at his arms to see every hair standing on end. Spinning around on his heels he caught sight of a massive storm cloud headed at them from out of the north. The storm was moving faster than their boat and would intercept them within minutes. He was forced to adjust course to the south.

~   ~   ~

Kukka was abruptly awakened by howling winds and driving rain. She scrambled for the mouth of the cave and took shelter. Peering up into the night sky confused the child. Stars were out in masse which meant there shouldn't be any storms and yet, lightning flashed all around her.

To make matters worse, the storm doused her signal fire so there would be no way for the Andersen's to know where she was. She clutched herself tightly and began to cry. A little at first, but those tiny tears were enough to burst the dam holding back her fears and she wailed alone in the darkness.

The child was between sobs when she heard a crack of lightning so close she could smell the sizzling ozone in the air. And then she saw the Andersen's boat careening through the rough seas with its jib alight. Kukka ran for the water's edge frantically waving her arms but stopped dead in her tracks. The big cat was following the boat.

The feline serpent slipped beneath the ebony waves and the seas fell silent. The boat was headed straight for a huge rock outcropping, and it was obvious from their tack that their rudder was of no use. Kukka was waist deep in the lake trying to warn Mr. Andersen when the boat struck a submerged boulder and stopped dead in the water catapulting its passengers into the darkness. Mrs. Andersen was the first out of the boat and slammed face first into a rock jutting from the lake. Kukka thought the woman looked like a rag doll as she cartwheeled through the air.

Sven Andersen never made it off the vessel and instead was impaled by a piece of broken mast. Kukka knew they were both dead along with any chance she may have of escaping the island. Dejected, she turned back for the beach and noticed something floating in the water. It was then she remembered the Andersen's had a baby.

Walking the bottom of the lake on her tippy toes Kukka made her way to the rock where Mrs. Andersen lay motionless. Blood ran in streams down the rock and into the water, so the child averted her eyes and tried not to cry. She was forced to climb over the dead woman to get to the bundle on the other side of the rock.

She plucked the soaking wet bundle from the lake and rolled the baby over in her arms. Kukka was amazed to see the baby's chest rise and fall with each breath. She was still alive. But sadly, there was a nasty looking gash from the baby's forehead to just above her ear where her skull had been crushed by the rock.

She turned away from the boulder to start back for the beach when the water began to swirl in front of her. Kukka tried to run, which was near impossible in the neck deep water while carrying an injured baby. The surface of the water broke, and she found herself face to face with the cat creature.

Mishipeshu sniffed at the air. These little ones were no danger. But she smelled the smallest one was gravely injured, and she eased in for a closer look.

Kukka trembled as the giant cat leaned into them, lapped out with its enormous, pink tongue, and licked the baby's wounded skull. Using her nose, she pushed the two children toward the shore and then turned her attention back to the boat. She let out a piercing shriek, slammed her tail down across the boat's midsection and then disappeared beneath the waves to retrieve what was hers.

Part Two

The New Owners

A red and white seaplane circled the cliffs of Grand Island several times before touching down into Murry Bay. On the last pass the pilot tilted the plane on its side so his passengers could get a bird's eye view of the shipwreck Bermuda sitting at the bottom of the bay below. After several long passes the seaplane's pontoons kissed the water with a gentle hiss as the plane glided up to the pier.

Gabe scratched at his two-week-old beard before climbing out of the plane to help the pilot tie her up. His wife Tara was waiting for them on the dock with a picnic basket cradled in her arms.

"You should have come with us mom, it was so cool," Travis, her soon to be teenaged son, claimed as he exited the plane and helped his father unload their baggage.

"She's too chicken. Mom would have screamed when the pilot tipped the plane," Amanda, her youngest and brightest stated with a squeal of laughter in her voice, and her face still flush with excitement.

"Your mother is not scared, she just prefers not to fly," Gabe said in his wife's defense.

"Yeah right, that's just another way of saying she's chicken," the gangly young man said coming up from behind them with an armload of his sister's crap while clucking like a chicken.

Travis referred to himself as a tweener because he was in between just about everything in his life. Between being a boy and a man, between hating girls and loving them, between bubblegum music and rock and roll. He accepted his perspective because it was who he was, but that didn't mean he had to like it. He was already an inch taller than his father's five foot ten but weighed fifty pounds less, so he resembled a male Olive Oyl.

Travis was wearing his father's favorite concert t-shirt from a Pink Floyd show earlier that spring in New York. The show was a big deal to his father, so he tried to embrace it in a show of solidarity. He listened to the album Obscured by Clouds half a dozen times before finally giving up. He would never get that type of music, there were no words in most of the songs and the ones with words he didn't quite understand. The boy was adult enough to reason drugs must have played a part in why people liked the music.

"Travis," Gabe said in a tone of voice that let the boy know to drop it.

A cloud of dust rose from the north as a battered old bus came barreling down the dirt road. The island was a rugged wilderness with limited roadways and anyone wanting a tour of the non-restricted areas could hire good old Mel to show them the sights, but those were few and far between. Mel was pleased to learn the lighthouse had been sold and that a family was moving to the island. Mel's taxi at your service, for a fee of course.

"So, have you been up to see the place yet?" Gabe asked Tara, stroking at his beard trying to sneak in a scratch his wife wouldn't see to avoid another of her patented *I told you so* glances.

"No, I was waiting for you all to arrive while enjoying the gorgeous scenery. Duke stopped on his way up to the lighthouse with another load of lumber. He said he will bring hardware and tools tomorrow. I still cannot believe you bought this place sight unseen," Tara said, her emerald eyes contrasting with her raven hair. She put on a smattering of ruby red lip gloss which completed the ensemble and grabbed her husband's full attention.

"It was a golden opportunity at a great price. Who wouldn't want to live in a lighthouse on an island? I mean, come on, we are going to be living in a lighthouse on the edge of a cliff. It is something out of a romance novel."

"Or a Hitchcock movie."

"And it wasn't quite sight unseen, I did see a photograph of the place."

"A fifty-year-old photo."

"Hush, you are going to love it."

"I will let you know how I feel when the snow starts to fly."

"Tara, you know I rented us a place in Munising for the winter."

Mel's dilapidated, brown, and rust colored bus came to a screeching stop with a hiss of the air brakes causing the rusted-out fender to flap in protest. *Bye Bye Miss American Pie* spilled out of the tri-fold door as the driver, an ancient man with leathery skin, leaned over in his seat and yelled out the open door even though Travis was less than three feet away.

"Mel's taxi at your service. Load her up, I'll take you up to your new house. Your bicycles have already been delivered," Mel, the driver and local tour guide said with a toothy grin. He adjusted his dusty Detroit Tiger's baseball cap that looked tattered and old enough to have been from the nineteen thirty-five World Series.

Gabe and Travis loaded the family's gear into the back of the modified bus and climbed into the passenger compartment with the rest of them. Mel double checked his passengers were all seated before easing the bus away from the docks and back out onto the dirt road heading north. A flock of seagulls ran in front of the bus until finally scattering to the wind, leaving remnants of their disgust at being interrupted all over the hood.

The children craned their necks out the window as the road wound its way around the cliff side to gaze at the aquamarine glow of Lake Superior below. Eventually the road angled away from the lake and toward the interior of the island. Soon the road was merely a two track so tight to the trees it forced the passengers to close the bus windows to keep from being slapped by branches. Travis peered into the deep, dark woods and could not help but wonder what dangers lurked in those shadows. On one hand, the threat of jeopardy was exciting, but on the other he knew they were real, not just something made up in Hollywood. He suddenly felt a sense of duty in protecting his little sister from the perils of the forest. So, he punched her in the arm.

"Ow. Hey! What did you do that for?" Amanda asked, rubbing the newly created sore spot on her bicep. "Mom, Travis hit me," she called out from the back seat.

"Well, what did you do to provoke him?"

Amanda clicked her tongue in disgust and moved all the way to the back of the short bus which was only two seats away from her brother. Travis felt a pang of guilt for hitting his sister harder than he intended. To compensate, he would have to be nice to her for the rest of the day and let her tag along with him regardless of if he wanted her company or not.

"Wow, this road is narrow, what happens if someone is coming from the other direction?" Gabe asked, leaning across the forest green seat to talk to the driver.

"They'd be ghosts I reckon," he said with a grin.

"Ghosts?" Tara asked.

"Nobody alive up here except for you people, and me of course."

"That is comforting," Tara said while tightly gripping her husband's arm.

"Don't mind me, I like to have my fun now and again. I'm driving faster than I should be, but I know there isn't anyone up here but you folks. Duke has already come and gone. And once the construction is over, there won't be anyone up here at all but you folks on this side of the island."

"That is what I was counting on, peace and quiet," Gabe said.

Gabe worked as a professor as well as being a published author working on several new projects, so he was always busy. Tara was an elementary school science teacher, so she was busy as well. Both were so caught up in their careers and lives they didn't realize they were not spending as much quality time with Amanda as they should be. It was not intentional; it was just a fact of life so Travis tried to step in as much as he could. But he was still just a boy himself no matter how much he would argue that fact to the adults.

A crystalline droplet slid from the corner of Amanda's eye and even though it tickled like crazy she was not about to wipe it off and give her brother the satisfaction even though she knew she overreacted, and her brother hadn't hit her as hard as she made it seem. In fact, it didn't even hurt. What hurt was that her mother didn't even pay attention to her cry for help. She was peering out the window when she spied movement three trees deep into the woods.

"Who was that?" she called out.

"What are you talking about?" Travis asked.

"There was someone out there in the woods, watching us."

"There is no one out there honey, it was just a reflection off the bus window," her father said in a comforting tone.

"It wasn't a reflection. I know what a reflection looks like. Someone was watching us."

"Mandy, there is no one out there, it's just your imagination," her mother added.

"You always say that, it's just your imagination, Mandy," the child said in a mocking tone. Under her breath she finished. "I'm almost eight years old. I know the difference between a reflection and a real person."

She moved to the other side of the bus and turned her back on her family. They were all cretins, every last one of them.

Mel turned his head and whispered, "I don't want to spook her, be she might be right, the islanders might be a little curious about their new neighbors and were just trying to steal a peek."

"Aren't they all way over on the western side of the island?" Gabe asked.

"Even though this island is more than twenty square miles, it is only a few miles wide and a bored teenager can make that hike in a couple of hours, even faster on bicycles. Whoever it was your daughter saw out there, I can assure you, they are harmless."

"I guess you're right," Gabe said with a smile. "Anyone else living on this island I should know about?"

"There is an old woman who lives in the forest at the southern end of Echo Lake. It is near impossible to get to her on account of there being no roads, not even a two track near her place. And she never leaves her property. Hell, I bet it has been more than two years since I laid eyes on her. For all I know she could have died in that old, decrepit cabin of hers," Mel explained.

"Died!" Amanda blurted out and leaned over the bus seat with her arms crossed and her eyes bulging wide. "Someone died in these woods?"

"No honey, no one died. I think Mr. Mel was just exaggerating," Tara said while giving the bus driver the evil eye.

"Your mother is right. I was just poking fun. There is nothing to worry about. Hey, I left a two-way radio and a charger in your kitchen. No telephones out here so it's the only way to contact me. There is also a radio to contact the Coast Guard with as well. But don't go calling them for a ride to the docks, from experience I can tell you they get pretty agitated about that," Mel laughed and cranked the wheel hard.

The bus pulled up the horseshoe driveway and continued around to the western exit before squealing to a stop. Seeing her new home for the first-time left Tara feeling a little underwhelmed. Gabe helped her out of the bus with an apologetic smile.

The concrete steps leading up to the front door were crumbled and there was a wooden plank laid across them to bypass their deterioration. The makeshift walkway was near useless because once at the top of the plank one still had to navigate a front door that hung cockeyed from one hinge. There were two small windows on the right front side and one larger one on the left. For all the good the windows did they were slightly more than useless. The glass was milky and streaked with decades old cobwebs blocking any light that may want to enter.

"I am not sleeping in that place, it's creepy," Amanda said, dropping her bag at her feet.

"Cool, we're going to live in a . . .," Travis stopped midsentence as a result of his father's sideways glance.

There were piles of brown paint chips at the base of each of the windows, undoubtedly the remnants of what were once storm shutters. The weeds, although dead, were waist high and six inches deep all the way around the building.

"What does that trail lead to?" Travis asked.

"It leads out to the utility shed and then further out to the cliffs."

"Cool, I bet the view is awesome from there."

"I don't want you kids wandering out there alone, either of you. The stairs are dilapidated and unsafe not to mention the cliff edge could be unstable. You saw all the boulder sized rocks in the water, well, they were once part of these cliffs. They could let loose without warning at any given moment, and you would plummet to the bottom."

"I got it dad, stay away from the cliffs. We didn't need a lecture," Travis said and went around to the back of the bus to carry another bag around.

Travis spotted a freshly mowed path one mower width leading from the driveway around to the back of the house, so he went to explore while his parents were, in their words, debating. His sister Amanda was right about one thing, this place sure was creepy. While in some ways that excited him, he still couldn't shake the foreboding appearance the lighthouse presented. To make matters worse there were dark clouds forming on the horizon and rolling toward them across the water. It looked as though their first night in this place was going to be a stormy one.

"Trav, I don't like this place," Amanda said coming up from behind him clutching her Scooby Doo plush doll firmly to her chest which was a clear indicator she was truly upset. Her clothes were all twisted so he knelt down and straightened her t-shirt for her.

He quickly shed off the startling she gave him and shot her a smile. "Hey, squirt, I'm sorry about that punch earlier. I didn't mean to hit you that hard."

"It's okay, it wasn't that hard anyway. You hit like a girl," she said with a sniffle. "I mean it, I don't like this place."

"I know it looks creepy right now, but it will look a lot better once the builders get it fixed up and painted."

"I wish they would have done all that before we got here."

"Me too, Mandy. Me too. There's a side door over here, help me get all of our bags inside."

The two of them went about the task of bringing the family's belongings from the bus to the side door but neither of them wanted to go in by themselves so they waited until all the bags were at the door before moving them inside together.

Gabe walked his wife out to the cliffs for a bird's eye view of Lake Superior. Tara could not help but be impressed with the scenery. However, she was a lot less enthralled with the rickety staircase zig-zagging down the cliff face to the water. Or to be exact, to twenty feet from the water because the last sections had collapsed into the lake some time ago. Down below a pair of seagulls shared a joke while a channel buoy's bell chimed in.

Distant crickets began to announce the arrival of sunset as the couple stood in awe of nature's glory. A radiant golden globe slowly descended on the horizon, moving faster and faster as it neared the boundary line until it was nothing more than a pea sized orange glow. A bruised orange blanket with streaks of angry purple pulled itself up over the sky while the brewing storm threatened to erase the canvas.

"It's not as bad as it looks," he said as they turned around and headed back up the trail toward the lighthouse hand in hand.

"It couldn't possibly be worse than it looks," Tara responded, trying not to sound too disappointed.

"You have to admit one thing," Gabe said, easing her around the side of the house where there was a clear view of Pictured Rocks off in the distance.

"Yeah, what's that?"

"The view is to die for."

Chapter Nine

Fireflies danced across the open field in front of the lighthouse. Gabe busied himself with lighting a campfire while Tara and the kids watched the trailing remnants of the sunset over the lake. Seagulls cried from the rocks below adding to the concerto of the night. The children's eyes lit up when they saw a small picnic table next to the fire jam packed with the makings of s'mores and hobo pies.

"I want cherry," Amanda said, reaching for the can of cherry pie filling and the box of graham crackers.

First, she put two generous teaspoons of butter into each side of the hobo pie iron, then she grabbed as many crackers as her tiny fists could hold and crumbled them on top of the butter. Two big dollops of cherry pie filling into each side completed the masterpiece. She closed the pie iron with the two long handles and clipped it closed. Before lighting the fire, Gabe stabbed several Y shaped branches into the dirt strategically placed around the fire pit, so Amanda carefully placed her pie iron into the crook of the branch and slid it slowly into the perfect position over the hot coals. She walked back over to the picnic bench and turned the dial on the egg timer for five minutes.

Tara opted for an apple filled hobo pie while Travis was content with a gooey, molten marshmallow laden s'more dripping with melted chocolate. Gabe popped the cork on a bottle of Riesling and poured two generous glasses, handing one to his wife. With the setting of the sun the night cooled off considerably, so the campfire felt that much more luxurious. Gabe looked around him and smiled, this was just what the doctor ordered.

Tara took a long drink of her wine and said, "Travis, could you please take your sister out and help her with her science project tomorrow?"

"Science project? But mom, it's summer," Amanda protested by crossing her arms over her chest. She was a comical sight in her brother's Groovie Goolies T-shirt that was many sizes too big for her. It was hard for Tara to maintain a straight face and austere demeanor when she wanted to pick her daughter up and hug her.

"Mandy, you know I want you to get three projects done over the course of the summer so you might as well get one of them done right away rather than procrastinate like you usually do."

"But mom, what does it matter if my homework is late, you can excuse me."

"I will not give you an excuse which is all the more reason to hand your work in on time. Besides, I hear your new teacher is a real stickler for the rules and I am sure she will not be playing favorites."

"I hear her new teacher is a real fire-breathing dragon," Travis remarked drawing a warning glance of *drop it* from his father.

"But mom, you're my new teacher, we're being homeschooled this year."

"So then let's get off on the right foot, shall we," Gabe interjected. "We're going to spend the entire year together working and studying without any interruptions, isn't that great?"

"I for one am really looking forward to no friends all year long," Travis said with a drawn-out sigh.

"You know your father is exaggerating, you are going to have friends to spend time with. Aside from the locals here on the island we're going to winter in Munising where there are plenty of children your age," Tara said, unpinning her hair and letting her long, dark locks fall down around her shoulders.

"I am not a child mother, I don't play with my friends," Travis said, got up from the fire, and stormed toward the lighthouse.

"Where are you going, Travis?" his father asked.

"I'm getting our tents. Mandy and I want to sleep outside since it looks like the storm has passed us by and it's going to be a nice night."

"Or is it because you two are too scared to sleep inside?" Tara prodded.

"Go ahead and laugh mom, but you didn't see the size of the spiders in there," Amanda said, concealing her devilish grin.

"And I swear I saw a rat when I put the food in the kitchen," Travis added, earning a soft punch of approval from his sister.

Tara's expression suddenly changed, and Gabe found himself having to stifle his laughter. He knew the kids were just jerking her chain, but it is what they did, and they did it to perfection. She turned to look at him through the undulations of the campfire and he shook his head vehemently back and forth. She was not sure who to believe and contemplated grabbing her own sleeping bag.

Once he was able to dispense with his sister's assistance, putting up the tents went much smoother. Within fifteen minutes Travis set both tents up and their bedding inside so he and Amanda returned to the campfire for another s'more.

"How many does that make?" Tara asked.

He shrugged.

"Well?"

"I don't know I wasn't keeping count."

"Last one," she said.

He shrugged again.

"Hey, where is the bathroom?" Amanda asked, rocking back and forth on the balls of her feet.

Gabe shined his flashlight over toward a small, ominous building tucked within the shadows fifty feet from the main house. "It is over there honey."

Amanda stood in the darkness with a look of confusion on her face, which was made worse by the flickering flames. She crossed her legs and started to bounce up and down.

"Daddy, I'm not kidding. I really have to go."

"I'm not kidding either, it's over there. Take a flashlight with you."

"And watch out for the crap monster hiding in the hole," Travis said.

"Gabriel, an outhouse? You didn't tell me this place does not have a bathroom," Tara said.

"Tara, it's just for a couple of days, three at the most before the contractors can get the plumbing working again. Come on, it will be fun."

"Yay, let's all take a dump into a deep, dark hole while fighting off spiders, and smelling hundred-year-old poo. It'll be fun, said no one ever," Travis shot back.

"Travis, don't you start. In fact, go with your sister and make sure there are no spiders in there before she goes in."

"Spiders? Can't I just go number one in the bushes?" Amanda squeaked.

"Spiders, Gabe? Really?"

"Come on, squirt," Travis said, taking his little sister by the hand and leading her through the shadows to the outhouse on the perimeter of the property.

Gabe gathered another armload of wood and checked on the tents to make sure Travis put them up correctly. He was a fine young man, but he sometimes liked to take shortcuts when it came to certain tasks, setting up the tents was one of them. He staked them both down, something Travis neglected to do. The winds on the cliffs could turn them into kites in the right conditions and he had no desire to have his children plummeting off the island on their first night.

"I was going to do that, dad," Travis said, walking hand in hand with his sister back to the tents. He took the rubber mallet away from his father and finished pounding in the tent stakes.

"I'm sure you were son. I just didn't want you to forget. The wind can get dangerous and unpredictable up here."

Travis lost all desire to argue with his father. His stomach hurt from that last s'more, and he wanted nothing more than to lay down.

"Holy shit!" Travis cried out.

"Travis Michael! Watch your language," Tara said.

"Something just hit me."

"Something hit you? What are you talking about?" Gabe asked. "Was it a bug maybe?"

"Whatever it was, was a lot bigger than a bug."

"Maybe it was a Phyllophaga, they can get pretty big," Tara said.

"A phyllo what?"

"A June bug."

"Mom, can't you just be normal once in a while instead of being Mrs. Science all the time," Travis laughed, his heart still pounding.

"Over there, something flew right by me too," Amanda said and ran over to her father.

Gabe gathered his frightened horde under his wing while scanning the night skies. He felt like his eyes were playing tricks on him and every single shadow was moving. And then he saw the source of their dilemma.

"Bats. They must be drawn to the bugs attracted by the campfire. They're harmless."

"Yeah, tell that to Lucy Westenra," Travis said.

"Lucy who?" Tara asked.

"From Dracula."

"What's a Dracula?" Amanda asked with wide eyes. She wasn't sure who or what it was, but since it had to do with bats, she was sure she wouldn't like it.

"Now who can't be normal Mr. Creepshow," Gabe said with a gentle nudge.

They spent the next half an hour watching the bats, or at least attempting to watch them as they swooped through the starlit sky. Amanda fell asleep so Tara carried her over to her tent and gently tucked her in.

"Holy shit!" she cried out as she turned back for the campfire.

"Tara Marie! Watch your language, there are children present," Travis said, mocking his mother.

As white as a porcelain doll she stood staring at the lighthouse with an outstretched arm pointing up to the lantern room.

"Honey, what is it?" Gabe asked.

She simply pointed up at the lighthouse tower where a man stood looking down on them. A light in the cupola was backlighting him lending a freakish glow to his face.

"Who in the hell is that?" Travis asked.

Gabe laughed and waved up at the man who waved back. "That, my dear, is Mr. Paul Rainbird. He's working on painting a mural inside the cupola of the lighthouse tower."

"You could have warned me," Tara said with a swat. "I nearly peed myself."

"I'm sorry honey. I didn't realize he was still here. I assumed he went back to the mainland for the weekend."

"Who in the hell is *he*?"

"Paul Rainbird, I told you about him. I served with him in Vietnam before I got wounded and sent home. He served another tour, but we ran into each other again at Woodstock of all places. You should remember that," Gabe said.

"I do remember Woodstock, do you?"

"Cute. I ran into him a few weeks ago at the cultural center in Marquette when I was up here scheduling the remodel with Duke, and we got to talking so I invited him to the island."

"Okay, that explains who he is, but why is he here?"

"Like I said, he is painting a mural for me in the work study up in the lantern room. He must have been working late and lost track of time. I told him he could stay with us instead of taking the ferry back and forth to the mainland every day."

"And just how much of this paint project is coming out of your book advance?"

"Nothing. Absolutely zero."

"What's the catch?" she asked.

"The catch is that we allow him to do some archeological digging in the forest with some of his students. He promised we won't even know he's here."

Paul Rainbird came down from the tower and made his way over to the campfire. Tara's first impression of the man was that he just left a peace protest. He wore a fringed buckskin jacket with a peace sign made from multicolored beads over the breast pocket. Across the back shoulders of the jacket was the phrase *98% fewer cavities with sex.* He was a rugged looking man with hard eyes, undoubtedly from his experiences in the war, but he was handsome underneath the rough exterior. He wore long, black hair, longer than Tara's which was braided into one long braid in the back. His face was splotched with earthen tones of paint. He reached his hand out to her with a big smile and dark, sparkling eyes.

"As much as I would love to stay and listen to you hippies ramble on about Woodstock for the next two hours, I'm exhausted," Travis said and disappeared behind the zip of his tent's door flap.

"Paul Rainbird. And you must be Tara, Gabe has told me so much about you. I apologize if I startled you," he said, offering his hand.

"A little, I will admit," Tara said. "We did meet once, a while back though it was a hazy weekend which seems like decades ago."

"Ah, yes, you were the chick at Woodstock."

"Yes, I was *the* chick," Tara said.

"Sorry, I guess I lost track of time and fell asleep while painting."

"How is the mural coming along?" Gabe asked.

"Quite well actually. I have Mishipeshu almost finished. I'll be starting on the Wiindigoo tomorrow."

"Fantastic."

"What is Mishipeshu?" Tara asked.

"Mishipeshu is a native legend of the lake, a water panther sort of like the Loch Ness Monster in Scotland I suppose, though no one has been able to capture the drenched cat in a grainy, highly suspect photograph as of yet," Paul explained with a chuckle.

"And just what does this Mishipeshu do?"

"According to legend, quite simply put, he protects copper under the lake."

"Protects if from who? And how does he protect it?"

"From anyone who wants to steal it I suppose. And those who are foolish enough to attempt the larceny are torn asunder by violent storms created by the copper tail of the beast," Paul explained.

"That sounds lovely. And Wiindigoo?" Tara said, unable to erase the sarcasm from her voice.

"Well, dear, that would be another native legend, but this one is a bit more sinister and involves a man-eating beast. It is one of the traditional stories I hope to learn more about. I sometimes question whether it is purely a myth born of a necessity to control certain behaviors not unlike many parables in the Bible or a living creature fabricated from the evil deeds of men."

"Behaviors such as?" Tara asked.

"Honey, are you sure you want to know about this stuff?" Gabe said with a poke which earned him a sour glance from his wife.

"Many of the tribes engaged in cannibalism, especially consuming their enemies after a battle to absorb their powers."

"That is disgusting and barbaric," Tara said.

"To an outsider, yes, I suppose it does seem that way. But for them, at that time, it was perfectly normal behavior, even celebrated behavior. Try not to judge people's past behavior by present day standards, it's not fair to either party."

"I'll bet the families of those eaten would have a much different perspective on the matter," Tara said.

"I believe this practice eventually lost favor amongst many people in many of the tribes, enough so that it became frowned upon by the majority. I believe this is when, in their infinite wisdom, the elders created the wiindigoo as a means to curb cannibalistic behavior by threatening practitioners with a fate far worse than death. While I wish to believe it's purely a work of fiction the fact remains that many peoples hold the same beliefs and myths. Tribes in the Pacific Northwest have a similar beast called a wechuge," Paul said.

"And all of this is going to be represented in the lighthouse tower?" Tara asked.

"Inspiration honey. You do know I'm writing horror fiction this go around," Gabe said.

"Writing it and living with it are two different things altogether. If you didn't want me in your writer's nook you should have just said so," she said with a smile.

"Come on up and take a look," Paul offered and headed for the door which led to the tower entrance.

The three of them climbed the spiral staircase up into the lantern room of the lighthouse which was much roomier now that the contractors removed the Fresnel lens and mechanics of the lamp. There was lumber laid out in piles on the deck around the room. In the center was a scaffolding that Paul was using to paint the interior dome of the cupola. The cupola was divided into four equal panels painted with a base coat of pitch black, one of which showcased the famed and quite colorful water panther which was near completion. The other bore a charcoal sketch of a mythical beast that Tara was not too keen on seeing in its finished state. The other two panels were still blank.

"I think I have reserved those for a rendition of Pukwudjininees due to the fact you are surrounded by forests. They are a lot like elves, sprites, leprechauns, fairies, pesky but good natured. And then Mishi-Ginebig, the great water serpent."

"So, more pleasantries," Tara said.

"Every religion and every culture enjoy a host of their own demons," Paul smiled.

"Come on out here onto the widow's walk," Gabe said, while opening the door and guiding his wife's head down and under the metal angle iron above the three-foot-tall hatch. He used his hand to keep her from banging her head on the low hanging transom.

"I will admit, this view is stunning," Tara said.

The smell of fresh paint hung in the air and the iron fixtures shone in the moonlight. The big dipper hung so large in the sky it felt as though one could reach out and grab the handle. The forest behind them was thick and still as there was not much of a breeze. Tara was in love with the view already.

"Sad though, isn't it?" she asked.

"What's sad about it?"

"That it's called a widow's walk. Women waiting for their mariners to return home, hoping their men's lives hadn't been claimed by the sea. Romantic, but tragic."

The trio wandered back down the spiral staircase and out to the campfire where the gentle snores of the children mingled with the melody of the night. The dense forest was ominous and foreboding in the diminished light and Tara felt a slight shiver, so she moved closer to the fire. A woman's scream split the night causing her to drop her wine glass.

"What in the hell was that?"

Paul laughed. "That was a red fox, a female from the sounds of it."

"What is wrong with her? Is she caught in a trap?" Tara asked, suddenly more concerned than frightened.

"No honey, she is just horny," Gabe said. "That is the shriek of response to a randy male fox. Soon we will have all sorts of little foxes running around here getting into the chickens."

"So, what happened to you two at Woodstock? Last thing I remember was singing along to Santana and then you two just disappeared," Paul asked, passing a newly lit joint to Tara.

"Mr. Party Animal here passed out just after Carlos finished Evil Ways and didn't wake up again until Leslie West started rocking," Tara said, taking a toke and passing the bowl to Gabe.

"In my defense, I drove us there, I was tired."

They spent the next half hour chatting about 'Stock and passing Paul's pipe around their tight circle.

"Mommy."

"What is it Mandy, dear?" she asked while trying not to laugh. The wine was good and the weed even better.

"I think there's a skunk by my tent and I have to go potty."

The three of them could not contain their laughter.

"What is so funny about me having to go pee?"

"Nothing squirt, come on, let's go. I'll make sure the skunk doesn't get you," Travis said and turned on his flashlight before leading his sister to the outhouse, stopping long enough to shoot a disapproving glance in his parents' direction.

Paul thought it best to put the bowl away and soon they ran out of conversation. The bottle of wine was drained and shortly after, their wine glasses were empty as well. Paul grabbed his bedroll and rolled it out by the fire while Gabe checked on the kids before taking his wife into the house. Tara had just enough of a buzz going that she would be able to fall asleep in her newly acquired haunted abode. Gabe tucked her in and headed back outside.

"So, how heavy is it?" Gabe asked, staring into the fire while finishing his drink.

"How heavy is what?"

"That Navy Cross."

"You heard about that, huh?"

"I saw a newspaper article in the Navy Times that listed recipients. I saw your name."

"It was no big deal," Paul said.

"The Navy Cross is a huge deal," Gabe countered.

"Yeah, well I only get to wear the medal because I'm the one who managed to survive," he said. He rolled over and away from his friend to effectively put an end to the discussion.

Gabe swallowed the last of his drink and called it a night.

Chapter Ten

The entire house smelled of sizzling bacon, maple and freshly brewed coffee, rousting Tara from a deep and restful sleep. She wandered out to the kitchen to find her houseguest and young daughter hard at work preparing breakfast. Amanda looked adorable standing on her tiptoes to check the eggs in the pan.

"Paul, did you just pour maple syrup on those eggs?" she asked.

"I did not pour, I drizzled, and it's not syrup, it's sap," Paul responded, his buckskin jacket having been replaced for a flour sack white shirt that hung on him like drapery.

"So, yes, you did just pour maple syrup on sunny side up eggs," she said, pouring herself a cup of coffee from the percolator on the counter which gurgled in protest.

Paul eased the dozen eggs out of the pan onto a platter and handed it to Amanda who struggled to get it to the table but still refused her mother's help. He set a plate of bacon on the table and drizzled maple sap across the

116

top of the meat. A plate of fried bread rounded out the feast. Tara picked up a piece of the irregularly shaped bread and gave it the once over.

"It smells delicious," she said.

"Zaasakokwaan, a childhood favorite of mine. I haven't made any for several years, so I thought what better way to share some of my heritage with my new extended family."

She took a bite. "Oh, my, that is much tastier than it looks."

"The rugged appearance is part of the charm. It beats Trenary toast any day of the week."

Gabe wandered into the kitchen and poured himself a cup of coffee followed closely by Travis who stood in the doorway of the kitchen rubbing the sleep from his eyes.

"Did I hear a woman scream last night?" he asked, eliciting a snap of his sister's head who trailed behind her brother while dragging her Winnie the Pooh blanket behind her.

"No, you did not hear a woman's scream. According to your father it was a horny fox."

"Mother, please."

"What does horny mean?" Amanda asked.

"It means . . . "

"Travis, have some breakfast," his father interjected before the boy could get started with some cockamamie explanation for his sister that would leave her even more confused.

Everyone but Paul sat stunned as a diminutive elderly woman shuffled into the kitchen, fixed herself a plate of eggs, bacon, and a piece of zaasakokwaan, doubling back for a second piece of bread before disappearing out the front door of the lighthouse. Tara stood at the window with a smile as the elderly woman glided out into the center of the yard, sat down cross legged in the grass to enjoy her breakfast.

"Paul? Who is she?" Tara asked, not turning away from the window.

The woman waved her arms toward the heavens like seaweed undulating in the currents while repeating the same phrase. While she might not have folded her hands in prayer or thanked the Lord Tara sensed her ritual held the same meaning. As soon as she was finished with her sacrament she began to eat, sharing her meal with any critter who happened along, mostly ants and seagulls.

"Oh, I apologize, I meant to say something last night, but I forgot. I hope you don't mind but I brought my aunt to help with the murals and also to consult on any artifacts I might find out in the forest. I wanted to ensure authenticity when painting our legends."

Tara shrugged and started in on her own breakfast. While there was not a lot of conversation during the remainder of breakfast there was a lot of lip smacking. Travis gathered up everyone's plates and put them in the sink to wash later when there was running water.

"Man, this stuff is way better than," he paused. "You said you're sticking around all summer, right?" Travis asked, picking at the scraps of fried bread in the cast iron skillet.

"Travis, you mind your manners," Tara laughed. "Although, I must admit Paul, those were the best eggs I think I have ever eaten."

"Why thank you, but the credit all goes to my ancestors. I'm simply keeping their long-held traditions alive."

As if on cue the contractors pulled up out in front of the lighthouse with a load of lumber and bathroom fixtures so Gabe went out to speak with the foreman to get a timeline when his wife and daughter would be appeased with an indoor potty arrangement. Paul poured a cup of coffee and headed for the lantern room to continue his painting while Tara and the kids busied themselves with Amanda's science project. Amanda gathered up her butterfly net and a Miracle Whip jar with the label peeled off. Travis punched a half a dozen holes in the top with the awl in his multi-functional pocketknife with one red plastic side missing. Out in the yard she unscrewed the lid and threw a handful of grass into the bottom before screwing the lid back on. They were headed for the perimeter of the forest when Gabe called out to them.

"Hey, Travis, if you go into the woods make sure to mark the trail."

"I know the drill, I've got the ribbon," he said, holding a spool of pink ribbon high above his head while wagging it back and forth.

The yard and meadow area of the lighthouse were large but wide open with not much butterfly enticing flora, so Travis and Amanda exhausted their butterfly hunting territory within the hour. Mel, the bus driver, and tour

119

guide extraordinaire had given Travis a crudely drawn map of the area surrounding the lighthouse which showed another larger clearing to the south. A hike through the woods seemed like a perfectly harmless idea to him, not so much to his little sister.

"I don't like it in here," Amanda said after they travelled less than fifty yards into the dense forest.

"Look, according to the map there's a clearing not too far from here. I know you're scared but look, you can see all the pink ribbons I have tied to the trees leading back to the house so there's nothing to worry about," he said while tying another three-inch strip of pink ribbon to a pine bough.

Travis was quiet and somber as they walked, he was trying to commit the terrain to memory as best he could. He would never admit it to his little sister, but he was spooked as hell himself. The forest was a lot denser than he expected and he knew if they got turned around, they could be in serious trouble. The trees and trail both narrowed to a path barely wide enough for the two of them to walk abreast. Several times the trail disappeared under a layer of dead leaves and brown pine needles, and they were forced to stop and investigate before being able to pick up the trail again. His pride drove him on ahead of his common sense.

"Travis, what kind of a fox has horns? I've never seen a picture of a fox with horns," Amanda said.

It took him several moments to catch his breath from laughing before he could respond. "It is just adult humor, ignore it."

"Adults are weird. A fox with horns, who ever heard of anything so preposterous."

Finally, after what seemed like hours of hiking, they came to a clearing that opened into a large meadow filled with patches of wildflowers. He tied extra ribbons around the place where they exited the woods so they wouldn't lose the trail back as the entire perimeter of the paddock looked identical. There was not a single rock, stump, overly large tree nor any other natural landmark to set the trees apart from one another.

Travis and his sister spent close to an hour searching the large meadow for butterflies but didn't see a single winged creature despite the cornucopia of spring blossoms. Travis found this odd and started to pay more attention to his surroundings. There was something not sitting right with him. It was too quiet. Deathly quiet.

"Travis," Amanda whispered.

"Why are you whispering?"

"There is something watching us," she whispered even softer.

"What are you talking about, Mandy?"

"Over there in the trees, I saw something flash," she said as she bobbed her head toward the tree line.

Travis tried to play nonchalant and pretended to be searching for bugs while keeping an eye on the area his sister indicated. It was several minutes before she was proven right, there was someone watching them from the woods. Continuing with his ruse he circled himself and Amanda closer to the person in the woods. His heart was thumping against his breastbone and there was a little voice in his head screaming at him to run but his pride prevented him from listening to it. How could he run away in front of his little sister?

"We can see you. What, are you some kind of peeping Tom pervert?" Travis called out, his voice betraying his apprehension.

"Yeah, we're not scared of you. My big brother will kick your butt," Amanda added to Travis' chagrin.

From out of the shadows two yellow-haired boys emerged into the clearing pushing two pedal bikes. The first to show himself was on a brand-new Schwinn Manta-Ray wearing a Natasha Fatale plastic Halloween mask while the older of the two, wearing Boris Badenov, rode out of the woods on his Sting-Ray complete with a shock absorbing seat and a stick shift dead center on the frame of the Apple Krate red bike. Travis was immediately jealous, and a little more nervous upon seeing their stalkers. There was something creepy about the masks they wore and not just because it was months before Halloween.

The larger of the two yellow-haired boys walked over to where Travis was standing with his chest puffed out and his fists balled up at his sides. He flipped his mask up to the top of his head, his piercing blue eyes filled with challenge. He smelled of Hai Karate cologne, the green kind that smelled of lime, the one that Travis hated.

"So, your big sister is going to kick my butt is she," he mocked Amanda's voice while his crystal blue eyes flashed a hint of ill intentions.

"He's not my sister, he's my brother," she puffed her chest out as well while Travis tried to shrink back into the shadows.

"How could we tell with that girly hair of his?" The smaller one asserted his dominance knowing he had more than adequate back up. The tough guy façade was not convincing coming from a bungling female Russian spy.

They reached an impasse in which the four of them stood in the center of the meadow staring each other down. Travis was not the fighting type so he ignored their insults as best he could and offered none of his own as to not fuel an already lit fire. Amanda on the other hand possessed no filter when it came to precarious situations and offered more than enough sass for the both.

"You are those new kids at the lighthouse, aren't you?" the older one asked, relaxing his demeanor a slight touch.

"Yes, so what of it?" Amanda stomped.

"You do know it's haunted, right?" the younger boy said, lifting his mask to reveal a sneer greasing his lips.

Amanda's aggressive posture was all but erased. "Haunted?"

"Yep, full of ghosts."

"There's no such thing as ghosts," she argued.

"Better hope your family doesn't disappear like the last people who lived there," the boy taunted while making spooky noises.

"There is no such thing as ghosts," she reiterated with a sniffle, wiping her tears away with her shirt tail.

"If ghosts don't scare her just wait until she meets up with the witch of Echo Lake, huh Greg," his older brother Frederico said.

"Witch?" Amanda squeaked. "Like in Hansel and Gretel?"

"Just like that story. She eats lost little children too," Greg said in a spooky voice forcing Amanda to wipe tiny tears from her eyes.

"Come on, fellas, she's just a kid. Don't scare her," Travis finally spoke up.

"What are you going to do about it?" The older boy stepped up so that he was chest to chest with Travis. Travis turned his head slightly in an effort to not make eye contact. "I didn't think so," he said, shoving Travis back with both of his hands.

Travis kept his balance despite the hard shove. His chest hurt but he refused to rub it and give the bully any satisfaction.

"Come on, Greg, let's leave these girls to play by themselves," the older boy said, turning his bicycle around and pedaling hard for the tree line with his little brother in tow.

Travis' heart sank and near panic set in when he noticed a handful of pink ribbons dangling from the boy's back pocket. To make matters worse, the sun started its downward arc over the tree line.

Chapter Eleven

The children wandered the perimeter of the meadow that ringed the forest for nearly an hour under the guise of Amanda's quest for butterflies, and Travis was starting to get extremely nervous. He lost all sense of direction and every single deer trail leading into the forest looked identical. He even lost track of where the two boys rode their bikes into the woods. Eventually he was going to have to tell his sister the ribbons had been taken down and they could be lost.

"Travis, I'm hungry let's go home," Amanda said. Immediately she recognized the look on her brother's face and uneasiness set in. "What's wrong?"

"Listen squirt, I don't want you to be scared but those boys took our trail marking ribbons, so I'm not really sure which way we came out of the woods and into this clearing."

"We're lost?"

"We're not lost. I'm just not sure which way we came in yet. I have to get my bearings straight. Look, we have a good four hours before it gets dark, probably more," he said, holding his hand four fingers deep up to the base of the sun and measuring down.

"That only works when dad does it. His hands are a lot bigger than yours. I don't want to be in these woods after dark," she said on the verge of tears.

Travis reached into his pocket and pulled out his compass. The lighthouse was on the northeast quadrant of the island so all they needed to do was follow a path that led in that direction. The problem was that most of these deer trails zig zagged back and forth, some even crossing one another several times.

"What is that thing?" Amanda asked.

"It's called a compass."

"What does it do?"

"It tells me which direction is north which then tells me where the lighthouse is," he explained.

"Is it supposed to be spinning around in circles like that?" she asked, scrunching up her face.

"Unfortunately, no. There must be a lot of iron in the ground here, it's messing with the needle."

"What are we going to do?"

"No tears squirt. We'll just pick the widest path and maybe once we are inside the forest we'll get away from the vein of iron and the compass will start working again. Those boys didn't have enough time to take down all of our ribbons so all we need to do is find one and we'll be able to find our way back to the trail."

Travis saw that the sun dipped in the sky indicating which direction was west. He led his sister into the dusky forest, checking the compass every so often. His instincts were right, after a hundred yards of walking the compass needle settled down and gave him a direction to follow which seemed to be accurate as the sun was hanging over his left shoulder so they must be travelling north. Now the trick was, how far off the path were they and would they know when they were on their way home. With his sister sniffling beside him he felt an overwhelming sense of duty to get her home safely. He wasn't sure if he would have been as brave as she was being when he was her age.

Travis was walking with his head down, paying attention to the compass when suddenly the ground gave way under foot. His leg punched a hole in the earth, and he dropped straight down to his crotch. He yelped in pain as his delicate pubescent organs slammed into the hard-packed ground.

"Travis, are you okay?"

He waved his sister off while trying to catch his breath.

"Did you break your jewels?" she couldn't help but laugh. She didn't get her own joke, but she heard him and his friends talking while playing in the yard. They all laughed when one of the boys got hit between the legs, so she took the opportunity to slip in a taunt of her own.

He simply nodded and waved her away again. Five minutes passed before he was able to catch his breath and extract himself from the hole. As soon as his leg pulled free of the fissure a stream of iridescent blue moths flooded out through the opening. They glowed a beautiful hue against the darkness of the forest.

"Quick, catch one of those things before they get away," he told his sister.

Amanda chased after the moths with her net while Travis tended to his scrapes and bruises. There was a piece of protruding metal near the hole which scraped up his knee and shin pretty badly. Once he dragged himself back to his feet, he realized he twisted his ankle, and it was tender, almost too tender to walk on. He found himself praying that their parents were out looking for them already.

"Look!" his sister said as she came running back over to him almost completely out of breath. She was holding up the jar with one of the blue moths inside. It was glowing so brightly that it lit up the forest like a lantern.

"That's nice," Travis replied without looking.

"What's wrong?"

"I don't think I can walk on this ankle. Not the way it is anyway," he said.

Amanda thought about this for a minute and panic set in. It was getting dark and if her brother couldn't walk that meant they would have to spend the night in the woods all by themselves.

"Wipe those tears squirt, it's not that bad. While I am tearing my shirt into strips you go out and find me some sturdy dead branches about this long," he said, holding his hands a foot apart. "And then get one long one I can use like a crutch."

While she was scouring the forest floor, he set about tearing his shirt into long strips. When Amanda returned, she laid a pile of sticks at her brother's side. He used the sticks and strips of cloth from his torn shirt to splint his ankle. She helped him to his feet, and he tried out the emergency patch up job.

128

"This will have to do," he said while trying to hide his wincing.

It had neared complete darkness and Travis was terrified. He had no way of knowing which direction to take them in and could end up wandering around in circles all night. The safest thing would be to hunker down and hope his parents were out looking for them. He knew his sister wouldn't go for that decision and would become inconsolable. The last thing they needed was a crying, distressed child beckoning predators to them.

"Look," Amanda said while pointing into the sky.

"What do you see squirt?"

"Isn't that the moon?"

"I do believe that is indeed the moon."

"Last night I was playing around trying to line the moon up with the lighthouse tower so I could see what the lighthouse looked like all lit up. The moon was behind the lighthouse over the water."

"So, all we have to do is walk in the direction of the moon. Good job squirt."

"It is not quite that simple. The moon moves about thirteen degrees to the east every night, so it won't be in the same place it was last night."

"Well thirteen degrees off is better than nothing. And you have been hanging around mom too much."

"Not if those thirteen degrees causes us to walk off the cliff," she said with her hands on her hips and a stern look on her face that definitely reminded him of their mother.

"We are not walking off any cliffs at this pace little sister," he said and tussled her hair.

As they headed toward the moon hanging in the sky while trying to judge thirteen-degree variation Travis was praying his little sister was right. She was pretty smart for an eight-year-old so under these circumstances he was not about to question her judgment. Besides, he got them into this mess, it was no problem letting her get them out of it. The more they limped along the later it got and the more severe he knew his punishment would be.

"Hold still," he said, putting a hand on Amanda's shoulder to stop her.

"What? Did you see something?" she asked, trying to hold back her tears.

"No, nothing to be afraid of. I'm just trying to see if I can hear mom or dad calling us. I'm sure they are pretty pissed off right about now. It's almost completely dark, so we've been gone about five hours."

"They can't be too mad, at least not at us. It's not our fault those mean boys took the ribbons."

She was taking the opportunity during the break in action to look at her newly acquired prize. She held the jar up to the moonlight away from her face. The moth fluttered to the opposite side of the jar, pressed itself against the glass and glowed brightly. Travis reached out and took the jar from her.

"Ow, that is kind of hot," he said, grabbing the jar by the glass side instead of by the lid.

"Hot? Are you just joshing me?"

"Feel it for yourself but be careful."

Amanda extended her delicate finger toward the glass. She was as wound up as a kitten preparing to pounce on a toy mouse. She just knew her brother was setting her up to scare her. But when she tapped the glass, he didn't startle her as she expected. And he was right, it was hot enough to hurt.

"That can't be right," she said.

As quickly as the moth started to glow it suddenly went completely dark. Amanda tapped on the glass, but it stayed dark.

"Did it die?" Travis asked.

"I don't think so, the wings are still moving."

Off in the distance, several rows of trees away there was a glow coming from a tree trunk. Amanda slowly held her captive in a jar up in the air and as soon as it was in line with the distant tree the moth in the jar began to glow. The glow in the distance faded into nothing but then reappeared on another, much closer, tree.

"Should we walk in that direction?" Travis asked.

"Why are you asking me? This is creeping me out."

Following the lead of the Miracle Whip moth they walked to where they saw the last glow. Again, the two moths communicated in an odd dance of light, so the children followed their cue once more.

"Travis, wait. What if they are leading us into a trap?"

"Mandy, they are moths."

"Moths that are intelligent enough to talk to one another," she pointed out.

"We don't know for sure if that is what is happening. This could all be some coincidence."

While the children were talking, they didn't notice the moths were flashing one another back and forth and that the moth outside the jar continued to move closer until it was only two trees away from them. Suddenly it sped across the expanse and plastered itself on the outside of the jar and laid completely flat. The moth inside the jar mimicked this and they both began to glow.

"That did not just happen," Travis said.

"I think they're talking to each other," Amanda added.

"No way in hell are they talking to each other, they're just moths."

"You're not supposed to say that word. And why not, all animals communicate with one another."

"But these are just stupid insects."

"They're not dumb enough to get themselves lost in the forest," she said with a grin.

The moth on the side of the jar stopped glowing and fluttered off in the darkness. After a few seconds it lit up again, resting on a low branch. The moth inside the jar glowed and then went dark which caused the moth on the branch to do the same.

"I think it wants us to follow it," Amanda said.

"We can't follow a moth through the dark woods," Travis said.

"But look," she said, pulling a protractor from her pocket. She held it up to the moon in the sky. "That moth is sitting exactly thirteen degrees west of the moon."

"Please do not do that in school, or at the park, or anywhere else for that matter."

"Don't do what?" Amanda asked, genuinely confused.

"Pull that science thing out of your pocket."

"Why not? And it's called a protractor."

"Because it makes you look like a dork."

"My teacher says it makes me look cool," Amanda argued with a smug grin.

"Yeah, well your teacher is mom, and she has to say that."

"Not mom, my other teacher."

While they were debating the coolness factor of science and her protractor the moth lit on another tree branch. Since the moth seemed to be guiding them in the right direction the kids decided to follow it, at least for a while. A hundred yards deeper into the woods both moths stopped glowing and both of them laid completely still and flat. A branch snapped off in the distance. Then another.

"What is that?" Amanda whispered.

"Put that jar under your shirt in case that moth starts to glow again," he whispered.

"Why?"

Travis shook his head and put a finger to his lips. An odd snorting sound echoed through the forest and a large shadow passed through the trees. Travis reached over and pushed down on his sister's shoulders indicating she should lie face down. He eased himself down with her.

"Is it a bear?" she whispered, her tiny hand trembling in his.

He shook his head.

"A deer? That kind of sounded like a buck snort."

"Shhhh," he mouthed.

Dead leaves and branches crunched as an unseen beast patrolled past them. Travis tried to contain his fear enough that his sister would not pick up on it. In the moonlight he could see tears streaming down her face, so it wasn't working.

The moth inside of the jar began to emit a high-pitched sound that sounded like a miniature human scream. Travis thought about killing the thing until it stopped, and then the sound was repeated deeper into the forest by one of the other moths not inside the jar.

Travis felt relieved when he realized the footfalls were moving away from them. A shriek split the night not more than twenty yards away and Amanda screamed. Her brother clamped his hand over her mouth and clutched her close to him. A familiar sound carried through the night air.

"Travis, Amanda," Tara called out through a tight throat.

"Mandy, honey," Gabe called out from one hundred feet away in the other direction.

Paul Rainbird called out for the children as well. Three flashlight beams cut through the dark forest as the searchers moved further away from the lighthouse. Gabe was using a high intensity beam and shined it high up into the trees hoping the kids might see it.

Tara was the first to cry out and take off running to her children who were limping through the forest. The others ran after her.

"Mommy, please don't be mad at Travis, it's not his fault," she said.

Tara didn't say a word, she simply hugged both of her children close to her chest.

Gabe took a moment to compose himself before he asked, "What happened out there? How did you get lost?"

"Those mean boys took our trail markers, that's how," Amanda said, wiping the tears from her eyes.

"What boys?" Tara asked as she held her daughter away from her to wipe her tears.

"I don't know. I think they were the same ones we saw watching us from the woods when we were driving up to the lighthouse. The older one tried to goad me into a fight," Travis said.

"But Travis wouldn't use his karate on him. He should have roundhouse kicked him like Bruce Lee."

"You know violence is not the answer," Gabe said. "But I will be giving their parents a good talking to."

"Blond boys, fifteen and ten or so?" Paul asked.

"Yeah, that's them," Travis answered.

"Sounds like the LaPierre kids Federico and Gregorio. Little bastonions if you ask me," he said, stopping himself short.

"What is a bastonion?" Amanda asked.

"Nothing you need to concern yourself about dear," Tara said, leading her daughter out of the woods.

"Their names are a bit pretentious, maybe it is not their fault they are little bastonions," Gabe said with a chuckle.

"What is a bastonion?" Amanda called back over her shoulder.

"Ignore your father dear."

"It is just another name for someone from the city of Baston," Gabe said in his best Thurston Howell the Third's voice which was lame at best.

Travis was limping so both Paul and Gabe grabbed a shoulder to help him along.

"What happened?"

"I am not sure. The ground gave way and my leg dropped into a hole."

"Maybe a dead fall," Paul said.

"No, I don't think so. I think I felt something metal under the branches when I was getting myself out of the hole. And something scratched my leg up pretty good too."

Within ten minutes they were back within the safe confines of the lighthouse grounds. Travis breathed his first sigh of relief in a long time.

"What is in the jar, honey?" Tara asked.

"It's a really cool moth, but he must be sleeping now," Amanda said.

"Why do you think it is sleeping?"

"Because he usually glows really bright. And he has a friend too."

Chapter Twelve

Minose knelt by a small, hand-carved grave marker behind her shack and chanted a prayer of protection. Not for her, but for the two children lost in the woods. Those mean boys who teased and harassed her put those new children on harm's path. She spoke to the marker in a language all her own.

"Kukka, you have been gone so long I barely remember you anymore. I have grown so old I barely remember me as well. I need your guidance," she said, fingering the large scar on the front of her head where the hair would not grow.

Minose felt the weight of loneliness crushing down on her. She spent her entire life not only on an island, far away from civilization but also in self-imposed solitary confinement in her dilapidated shack far removed from human interaction. And while she knew a few words of Finnish and some English most of her vocabulary was made up of grunts, clicks and other mimicked sounds, but she understood the thought she was trying to convey.

Besides, when you are a solitary creature there is no need for communication.

"I did like you said and stayed away from the other people on the island but now I fear I must leave this place for those children's sake. I cannot let the monster take them as it has taken everyone else on this island. I need to know what to do."

Minose paced back and forth waiting for a sign, something to guide her way. She spent decades on this island completely alone since she was not much more than thigh high. First the monster took everyone else, and then the fever took Kukka.

She regaled herself with the memory of Kukka's tales of bravery during her escape from the monsters before she found Minose. Her mother was a cook at the consortium's camp and her father a hardened miner with coal for eyes. Both were killed, mutilated by the ferocious beast. But not Kukka, she ran like the wind never looking back just like her father instructed her to do.

She hid down on the beach for hours when she finally spotted the small schooner, but it was being chased by the fearsome beast who lived beneath the cold waves. The captain of the vessel misjudged the water's depth and hit a rock, splintering the hull of the small boat. Minose was but an infant when Kukka plucked her from the icy waters of Lake Superior after her parent's boat hit the rocks and sank while trying to escape the island. This was according to her savior who was not much more than a child herself and relayed to Minose with only hand gestures and drawings in the sand.

Long ago, before Minose was even old enough to remember, Kukka made many trips under the cover of darkness to steal supplies and building material from the destroyed camp. She herself was just a child so it was grueling work, but eventually she was able to construct a shelter for them that saw them through that first winter. In addition to the building supplies she managed to gather jars of food and more importantly, seeds. Come the following spring she planted corn, tomatoes, peppers, and an assortment of squash.

Kukka somehow managed to keep not only herself but the child alive through four winters before succumbing to a fever. She taught the child how to garden, forage, hunt, and fish during those short four years. Being an attentive pupil, Minose managed to glean enough information to keep herself alive on the island alone for nearly a century. The biggest reason for her survival was that she kept to herself and did not go near other people. People carried disease, but most importantly, people carried hatred in their hearts.

The old woman sighed and leaned over her rain barrel to peer at her reflection through milky eyes. She hacked out a wet laugh at the memory of those two yellow haired kids running scared at the sight of her when they ventured too far away from their home. Her mane of white hair tamed only by her fingers and a piece of glass from a broken window undulated in the breeze as if it possessed a life and mind of its own. Her skin was leathered and ghostly pale, bearing a multitude of nasty scars from wounds healed without proper medical treatment. She had grown old, much, much older than

Kukka was when she left her all alone on the island. Her reflection was the sign she was looking for. She would only frighten those poor children worse than they already were.

Although she could not read or write she managed to find books with pictures while scrounging around the hunter's camp. Many were too wet and moldy to be of any use as she hadn't dared go near the dreadful place for years after the attack. Nonetheless several of the tomes taught her better ways to garden, make fire and other essential tidbits of knowledge Kukka was unable to impart due to her own youth and inexperience.

As she grew, she also grew a little more brazen and ventured further away from her camp, though those were very rare occasions. But when others moved to her island, specifically the yellow haired boy's parents, she learned to pilfer, but only what she absolutely needed. That was before the boys were born. After they came along, it became much more difficult but by then she was much too old to even care.

Minose continued to pace circles around her encampment. Those children needed her help, but she was too afraid to venture out after them. Besides, what good would a near-blind, old woman be to them. No, she had not seen any sign telling her she should get involved. Let nature run its course, it always did.

She ladled a cup of water and sat down on her favorite log and pondered current events. Movement in the trees caught her attention and she began to scan the limbs as best as her tired old eyes would allow. And then an unfamiliar song carried on the wind, there was a bird in the tree she had yet to catalog.

"Come down here little fella. I won't hurt you," she called out in her broken dialect.

The little bird dropped down out of the higher limbs and came to rest not much more than ten feet above her head where it warbled at her. Minose mimicked the bird the best her aging voice and lack of teeth would allow. Her new feathered friend hopped sideways down the limb a few feet and sang out a gleeful song.

She went inside her raggedy shack and brought out some stale homemade bread she was saving for just such an occasion. Minose put a piece of hard, dry bread between her palms and rubbed them together, breaking the bread into bird sized pieces. The critter reacted as if it knew it was dinner time and slid down the limb closer to her but was still reluctant to fly down to the ground. It was then she noticed the poor creature's wing was broken.

A small tear drop formed at the side of her eye and she sighed. She hated to see anything suffer. Reaching her cupped hands as high as she could she tried to coax the little creature down to her, but it still would not take the plunge. The sun was setting, and darkness was chewing away at the day, so she sighed, gathered her things, and started inside. Then something extraordinary happened, the bird began to glow, just its eyes at first, but then the leading edge of its wings illuminated as well.

Minose hurried inside her shack and retrieved her spyglass, a trinket she found while rummaging through the old camp at Echo Lake. It was bent and the lenses were cracked but if she held it just right it allowed her to see with a young girl's eyes instead of her old, worn-out ones.

"My, you are pretty," she clicked and held her hand out palm facing up toward the moon. "Don't be scared."

The little blue bird was something to see. It was a species not in her book and not one she had ever encountered before. Its beak was longer, like a wren, but she knew of no blue wrens. Especially none this sparkling shade of blue. The coloring on its wings began pulsating, slowly at first, but then more rapidly. Minose focused her spyglass on the little bird, but the light was blinding at that magnification, and she was forced to lower the glass. It was then she noticed the little bird was joined by a friend. Several minutes later there were half a dozen little blue birds sparkling on the tree limb.

She sat down cross-legged in the wet grass and lost herself in the colorful wonderment. It was as if her entire life had been leading up to this point. The beauty of these iridescent creatures as they flittered about above her head in a wonderous show was worth the lifetime of bleakness spent thus far. It was magical, just like in the book Kukka would read to her every night all those eons ago.

Her heart thumped against her chest with each movement the tiny birds made as they inched closer to her until finally one lit on her knee. She put her hand out and the tiny bird not much bigger than her thumb hopped into her palm to peck at the breadcrumbs she offered. She was ecstatic when the creature allowed her to stroke its tiny head with her crooked finger. A second, then a third little bird joined in the communal meal. Yes indeed, all her life's trials and tribulations led her to this one glorious moment.

Minose was lost in the heavenly moment when the air around her suddenly exploded into a flurry of cacophonous kinetic energy as hundreds of tiny birds dropped from the trees to swirl around her in a dazzling array of color. At first, she was charmed by the mystical display but then she was touched with a tinge of fear at their sheer numbers.

Then all at once the birds stopped zipping about and lit on a single branch nearest to her. The little bird in her hand looked up at her and began to warble the most beautiful song she had ever heard. She leaned her head back and closed her eyes, enraptured by the harmonious melody.

She slowly raised her hand up to her face and with her eyes still closed found the bird's miniature head and gave the creature a gentle kiss. Several moments of silence passed and she became worried she scared it and it had flown away but then she felt a delicate tap on her lips. And then another.

Again, there was a long pause and Minose feared the creature may have become bored and flittered away, so she slowly opened her eyes and was captivated by the sight before her. Even through her milky eyes she could see hundreds of the little blue birds hovering in front of her, casting a blue haze all around her. The bird she kissed was hovering closest to her face igniting a smile unlike any she had ever smiled before in her life.

The old woman's heart was like that of a child's, and she spread her arms wide in a gesture of embrace. The birds seemed to understand this and in turn they zipped in and zipped back out, stopping long enough to tap her lightly with their beak as if to kiss her. In a dazzling display they began to circle her, slowly at first, but picking up their pace with each revolution until they covered her in a shroud of hazy blue pigment.

Faster and faster, they flew until leaves began to swirl around her ankles caused by their turbulence. They inched upward from her lap to her chest where the drumming of their tiny wings made her stomach feel funny and she giggled. Minose crossed her arms over her chest and hugged herself while watching a miracle being performed in front of her.

The birds increased their speed and moved even further up her body until they fashioned themselves into a blue halo encircling her head. She was a princess just like in the story books. Her long, fluffy white hair began to float up off her back and shoulders until it was standing straight out around her. She was giggling loudly now but her laughter was being drowned out by the beating of a thousand tiny wings.

"Ouch, be careful," Minose said as one of the birds darted in and grabbed a tuft of her hair in its talons during its flyby.

Another did the same, then another until Minose screamed in pain. She tried to shoo the birds away by swinging her arms at them but some of them broke away from the flock and began pecking at her hands and face. Within seconds blood was running down her face and arms in rivulets. More birds grabbed tufts of hair and soon locks of her hair were being ripped out by the roots. She tried to get to her feet and run for the safety of her shack but the weight of all the birds combined would not allow her to.

Blood freckled her face as more and more tufts of hair were ripped from her scalp. Her screams were choked off by the sheer force of the birds twisting her head around to the left stretching the skin of her neck so taught she feared it would rip. She struggled to bring her head back to the center but the harder she fought the faster the birds flew until finally her aging bones gave out and her neck snapped. The birds continued their bombardment, keeping her dead body held in the upright position as they whirled. Faster and faster the avians flew in their frenzy until they reached a crescendo and Minose's head completely separated from her body with a wet, sickening pop.

The old woman's body fell limp as the birds flew away into the night dropping her head in the forest as they dissipated into the wind.

Chapter Thirteen

Paul was up before everyone else except for Travis who was sitting at the kitchen table looking exhausted. Paul started cracking some eggs into a mixing bowl.

"Couldn't you sleep?" he asked.

"Off and on. The pain in my ankle woke me up every time I rolled over in bed."

"You need to elevate it, and while you're at it, get some ice on it to bring down the swelling too," Paul said, scooting a chair across the kitchen where Travis could rest his tender ankle.

Paul mixed up some bread dough in another bowl with a generous amount of cinnamon and his secret ingredient, wild clover honey. He spooned the mixture into a hot cast iron skillet. The small kitchen erupted with the sizzling of the bread and the aroma of caramelizing honey wafted in the air.

"Paul, what kind of animals are on this island?"

"Well, Travis, there are squirrels, chipmunks, mice, which means there is probably a horny fox or two. All kinds of birds make their way out here, though you wouldn't know it with all the seagull squawking drowning out the warblers."

"What about something bigger than that?"

"You mean like bears?"

"Or wolves," Travis said.

"I think there might be a transient population of bears and wolves here, but they migrate with the passing of seasons. Not too many stick around for the spring thaw, there's not much to hunt here on the island, not anymore, I don't think. But it's not impossible for a stray to call the island its home. Why do you ask?"

"Any cats?"

"Housecats?" Paul asked, confused as to why the boy would be concerned about a tom cat prowling the woods.

"No, wildcats. Panthers, cougars, bobcats that sort of thing."

"Nothing larger than a bobcat I would imagine. But no, no cats this late in the season. Bobcats will swim, but generally not this far out without a good reason. Why do you ask about cats?"

"I heard something out there in the woods last night, something that sounded catlike."

"Catlike how?"

"I don't know, a kind of growl, I guess. It reminded me of an old stray tomcat we used to have prowling around our house. What did you mean by not much to hunt anymore?"

Paul sat down at the table and began cutting oranges in half and then grinding the halves on a juicer into a glass pitcher with a frosted image of the Kool-Aid man. He set the rinds aside which he would use later to try and coax an oriole or two to the island, possibly even some hummingbirds as well.

"There used to be a hunting lodge on the island more than seventy-five years ago. It was a consortium of rich men who brought exotic animals to the island for their sporting pleasure. Not very sporting if you ask me."

"Exotic? Like lions and tigers?"

Paul laughed. "No, like elk, caribou, and moose. Big game animals not native to the island."

"And wolves?"

"No, I don't think they stocked wolves, but the introduction of non-native prey like moose could have coaxed a hungry wolf or two over here on the ice bridge. But they would be long gone by now."

Paul served two sunny-side-up eggs, two pieces of fried bread and a glass of orange juice to Travis. He started the scrambled eggs in the now empty pan and sat down with a plate of fried bread saturated with maple sap for himself.

"What makes you ask about wolves?"

"I think there was something stalking us out there in the woods last night. Whatever it was, it was big enough to snap branches when it walked. I would imagine a big cat would be much stealthier than a wolf."

"Don't be fooled, wolves can be quite stealthy when they want to be."

"I see," Travis said, focusing on breakfast instead of an island chocked full of wild beasts.

Paul recognized the boy's expression. "It was probably just those two miscreants. Just between us, you should have gone all Chuck Norris on them."

"Didn't Bruce Lee kick his butt?"

"That is not the point," Paul said, not wanting to admit he didn't even know who either of the two men were.

"So, you don't think there was a wolf out there in the woods?"

"Not likely. I tell you what, after breakfast we'll go back out there, and I'll see if I can spot any animal tracks. Or human, which is what I suspect. I'm sure it was nothing more than a couple of Bastonions," Paul said with a grin.

The remainder of the morning proceeded without incident. Tara attended to her son's wounds with stinging Bactine which almost caused him to blurt out a few inappropriate and frowned upon explicates. By the time she finished he was able to walk much better, but it was still painful and hard to walk without a lot of discomfort.

"That's one heck of a laceration, Travis. We're going to have to find that area and mark it before someone else gets hurt," Gabe said.

"I'm not sure if I can find it again. We got pretty turned around in there."

Amanda held her jar up in front of her and said, "Maybe the moth can lead us back there."

"Why on earth would you think your moth could lead us back to where Travis injured himself?" Tara asked.

"The moths led us out of the forest to you."

"What are you talking about?" her mother asked.

"She's just talking nonsense," Travis injected.

149

"I am not, and you know it," Amanda said and stormed out of the room.

"What is she talking about Travis?" Gabe asked.

"It was just a strange coincidence, dad."

"Feel free to elaborate," Gabe said which was his polite way of telling his son to spit it out.

"When we were lost, I mean really lost, a moth that wasn't in the jar fluttered out into the forest away from us and landed on a tree. It started to glow and the moth that was in the jar glowed in unison. When we followed the first moth it repeated the process, leading us through the forest."

"Travis, honey, moths do not communicate, at least not like that," his mother said in her best science teacher's intonation.

"Hey, you guys asked. Don't shoot me, I am only the piano player," he said and stormed out of the house letting the screen door slap behind him.

Travis wandered along the cliff edge enjoying the cool morning breeze. His ankle started to throb, so he stopped to rest. The scratches on his leg were itching like crazy. He peeled back the bandage to scratch the edges of the wound and was startled. There were already signs of healing, much more than there should have been. Queasiness reached up and grabbed him so hard he nearly lost his breakfast in the shrubbery. He had been feeling off ever since the previous night. Something wasn't right about what happened in the woods.

"Hey, champ, what do you say we try and locate where you fell into that hole last night?" Gabe called out with Paul at his side.

When Travis turned to face them, a sensation washed over him, and his knees buckled. He was able stay on his feet but just barely. A lone moth pulsated a glowing blue light at the perimeter of the forest where the trail led into the woods. On one hand he was relieved to see the moth so that he could prove himself right and on the other, he was frightened of the truth.

"No, but I bet he can," he said, pointing to the moth who was flat against a tree at the edge of the forest.

"What are you talking about?" Gabe asked.

"The moth, from last night. It's sitting at the edge of the trail," Travis pointed.

"Has that boy found your stash?" Paul leaned and whispered to Gabe.

Gabe laughed. "I hope not. What in the world are you talking about, son?"

Travis walked over to where the moth was lying tight against the tree with its translucent blue wings splayed out against the smooth white bark of the birch tree. The moment he stretched a cautious finger toward the insect it fluttered off three trees deeper into the forest and lit on another tree. The men followed behind, not quite sure of what they were witnessing. Travis and the moth repeated their impromptu dance and the party moved deeper into the forest.

"Hang on Travis, we're getting pretty deep into the forest already. I can't even see the lighthouse anymore," Gabe said and started tying off ribbons to the tree limbs.

"Lot of good that did me yesterday," Travis said, following the moth another six trees deeper into the woods.

"That reminds me, I am going to have to go have a talk with those boy's parents. What they did was extremely dangerous and could have ended up with much worse results than scared parents."

"Please don't do that dad."

"Why not?"

"Put yourself in my position, would you want your dad fighting your battles for you?"

"I suppose not. But next time, Grasshopper, use your Kung Fu. I have spent good money on those lessons."

"It's not Kung Fu dad. And it is all about self-control and ultimately defense if needed and only when absolutely necessary."

They continued to banter back and forth for another twenty minutes while allowing a moth to lead them deeper into the forest. Paul was keeping an eye on the ground away from the small path while contemplating what Travis said about panthers and wolves at breakfast. The forest carpet was most definitely disturbed recently by something much larger than chipmunks and squirrels. What concerned him was whatever had disturbed the ground was bigger than a wolf, much bigger.

"We must be getting closer," Travis said.

"Why do you think that?"

"Look, the moth is glowing."

Gabe could not believe what he was seeing. The aura around the moth was glowing with such intensity that it hurt his eyes to stare directly at the creature. This was unlike anything he had ever seen. He glanced over at Paul who sported a dumbfounded expression as well.

"What do you make of that?" Gabe asked.

"I don't make anything of it," Paul responded with a wrinkled brow.

The moth floated six feet above their heads and began circling the group. It expanded the circumference of its flight pattern little by little, growing brighter and brighter with each pass. Suddenly it darted fifty feet down the small deer trail where it resumed the circling pattern. The three of them shrugged and followed the moth.

"Well, I'll be damned," Paul said, bending down to pull a scrap of torn fabric from a piece of metal buried beneath the dirt. He brushed debris away to reveal a metal panel next to a small hole in the earth.

"Did that moth just lead us to where we wanted to go?" Gabe asked.

"Or maybe it led us to where it wanted us to go," Travis said nervously. "I think the moths came out of that hole last night, and there were a lot more than just the two of them."

"Do me a favor, don't tell your mother about this, at least not until we figure out what in the hell just happened."

"You got it dad. I'm not in the mood to play twenty questions with her anyway."

As a dog might do, the moth fluttered out of the way and perched on a branch watching the men as they cleared deadfall and other debris away from the hole. While Travis and his father worked at pulling dead branches away from the metal structure Paul wandered off away from them.

"Is this about where you thought you saw something in the trees?" he called back to them.

"I never really saw anything, I just felt like we were being followed. Shadowed would be a better term," Travis said. He positioned himself where he best thought his leg had fallen into the hole. He then walked the path, stopped, and looked around him in all directions before he pointed to a spot in the trees. "Over there I think."

Paul wandered a few more tree rows deeper into the woods and walked back the way they came. He didn't expect to find anything, chalking the boy's sensation up to his overactive, teenage imagination and he almost stepped on the tracks in the loose dirt. He bent down and carefully blew away the top layer of pine needles and dirt. There was definitely some sort of animal tracks, but they were completely unfamiliar to him.

Something glimmered in the sunlight that pierced through the tall trees and caught Paul's attention. Careful not to disturb the tracks he found he skirted the area until he made it over to the shiny object. Again, he delicately blew away the top layer of debris, which was mainly dead pine needles, to reveal a piece of copper lying on the ground. A jolt of excitement rippled through him; this was precisely the kind of thing he was hoping to find on the island. He never imagined he would find something so significant lying right on the surface without having to dig. He slipped the glimmering sheet of copper into the breast pocket of his shirt.

"Gabe did your wife bring her science stuff with her?" Paul asked while walking back over to the deadfall pile.

"Science stuff? Such as construction paper dinosaurs? You do know she teaches elementary school, right?"

Travis laughed and Paul joined in once he realized the absurdity of his question.

"Okay, you got me there. Specifically, do you think she brought materials to make plaster of Paris molds?"

"You found tracks, didn't you?" Travis asked, quickly getting to his feet.

"Simmer down, Travis, I'm not even sure what it is I found. The ground is too loose to be able to identify them from sight. It very well might be the work of an overzealous chipmunk. I need to see if your mother has any material I can use to make a cast of the prints."

"We've done all we could here without tools anyway so let's say we go back to the lighthouse and find out if Tara has what you need," Gabe said, dusting himself off from pine needles and black dirt.

Paul marked the area of the tracks by marking the trees with pink ribbon, but he also stabbed a few fallen pine boughs into the soft earth around the tracks. Their winged tour guide was nowhere to be found on the return trip. Travis continued to swivel his gaze from the trees all around them but didn't see the moth anywhere. The trio were glad to see lunch was ready when they got back home.

Tara made quite the spread for lunch. On the picnic table there was a plate of bacon, a plate of sliced juicy, ripe red tomatoes, another with perfectly toasted homemade bread, another with thinly sliced cucumber in red wine vinegar with celery seed and a jar of Miracle

Whip. The four of them sat eating while Amanda sat at the other end of the table by herself studying her captive in a jar.

"I think it's sick mommy," she said, holding the jar out in front of her. The moth inside was flat against the glass and completely dark.

"Maybe it's hungry," Travis said.

"Or maybe the poor thing isn't getting enough oxygen. Why don't you open the lid honey?" Tara said.

"But it will fly away."

"It wasn't meant to live in captivity anyway, Mandy. You have enjoyed it long enough. The most prudent thing would be to set it free before it dies," Gabe added.

"Can't you just talk normal dad you are not writing one of your books. Sheesh," Amanda said with a smile and began to unscrew the lid.

They watched as the moth inside the jar sprang back to life with irradiance. It fluttered out of the jar and into a holding pattern above the picnic table, mimicking the moth in the forest. Within minutes there was a glow from across the yard. Tara sat in amazement as she watched the two moths somehow communicate with each other through what could only be described as a crude form of Morse code. The second moth joined the first and they made several circular paths before both of them settled back into the open Miracle Whip jar together.

"I will be the first one to say that was strange," Tara said, the first of them brave enough to speak.

Each moth moved to an opposite side of the of the jar, laid itself completely flat and splayed out as much as it possibly could before slowly starting to glow. They each increased in intensity until they were blindingly bright. They pulsed several times before they began a spectacular light show. While glowing an iridescent blue they also began to emit a beam of deep indigo at the very edge of their wings. One moth sent their indigo beam spinning slowly in a clockwise manner while the other did the same, only counterclockwise. With each pass the bead of blue light sped up until it was a steady stream on the trailing edge of their wings.

Suddenly Zappa jumped up from his nap with a yelp and went running to the far end of the yard. The golden retriever dropped to the ground and buried his head beneath his paws and whined.

"What in the hell was that all about?" Gabe blurted.

"Zappa reacted as if there was something hurting his ears," Tara replied.

"Moths don't make any sound, do they mom?" Travis asked, his voice shaky and cracking.

"None that I was aware of. But if they do, it's beyond human audible ranges."

"Not dogs though," Amanda added.

"Mandy, honey, put the lid back on the jar please," Gabe said, not sure why he felt they would be safer with the insects trapped inside.

They went about clearing the picnic table without another word. Food was taken back into the house and the paper plates were tossed into the fire pit. Gabe went out to the shed and loaded some tools into an old, rickety wheelbarrow.

"Tara."

"What is it, Paul?"

"I know this will sound strange, but do you have any casting materials here?"

"Do you mean like for making molds?"

"Yes, exactly."

Suspicious she asked, "What do you need to make molds of?"

"I found some tracks out in the woods that I can't identify. I thought if I make a mold of them, I would be able to tell what kind of animal made them."

"What do you think made them?"

"Travis seemed to think a wolf was out in the woods following them last night. I looked at the tracks but while they are similar to a wolf's or dog's, there was something not quite right about the track."

"It was probably smudged by another animal. I'll get you some plaster of Paris to take with you. All you will need is some water and something to mix it in," she said, digging through a box labeled in thick, black marker, SCHOOL SUPPLIES.

"Fantastic. If anything, it will set my mind at ease. I didn't think there were any wolves on this island, but maybe I was mistaken," Paul said, filling a goat skin bag with water from a jug in the kitchen.

"Make sure you let me see those casts once you make them," she called after him as he trotted out to meet Gabe and his rickety wheelbarrow.

Chapter Fourteen

As soon as Paul was finished mixing the plaster, he poured several different casts of the prints he managed to locate. While scouring the forest floor he found a few more of the odd-looking pieces of copper as well. Once the molds were poured and drying, he went over to lend Gabe and Travis a hand digging out the chunk of rusted metal. Gabe broke two large tree limbs and a shovel handle trying to move the object.

"What the hell is this thing?" Gabe asked, panting to catch his breath. "It won't budge."

"It looks like a door of some kind."

"But there isn't a locking mechanism anywhere on the outside that I can see."

"Maybe it is bolted from the inside," Travis offered.

The three of them continued to clear away all the debris until the only thing left was the large square bunker door. The hatch was sealed tight and there was no way they were going to be able to pry it open with hand tools.

"We need a cutting torch or something," Gabe said.

"Or we could just leave it alone. Mark it as dangerous and go home," Travis said.

"Where is your sense of adventure?"

"It stayed on the mainland with your sanity," Travis quipped.

"I think I am with the kid on this one. It sure seems like a lot of work getting this thing open. I would hate to get it open and want nothing more than to close it again," Paul said.

"Like Pandora's box."

"When did you start paying attention in your mythology class, Travis? Aren't you guys even the least bit curious?"

"Of course, I am, but I'm also practical. And I'm getting hungry."

As they were packing up the tools Gabe saw something deeper into the woods. There was one of the unique moths lying on the ground, but it wasn't moving. He bent to pick it up, but it crumbled into dust in the palm of his hand. While squatting down he caught a whiff of something that didn't smell quite right. It smelled of decay, but not like rotting leaves or other forest fodder. This smelled of human decay.

"Paul, come over here for a minute would you please?"

Paul checked on his plaster, saw it wasn't quite set up yet and went over to where Gabe was squatted down on his haunches.

"What did you find?"

"Smell that, what do you smell?" he asked, holding the crumbled remains of the moth up to his friend's nose.

"What in the hell is that?"

"It's one of those moths, but it was dead. When I picked it up it crumbled into this black powder."

"Why does it smell like that?"

"Do you recognize that smell?" Gabe asked.

"No, and I am pretty sure I am glad that I don't," Travis said, taking a whiff of his father's hand against his better judgment.

"It's human decay," Paul said.

"You mean like excrement? You had me smell someone's poop?"

"No, more like a dead body," Gabe added with a reserved chuckle.

"Specifically, it smells like rotting human flesh. Why in the hell would a dead moth smell like a dead body?" Paul asked.

"I don't have a clue in the world, but I think we need to get those moths of Mandy's to the university," Gabe said.

The forest became noticeably quiet and still. The wind in the trees died down and there were no birds chattering about. Both men were lost in contemplation when Travis spooked them both.

"Hey guys," he called out and then laughed when he saw that he startled them.

"Nice bit of subtlety son. What is it?"

"I found something next to the hole I fell into."

Travis pointed out a small hole not much bigger in circumference than his leg a few inches from the corner of the hatch. Gabe and Paul cleared away debris from the hollow and shined a flashlight into the cavity.

"Look there," Paul said, point the light. "Doesn't that look like a concrete wall?"

Gabe grabbed the spade and slowly chopped away at the small opening until he created enough room to jam the shovel into the concrete. The hole looked too deep to drop down into, so he attacked the wall from the side. After a few strikes it started to crumble. Gabe, Paul, and Travis took turns whacking away at the wall until they were able to punch through. Paul shined the light into the hole they created.

"Look, over there, it looks like there is a bar mechanism locking the doors. See if you can push it with the shovel," Paul said.

They spent another hour taking turns holding the shovel and banging on the end of it with logs they scavenged from the forest. Finally, the bar shrieked in defiance as enough rust was knocked loose to allow it to loosen. The door was not only heavy, but the hinges were rusted, so it took the three of them several tries before they were able to lift it open. They swung the hatch high and over to the side before dropping it with a resounding crash.

Suddenly the forest was permeated with the smell of death and decay. But this was not fresh death, no, this was stale death. Death that had been dead an exceptionally long time. They eyeballed the rickety stairs leading down into the cellar, not one of them wanting to be the first to brave the descent.

"Travis, you wait up here. I have no idea what condition those stairs are in," Gabe said.

"You'll get no argument from me," Travis said as he backed away from the entrance.

Paul shined the light while Gabe descended the stairs one step and a time. He stopped at each step and tested it by stomping down before putting all his weight on the step. Every one of the steps creaked and groaned in protest but held fast all the way down to the first platform. Paul followed behind after securing a rope to the hatch framework and dropping it down to the bottom.

They repeated the process down to the next level and then the next. At the last landing, the cellar opened into a very large room. Paul battled with his fears with every step as his mind catapulted him back to tunnels beneath the jungles of Viet Nam.

"Gabe, I'm not liking this one bit. It took me a very long time to get that smell out of my head," Paul said.

"Something died down here. Probably an animal of some sort."

"How did they get through that barred door?"

"I guess that is something you and I have to figure out. Up for a Hardy Boys mystery?"

"I think you guys will end up being more like Scooby Doo," Travis called down the stairs with a chuckle.

Paul panned the flashlight beam around the room from corner to corner, but the beam was weak, so it wasn't doing a very good job illuminating the room.

"Should we go all the way down?"

"Are you crazy, Gabe? We have no idea what's down there, and this flashlight is a piece of shit."

"Hold it, swing that flashlight back to the left," Gabe instructed.

"Did you see something?" Paul asked, unable to mask the nervous tension in his voice. He knew if there were some wild animal down there, they would never make it back up the stairs before the animal would be able to catch them.

"For a war hero you are not very brave," Gabe said and gave his friend a playful punch to the arm.

"Yeah, well this native does not do ghosts."

Gabe reached out and stopped Paul's panning of the flashlight to illuminate a small corridor. The pair of them continued on through the large, empty room and into the hallway where Paul stopped to shine the flashlight into the next room. The beam illuminated a pile of something on the floor.

"Is that what I think it is?" Paul asked.

"Yes. Let's go back to the house and get Tara."

"Sounds like a plan to me, I've had enough of this place for one day," Paul said, wasting no time getting back up the stairs and into the open air.

On their way out of the forest Paul gathered up his plaster casts and carefully tucked them away in a well-worn work rucksack before the three of them headed back down the trail toward the lighthouse. The hike back was somber and quiet. Travis couldn't shake the feeling that the forest was watching them.

Travis finally gathered enough nerve to ask, "Dad, what did you guys see down there? You both seem kind of spooked when you came back up."

"To be honest, Travis, we didn't see much of anything. It was too dark," Gabe said.

"Why do you always think you can lie to me? You saw something down there and it has the two of you spooked. I'm a big boy. I can take it."

"Bones," Paul blurted out. "We saw bones."

"Cool, what kind of bones?" Travis said with wide eyed enthusiasm.

"I don't know, we didn't go any further. Like I said, it was too dark."

"Were they people, I mean human bones?"

Gabe ignored his son's rapid-fire questions until Travis became angry enough to give him the silent treatment which was precisely the outcome he was hoping for. The sun was already on its descent when they broke free from the woods and onto the lighthouse lawn. Tara and Amanda were playing croquet, the wooden balls clicking and clacking in the pre-summer air. Tara walked up to meet them and gave her husband a gentle kiss after finding a clean spot on his face.

"I missed you," she said.

"Croquet? You must have been desperate."

"The contractors were making one hell of a racket inside, so we came outside to enjoy the sunshine. I brought the hammock outside too if you're feeling energetic enough to put it up."

"Sure, I could use a nap," he said.

Gabe's face took a serious turn. He rotated so that his back was to the children. He gripped his wife firmly by the shoulders and made eye contact with her.

"What's wrong honey?" Tara asked.

"We found a cellar out in the forest. Actually, less of a cellar and more of a bomb shelter. It was a pain in the ass, but we finally got the door open."

"Why on earth would you do such a thing? Men and their curiosity," she said with a nervous smile.

"It was a little more complicated than that. First, do you know of a species of moth that reeks of human decay?"

"I'm not sure about that. Moths do use their olfactory senses when mating but I've never heard of a stinky moth. Maybe you were close to a dead fungus, the stinkhorn can smell like decaying flesh. Though I would have to check to see if there would be any of them on this island."

"That is one possible explanation. Okay, now for the biggie. Relax and stay calm when I tell you this."

"Gabe, just spit it out."

"You're going to get excited and bounce around. And then you're going to get scared, and I'll have to deal with all that," he said.

"How much grass did you smoke back there in the woods? You didn't get stoned around Travis, did you?"

"I am not stoned. Though that does sound like a particularly good idea right about now. We found something in the cellar, Paul, and I."

"Gabe, I swear, if you do not spit it out, I am going to throw all your stash over the cliff."

"Bones. There were bones down in the cellar."

"Bones! What kind of bones? Did you bring any back with you? Were they human? Please tell me they were not human bones," she fired off in rapid succession.

166

"They were white."

"Gabe, I swear, if you continue to play with me," she said, reaching out to tickle his ribcage.

Travis put his foot on a croquet ball and "kissed" Amanda's ball fifty feet across the other side of the yard. Both children went chasing after it with peals of laughter. Paul disappeared inside the lighthouse and was upstairs in the cupola. He waved, held up a paint brush, and disappeared as quickly as he appeared.

"To be honest, honey, I'm not sure what I saw. It was pitch black down there and the only light was from a flashlight with weak batteries."

"What did you see?"

"Like I said, bones."

"A pile of bones?"

"No, more like they were laid out in a skeleton."

"Gabe, you're the anthropologist, not me," Tara said.

"Social anthropologist. You're the scientist."

"You still took anatomy and biology. What in the hell did you see?"

"A skull. I saw a human skull alright."

Chapter Fifteen

The morning came much too abruptly for Gabe's tastes. The sun beaming through the window was almost as rude as the contractors who were nailing shingles to the roof and running power tools on the lawn under the bedroom window. The sounds of progress, the driving impetus behind his desperate need to escape civilization in the first place. Thank goodness, he thought to himself, this is only temporary.

"Good morning, Duke," Gabe said, offering a cup of coffee to the man in charge of the remodel and the purveyor of noise.

"Good morning, Mr. Roster," Duke said, reaching out his beefy hand with fingers the size of bratwurst to accept the steaming mug.

Duke was about the healthiest fifty-year-old Gabe ever met. He still sported a full head of golden curly locks which were made to look much lighter due to his deep, dark tan from working outdoors most of his day. First glance would make one believe he was a surfer from the California beaches rather than a hearty Yooper from the great white north. The day was warming up, so he had traded in his Carhartt bib overalls for a pair of cut off blue jeans.

"Call me Gabe," he greeted with a fist shoved in his eye socket rubbing out the sleep.

"Sorry Gabe, did we wake you?"

"Not any more than the sun did. I'm not used to sleeping until sunup, it felt good for a change."

"Good news, your plumbing should be all set by mid-morning."

"That is great news, we're all getting a bit gamey. My wife and daughter are getting more than a wee bit testy," he said, having seen Tara walk up within ear shot.

"Did I overhear that we're going to have running water today?" she asked with an optimistic smile while pulling a Michigan Tech sweatshirt over her head. It may have been summer in most parts of the Northern Hemisphere but in the Upper Peninsula of Michigan summer mornings could convince a person it was still winter. She cringed at Duke's shorts and thought he must have been freezing.

"Yes ma'am. I sent a water sample over to the mainland for testing. We should have results back in a few weeks, so until then, it is best to continue ferrying your drinking water over. I instructed the men bring over a replenishment stock of potable water which should last you a month or so."

"What would taint the well water way out here?" Tara asked.

"Heavy metals mostly. You are sitting on top of one huge mound of ore. When you break through into the water tables you can drop heavy metals from the surrounding rock into the water table. It's just a precaution. I'm sure the water is fine."

"What are the chances of waterborne parasites or bacteria?" Tara asked.

"There is always a chance, but I would wager the chances are pretty slim. Rest assured, the lab will be testing for those as well," Duke said.

Gabe went inside, poured them all another cup of coffee before rejoining Tara and Duke for a walk around tour. He told them the roof would be done by the end of the week and then they could get started putting siding up. From there they would move inside to finish the kitchen, bedrooms and upgrade the wiring to meet current safety codes.

"Hey Duke, what do you know about the history of this island?" Gabe asked.

"Not much other than local legend."

"Local legend?" Tara asked.

"I'm sure you know all about the rumors of the lighthouse being haunted," he said before he noticed Gabe slashing at his throat.

"Haunted? I haven't heard even the slightest peep about that particular local legend. Gabe, do you know anything about this?" Tara asked.

"May I plead the fifth?"

"Absolutely not."

"Duke, why don't you share your version of this story with us, I'm sure it's far more accurate than the little snippets I have heard," Gabe said.

"There is not much to tell really. I'll give you the cliff notes. Sometime near the turn of the century the assistant lighthouse keeper was found dead in a lifeboat adrift out on the lake. The keeper and his wife were never found. There were a lot of rumors, theories, and speculation about what happened but not even one was ever substantiated. In their defense. back then they did not have the luxury of a bald, lollipop sucking crime solving cop on the case either."

Tara turned and looked at Gabe, he could see that the wheels were turning. He thought about telling her how amazing she looked but her sweatpants and sweatshirt would not let him get away with that ruse. He saw something else in her eyes that worried him.

"Bones. Gabe, tell Duke about the bones."

"I never even thought about that. The main reason I asked you about the history of the island is because we found an underground cellar, more of a bunker, out in the woods about a mile or so I would estimate. I was wondering if maybe it was built during the second world war as a bomb shelter. We found human remains in the bunker."

"Sorry, I have never heard of any cellar, basement or bunker anywhere on this island. There wasn't any major construction on this island during the war, most construction workers joined the military and weren't even around, so I can assure you it wasn't built during those years. Maybe an animal got inside an old root cellar and died."

"That's quite possible. It was pretty dark, maybe my eyes were just playing tricks on me. But the place is a lot sturdier than a plain old root cellar, it's actually constructed with concrete walls."

"I have definitely never heard anything of that sort being on this island and my family has had a hand in building pretty near everything on this rock for the past hundred years or so. Tell you what, because I love a good adventure let me finish up here today and later, I'll use the tractor to bring a small generator and some work lights out to your hole in the ground."

"I would appreciate that, Duke. It just might set some minds at ease around here."

"Who knows, maybe after all these years we can finally solve the legendary murder mystery," Duke said and instantly regretted his words from the look on Gabe's face.

"Murder mystery? Who said anything about murder?" Tara said.

"Duke is only pulling your leg. Right Duke?" Gabe said.

He laughed. "I'm sorry, I just like to have a little fun with out of towners when it comes to local ghost stories. I find them ridiculous myself. No great mystery here on this island, just a lack of all the facts. We'll get it all sorted out, I promise you," Duke said. His attention was stolen by one of the men working on the roof waving frantically and he dashed off.

Everyone went off in their own separate directions, each with some master plan for the day. Gabe pulled the lawn tractor out of the utility shed, gassed it up and showed Travis the basics before sending his son off to mow the gargantuan lawn. He was proud of himself that during the entire time showing his son the ropes he made not one single comment about the colossal zit on the boy's face.

Gabe tried to putter around in the shed with this and that but knew Tara would be waiting for an explanation, so he got into his stash for a quick bowl to take the edge off.

Paul was lying on his back in the lantern room putting the finishing touches on one of his pukwudgies. The mischievous imp looked back at him with wild, staring eyes while his pointed tongue tested the sharpness of his spindly teeth.

"What is that thing?" A little voice echoed from behind him.

"Amanda, you shouldn't be up here, those stairs are dangerous," Paul said.

"But what is it?" she asked, ignoring his adulting.

"It is called a pukwudgie."

"Is it real?"

"To some people, but to me, they are just imaginary. Like this one, he only lives in my imagination."

"Why would someone imagine something so mean looking?"

"According to Anishinaabe legend they are not really mean, just obnoxiously playful."

"What does Anisibe mean?"

"Anishinaabe. In English it means the good humans. It's a name for my people," he explained.

Amanda pursed her lips and tilted her head to one side. It was obvious she was lost deep in thought.

"Mr. Paul isn't war bad?" she finally asked.

Even though he felt he was being led into a verbal trap by a seven-year-old he chose to answer truthfully. "Yes, Amanda, war is very bad," he said, hoping a simple answer would suffice even though he knew better.

"But Mr. Paul, you were in the war, weren't you?"

"Yes, darling I was."

"And you said that you are a 'Nishnabe, right? And 'Nishnabe are good humans?"

"I see where you are going with this little one. Yes, I am of the Anishinaabe people. And yes, while war is bad and Anishinaabe means good humans, not everything is black and white and easy to understand as simply good or bad. Life is filled with contradictions and forked paths," Paul said.

She shrugged indifferently as if he answered her question with an acceptable answer. Her eyes sparkled with childhood enthusiasm causing Paul Rainbird to smile big and wide.

"What is noxious and why does it play?"

"If you are referring to the pukwudgies, they are obnoxiously playful and what that means is having fun at another's expense."

"You mean like when Travis picks on me or tells me scary stories."

"Exactly like that."

"So, then Travis is a Pukmathingamajig?"

"Following your logic, Travis is indeed a pukwudgie."

"And he's got a zit just like that one there," she said, pointing with a grin spread wide across her face accentuating her deep dimples.

"You better head back downstairs, I don't think your parents would be too pleased with you climbing that big ladder all by yourself."

"Mom doesn't mind. She sent me up here but now I can't remember why," she said. Her eyes drifted up into her skull as she thought long and hard. "Oh, yeah, mom said to tell you that lunch was ready," Amanda finished and bounded down the spiral staircase with grace and ease.

Paul finished up the creature he was currently crafting and put the lids back on his paints. He then put his brushes into a jar of turpentine before heading down himself. He stopped, took a long look around the room and felt a sense of pride wash over him. He was doing his people an honor keeping old legends alive, even if most of them were scary as hell. He made a mental note to remember to get Noona's opinion later.

"Mmmm, that smells good," he said while washing up at the kitchen sink. "And it sure is nice to have running water, isn't it?"

"Thank you, and yes, it sure is. I might go take another shower after lunch just because I can," Tara said, setting a bowl of salad on the table.

Gabe came in, washed up and did his best to avoid eye contact with his wife. Travis followed closely behind smelling the house up with the scent of freshly cut grass and gasoline fumes. A snap of his mother's fingers sent him to the bathroom where he washed up as well.

Travis looked into the mirror and saw a third eye in the middle of his forehead. The damned zit was an even angrier red from just a couple of hours ago and had already grown to the size of a pencil eraser. That was bad enough, but what really alarmed the teenager was the fact that this zit did not have the normal white puss sac grossing him out, it was blue. The same color blue as the moths and when he touched it, it wriggled and caused him excruciating pain like something was stinging him in retaliation of his intrusion.

Travis pulled the first aid kit out from under the bathroom sink. He doused a few cotton balls with alcohol and squeezed them out over the zit, being careful not to get any into his eyes. He unwrapped a gauze pad with adhesive and put that over the zit. While it would not limit the questions about why he wore a bandage on his face, it would curtail the questions he would have to field concerning a blue zit.

They all made sandwiches, buffet style, and enjoyed a side of crisp, cold salad with Hidden Valley Ranch Dressing. Amanda finished before everyone else, wiped a sleeve across her mouth and ran out of the door sporting a cherry Kool-Aid moustache. Travis bolted out of the door as well and within thirty seconds the lawn mower engine fired up and drifted away. Gabe tried to slink out of the house with the kids, but Tara jabbed a finger at his chair telling him to stay seated.

"Murder mystery?" was all that she said.

"I think that is my cue to vamoose." Paul started to get up, but another finger from her put him back in his seat.

"Honey, no one was murdered."

"Then what was Duke talking about?"

"Nearly a hundred years ago the lighthouse keeper and his wife vanished without a trace. That is the just of it."

"The just of it? People do not just vanish, and other people do not use the term murder unless there is more to the story."

Paul said, "The story also has it that the assistant keeper was found in a lifeboat in pretty bad shape. He was dead."

"Who do they think murdered him?"

"There was a lot of speculation, but no one was ever charged or arrested. In fact, no one really knows what happened out here," Gabe said. "Besides, even if someone murdered the assistant keeper, they are long gone and long dead by now. Case closed."

"You should have told me, Gabe. You can go play now," she said with a dismissive wave of her hand and a smile. Gabe didn't wait for a second offer.

Tara got up from the table, went into the other room and brought a small cardboard box as well as several books back into the kitchen with her. She pulled the plaster casts Paul made of the tracks out of the cardboard box and arranged them all on the table.

"Now, it's your turn. Are you screwing with me or are you just that terrible at making plaster casts?"

"I'm not sure I know what you are referring to," Paul said in his own defense.

"These prints do not match any animal known to man in this region, or any other for that matter. I even checked the Amazon rainforests."

"What are you talking about? That's not possible."

"That's exactly the point I'm trying to make. Did you and Gabe smoke a few bowls out there in the woods and concoct a plan to screw with me? I might be a little naïve, but not this gullible."

"Tara, I'm innocent. I simply poured the plaster into the impressions in the ground and made casts. Hell, I didn't even look at them when we got back here," he said, picking one up and turning it over in his hands while looking it over.

"Look, two hundred pages in this book, over three hundred in this one and the third is even bigger. Those prints do not match any prints in any of these reference books, not even the National Geographic.

The plaster casts Paul made presented conflicting elements. While feline in nature there were several anomalies that could not be explained.

"I think you guys are trying to pull an elaborate prank, but be warned, I'm much smarter than either of you two Neanderthals," Tara said with a smile that didn't let Paul know whether or not she was joking.

"Honestly, I have no clue what you are alluding to," he said, putting his hands up in the air to declare his innocence.

"Look," she said, opening a folder filled with photographs of paintings and drawings he brought with him for reference when painting the murals. "Aren't these suspiciously similar?"

He studied the photographs and artwork while comparing them to the plaster casts. She was right, the similarities were uncanny.

"Okay, now who is pranking whom?" Paul asked.

"So, you are just going to continue with the charade?"

"Are you really suggesting what I think you are suggesting?"

"I am not suggesting anything. I am flat out stating that you and my husband, who is sleeping on the couch tonight by the way, have concocted this whole thing."

"Forgive me, but I'm not sure I understand what this whole thing even is?"

"Paul, are you trying to tell me that you do not see that these plaster casts you made look remarkably similar to the print that this Mishipeshu creature would leave?"

"What in the heck are you talking about?" Paul said, sliding the photos and casts toward himself.

The casts definitely resembled that of a feline more than a canine. The most obvious culprit in Paul's experience is that they were made by a lynx, but they were much deeper than the normally soft footed cat would leave. And they were bigger than any lynx he knew of.

"Well?" Tara asked after several minutes.

"I would be willing to wager they were made by a lynx, but a large specimen indeed. These prints are bigger than even a cougar would leave, but the pads are rounded like a lynx," Paul said.

"Okay, so it was made by a larger than average sized lynx, but one with webbed feet?

"I could have messed up the print when casting it. Maybe I pulled them out too early and they shifted."

"That explains the webbed feet, but what about this mark right here?" she asked, jabbing a finger at the cast on the table.

Paul looked at it for several minutes before asking, "What is it I am looking at?"

"I can't say for certain, but that mark looks like it was made by a spur, something a lynx would not have."

"A spur? Like on a rooster?"

"Exactly. And here, at the edge of the print, there is a hard line in the ground made by something rigid."

"Do you think something like this could have made those grooves?" Paul asked, pulling one of the pieces of copper from his pocket and dropping it on the table in front of Tara.

She picked up the shiny piece of metal and turned it over several times in her hand. The piece of copper looked more organic than metallic to her. Tara held it to the light at different angles to reflect the light which cast bluish-green hues on the ceiling. To her, it resembled the scale of a fish, though she was not prepared to admit that out loud.

"Mishipeshu?" she said barely above a whisper.

Paul shrugged.

~   ~   ~

Gabe stood out on the cliff edge watching the seagulls dance on the wind when Travis came up from behind him. He put his arm around his son and resisted the urge to ask him about the zit.

"All done with the lawn already?"

"Naw, Duke needed the tractor for a minute, he said he was going to take a generator and some lights out to the cellar thing we found."

"That's good. Listen, I know you're not going to like this, but I would like you to stay here with your sister when we go look at this place tomorrow. Your mom has insisted on going and we can't leave Mandy here by herself."

"That's perfectly fine with me, dad. I'm not too fond of that hole in the ground anyway."

"Tell you what, why don't you get my brand-new fishing pole from the shed and let her use yours. According to the map there is a big lake further south from here. But be careful, don't get lost this time, please," Gabe said.

"Dad, I don't care if it hurts mom's tree-hugger feelings or not, I'm marking the trees with something permanent this time."

They listened as Duke doled out a list of chores to the roofing crew and then went around back to do the same to the crew working on the landscaping. Even though they stood three hundred feet above the lake, echoes from the waves crashing against the boulders below caressed their souls.

"Dad?"

"What son?" Gabe asked, sensing a degree of seriousness from his usually sarcastic and snappy son.

"I overheard you guys talking the other night. Paul kept saying you guys met in the war, but I thought you were in the Navy?"

"I was in the Navy, but I was assigned to the Marines as a combat medic in country. That's where Paul and I made our first acquaintance."

"He said something about you saving his life?"

"He was being a bit melodramatic. I patched him up, that's all."

"So, did you see guys die?"

"A morbid question, but yes, men die in war and it's often in the company of their medic when that happens," Gabe said in a tone of voice he hoped would dissuade his son's line of questioning.

After a long pause in the conversation Travis asked, "Did you carry a gun?"

"Yes, Travis, I carried a gun. Not at first, but after being caught outside of the camp perimeter by myself once or twice I thought it prudent to be armed if I wanted to make it back home to you and your mother which was my first priority."

"Did you ever have to kill anyone?"

Gabe looked at his son and fought back his tears. "Would it make a difference about how you see me?"

"No. Well, maybe a little, but not in a bad way."

"Let's just say I did whatever was necessary to get back home to my family in one piece. How about neither one of us think about that anymore."

Travis nodded softly.

Chapter Sixteen

Duke loaded up the generator, two sets of work lights on stands and one droplight onto the small trailer hooked to the green and yellow John Deere lawn tractor. He also loaded a couple of framing hammers, nails, and braces to shore up the stairs and walls if needed, two five-gallon gas cans, a gas can with pre-mixed chainsaw gas and finally his trusty Stihl chainsaw with a sixteen-inch bar. He was not more than fifty yards into the woods before he had to drop the first sapling to widen the trail.

The day was turning out to be a scorcher which aggravated the black flies which in turn annoyed the hell out of Duke. After cutting down yet another tree in his way he rolled his sleeves down and put on his fishing hat complete with mosquito netting. The next time he stopped, Duke donned gloves as well. The vicious little bastards were highly skilled in finding the smallest piece of exposed flesh and were taking full advantage of the fortuitous feast brave enough to traipse through their feeding ground. He cursed his choice of shorts as his legs were bearing the brunt of their onslaught.

A little over an hour later Duke was finally at the bunker. The path was too tight for him to be able to turn around, so he unhooked the trailer and pushed it into the woods out of the way before turning the tractor to face back toward the lighthouse.

The first thing he unloaded was the generator which he placed near the bunker opening but with the exhaust pointing away from it. He checked the gas, spark plug and oil before setting the choke and pulling hard on the T handle. It sputtered the first try so he choked the engine a little more and gave it another pull. She coughed once in defiance but then began to purr like a contented kitten.

Duke hooked up the drop light and lowered it down into the hole a few inches. Gabe would be able to use it to inspect the stairs to make sure they were safe. Once he was satisfied with the set-up, he turned off the generator and covered it with a tarp assuming Gabe and crew would not be going down into the cellar until morning.

He was sitting on the tractor enjoying an ice-cold soda before heading back to the lighthouse when he spotted a cluster of the moths Gabe told him about. He didn't believe a word of the story when he first heard it because he had never seen a moth that looked like what Gabe described anywhere, let alone up here on the island. He chugged down the rest of the soda, put the empty bottle in the cooler and jumped off the tractor.

Once Duke was standing above the moths, he didn't see what Gabe had gotten all worked up about, they were just moths. Plain old, ordinary moths. Suddenly the pile of moths began to tremble and every single one of them crumbled into a fine black powder. From beneath the powder emerged a midnight blue, translucent lizard of sorts that was smaller than his pinky. The creature had large, bulging eyes that lent a curious expression to its face.

Duke dropped down to his knees, leaned his face into the tiny creature and said, "Well aren't you just the cutest little thing. Where on earth did you come from?"

The lizard craned its neck to look up at him while flicking its tall, broad tail rapidly back and forth like a dog happy to see its master. In fact, the impetus of the tail's motion lifted the lizard's feet off the ground. Just a smidgen of pink appeared from the crease that served as its mouth. Duke slowly extended a finger, not wanting to scare it away. As he got closer to the lizard a thin line began to glow a beautiful shade of blue and tiny spines erected along its backbone as what Duke speculated was a defense mechanism. A shiny, viscous fluid coated the animal from nose to tail.

"So, you are not a lizard, which means you must be some breed of salamander, an amphibian maybe. Hey, don't look at me like that, I may be just a hammer swinger, but I do know a thing or two about this island. And one thing I do know is that you do not belong around here. I think I will have Tara take a gander at you," Duke said and got up from his knees.

As he was walking over to the tractor wagon to look for something to put the creature in, he looked back and was shocked to see the salamander was following close on his heels. He reached down but the salamander rapidly retreated. Without warning the creature's tongue shot out several inches and landed a stinging blow on Duke's finger.

"Ow, shit! You've got a heck of a sting there little buddy," he said, rubbing a sore, red spot that developed along his index finger where the animal's tongue made contact.

Duke rummaged around on the wagon looking for a container to put the little lizard in when a familiar, overpowering sensation washed over him.

"Damn, little guy, what is in that tongue of yours, I have to piss like a racehorse," he said as he walked over to the nearest tree and unzipped his fly.

His knuckle was swollen to twice its normal size and he was more than a little concerned about what sort of venom this creature might have injected him with. He was having a difficult time urinating while being distracted by the throbbing appendage. He glanced down to see that the salamander crawled up his leg and was but an inch from the head of his penis. Suddenly the vicious little tongue lashed out again, this time striking the ultra-sensitive flesh of his frenulum. Immediately his penis began to swell to the point Duke thought it would burst. Before he could even scream out the unthinkable happened.

The salamander leapt up into the urine stream and into Duke's urethra. In a panic he grabbed at the creature but the spines along its back bristled up. The creature's spines pointed backward toward its tail making it impossible for him to pull it out as the spines locked themselves into his flesh. He pinched down hard on the animal's tail, but it broke off and the salamander was able to complete its breech. A little nubbin of amphibian flesh wriggled on the ground at his feet for several seconds before it transmuted into a tiny pile of fine black soot.

Duke ran for the tractor in a panic. He didn't know what the hell this thing was, but he knew he needed a doctor and fast. Internally he was on fire. The salamander was flicking its demonic tongue out in rapid succession against the walls of his bladder as if it were trying to break through the elastic shell.

Panic set in the moment he realized the parasite somehow made its way into his scrotum. He clutched at the loose bag of wrinkled skin and managed to grip the creature between his forefinger and thumb through his scrotum. He tried with all his strength to crush the thing regardless of the pain it caused from the spines needling into him. In defense of Duke's attack, the creature's venomous tongue lashed out and struck a delicate target. His right testicle was immediately aflame with debilitating pain that careened through his entire body and dropped him to his knees. Another tongue lash struck the left testicle and Duke vomited. In a sheer panic he managed to make it back to his feet where he ran blindly through the forest. A tree root tripped him, and Duke hit the ground hard enough to knock the wind out of him.

As he writhed in agony while clutching his groin, he saw the forest floor in front of him begin to flutter. Dried leaves shuddered and were cast aside by dozens of the radiant salamanders who marched toward him in unison. Duke flipped over on his belly and began dragging himself by his elbows. He managed to make it nearly fifty yards into the forest before the multitude of creatures descended upon him.

The first one shot its tongue to the back of his knee and within seconds the joint expanded to twice its normal size. Duke slapped his palm down on one of the creatures, killing it instantly. He raised his hand for another blow, but another creature's tongue found the crook of his arm, rendering that joint useless. He looked over in horror as his elbow continued to expand until he felt the cartilage in the joint burst. His right knee was the next joint to succumb to the mounting pressure.

Duke opened his mouth to scream, and a handful of the amphibians raced into the open orifice stinging the back of his throat repeatedly. An attacking pair crawled into each of his ears and two more into his nostrils, within seconds they invaded every single cavity of his body.

After several minutes of agonizing, mind-numbing pain his ears exploded, sending an intense shock wave reverberating throughout his entire body unlike anything he had ever felt before. Mercifully, his throat swelled to the point it choked off his blood supply and airway causing him to pass out before the swelling snapped his spinal column. Duke's body was ice cold long before the creatures were finished feeding.

~   ~   ~

"Have you ever seen anything like it?" Gabe asked as they sauntered through the forest.

"Honey, I think you are embellishing a little."

"No, I'm not. I swear, after Mandy falls asleep those moths leave the jar and flutter about for hours. And just before she wakes up, they flutter back into the jar."

"Gabe, I am officially calling that story pure bullshit," Paul said, passing the joint to Tara.

The three of them were enjoying a decent buzz, but it was more out of necessity than recreation. While their mood was light and airy on the outside, inside they knew they were going to investigate remains, possibly human and quite possibly their deaths were suspicious. And that required a somber note to the affair.

Each of them was lost in their own little world, Paul was looking up into the trees at the sunbursts peeking between the leaves and pine needles. Gabe was busy trying to fill the pipe and Tara was watching the ground, looking for anything unique she could share with her daughter that might somewhat interest the child. They were so preoccupied with their own thoughts they almost walked right into the tractor as a group.

"What in the hell?" Gabe said.

"It looks like Duke parked for an easy egress."

Gabe walked over to the bunker and peered down into the darkness. After several minutes of not seeing or hearing anything move, he called out.

"Duke. Hey, Duke, are you down there?"

"It looks like he hung one of the work lights. I'll fire up the generator," Paul said.

It only took two pulls on the cord and the generator started which in turn illuminated the dark chamber. Gabe slowly lowered the work light until he could see the bottom before making his way down to the

189

first landing while carrying one of the light stands. Paul followed, checking the integrity of each step one by one. Every so often he would pound another nail into the woodwork just for good measure. Neither of them was too comfortable with how far down the stairs descended into the earth. The bunker was old, ancient in fact and the threat of collapse was a real possibility. Once they were at the bottom Tara lowered an extension cord down to the bottom and Gabe plugged in the light tree.

The first chamber exploded with light, and they were relieved to find it void of life. Gabe positioned the light in one of the far corners to illuminate the room as completely as possible before returning to the surface for the other tree of work lights. Once he had the second set of lights plugged in and working, he and Paul moved down the small, dark corridor to the room Paul and Gabe visited on their first entry into the void. The new illumination of the room lent credence to their original assumption that there were human bones in the bunker. From what Paul could see, canine as well. The two men stood in silence while absorbing the scene.

After several minutes of silence Tara called down, "Is it safe for me to come down there?"

"Just take it slow and bring down the Polaroid camera, with extra film if we brought any."

Tara's footsteps echoed throughout the concrete chamber as she descended into the pit. Her last few steps were slow and methodical as she tried to brace herself for what she was about to encounter. Was this a burial site? Was there truly a pile of human bones down here? As she descended the last two stairs and rounded the corner, she faced a scene she hadn't prepared herself for. An empty room for the most part, save for the tree of work lights and a lot of dust. She followed Gabe's voice and the column of light, through the small passage to where the men were waiting.

She was taken aback by the scene in front of her. On the floor at the foot of a mattress pulled from one of the two sets of bunk beds were two skeletons still arranged exactly how they had died. One human, a male which she determined by bone structure and what appeared to be a dog. On the bed was what she deduced to be a woman's skeleton at her first glance of the pelvic bone. Tara was perplexed indeed.

"What is this place? Some sort of bomb shelter?" she asked.

"Possibly, but it looks too old to have been built only thirty or forty years ago," Gabe said.

"Did these people just starve to death?" Paul asked.

"No, I don't think so. They died in a great deal of pain I would imagine. Look at their open jaws, and the scratches on the floor. Whatever happened to them happened fast and it caused them a great deal of agony."

"Why wouldn't the dog have just run away?" Paul asked.

Tara bent down and inspected the skull of the canine more closely.

"Just as I suspected, this was not a dog, this was a wolf."

"Did they get themselves trapped down here with a wolf who attacked them? And once it finished eating them it simply starved to death?"

Tara walked around the bones, circling the remains several times. She didn't have a clue what to make of this. But she did know the wolf did not attack the people.

"No, if the wolf would have attacked them there would be teeth marks somewhere on at least one of the bones, but there isn't anything to indicate that is what happened. And there would be stains where they bled out, but these people did not die from blood loss. It is almost as if these two, the man and the wolf, knew what was in store for them and simply chose to remain in each other's company when it happened. See here, the man's arm was around the wolf's neck."

"He was hugging the beast as they died?" Paul asked.

"It appears that way. It's simply my first impression, I'll take photos and study the scene further," Tara said, her voice betraying the fact she was both fascinated and excited, but also a bit frightened.

Gabe was standing over the bed peering down at the woman's remains. There was something different about the way her bones were arranged. Something that just didn't make any sense.

"Why are her ribs positioned like this? It would seem to me that they would have collapsed here, and not over there, and they also appear to be upside down," Gabe said, pointing his finger at each of the ribs.

Tara walked back and forth from each side of the bed looking the remains over while making sure she didn't

192

touch anything. She knew they were not going to like her answer.

"Because her stomach burst open."

"You mean she was pregnant?" Paul asked.

"No, there are no fetal bones in this human stew. Every one of these bones came from her and her alone."

"What are you saying, Tara?"

"Gabe, I can only tell you what I see and what I see is that her stomach literally exploded blowing her ribs outward and away from the body."

Tara started taking Polaroid photos of the bones trying to distance herself mentally that these were once living, breathing human beings. There was a reason she never went to med school, she hated anything to do with living trauma.

"Could it have been gas?" Paul asked, startling his two cohorts and forcing a smile on both of their faces.

"Like she ate too many beans?" Gabe asked jokingly.

"No, like a poison gas. Maybe she ate something that reacted inside of her and released a poison gas into the atmosphere."

"I guess that is one possibility, but I would think she would have been in discomfort and the relationship of her bones do not validate that theory. She was not in pain, not the kind of pain that dying from poison would bring on or she would have been in the fetal position."

The lights flickered and Gabe walked over to the stairs to listen. The generator was running out of gas.

"I better run up and gas up the generator. I can't believe we have been down here this long," he said while checking his Timex.

"While you are up there grab my bag, I want to get a closer look at these bones and I don't want to move them," Tara said.

"Okay, but fair warning, I'll have to turn off the generator for a minute or two while refueling so you guys will be in the dark down here," Gabe said and bounded up the stairs before the machine ran completely out of gas.

His footsteps still echoed on the stairs when the lights flickered one last time and went out, plunging Tara and Paul into darkness. There was only ten or fifteen seconds before Paul switched his flashlight on but during that time, she didn't think her heart beat one time. Tara was not sure if it was her eyes playing tricks on her, but she swore she saw a tiny blue light flash by her in the darkness before disappearing.

What felt like an eternity in darkness ended and the lights snapped back on. Gabe was back downstairs with Paul and Tara in a matter of minutes. He set a large bag of equipment down on a small dresser near the bed. The old antique wobbled a little under the weight.

"Look at the furniture in this room," Paul said.

"It sure looks old, doesn't it?" Tara said.

"Antique, like really antique."

Tara pulled a couple of magnifying glasses and finally a microscope out of her bag and set her equipment down on the floor near the bones. She also pulled a small battery powered lamp from the bag.

"No wonder that damn thing is so heavy," Gabe said. "You brought your entire science lab with you."

"What do you intend to do with that thing?" Paul asked.

"I am going to examine the bones."

"You can't touch them."

"Why not?" Tara asked.

"They could be toxic," Paul said.

"If they were that toxic then we would already be sick, or worse."

"But these people may have been murdered. We have to alert the authorities, let them touch the bones," Paul said.

"I am not going to touch them, simply examine them," Tara said, sliding the microscope up to one of the metacarpal bones of the male on the floor. She removed the stage portion of the microscope so that she could slide the piece of equipment over the bone without touching the bone itself. "Besides, don't you think you are being a little melodramatic, Paul?"

"Not in the least. Something is dodgy about this place."

"It was probably nothing more than a bomb shelter built during World War Two and these people locked themselves in out of fear. They probably starved to death," Gabe said.

Paul ignored them and wandered about the cavernous bunker looking at all the furniture. It was ornate and old, much too old to have been built in the nineteen forties. No, this was still made with peg and dovetail construction popular in the eighteen hundreds. He shined his flashlight under the larger bureau closest to the mattress on the floor. There was something under the piece of furniture.

He went back topside for a minute and returned with a prybar. Paul fished around under the bureau until he hooked onto something and pulled it toward him.

"What did you find?" Gabe asked.

"It looks like some kind of journal. It must have gotten kicked under there somehow," Paul said, turning the leather-bound tome over in his hands. He thumbed through the first several pages which was a log of the lighthouse's day to day operation. "Can you tell how old those bones are through that gadget of yours?" he asked Tara.

"I can give a rough estimate, but that would be an extremely rough estimate. Why do you ask?" she replied, raising her eye from the eyepiece to look over at him.

"Because I think we may have found the missing lighthouse keeper and his wife."

"What on earth gives you that impression, Paul?" Gabe asked.

"This journal," he said, tossing the book across the room to Gabe who thumbed through the first few pages of log entries.

"As far as I can tell without using the proper equipment, this looks authentic. But it can't belong to these people, can it? That would mean they have been down here nearly a hundred years."

Tara was busy investigating the bones. She didn't like what she saw so she put lens cleaning solution on the top and bottom eyepieces and rubbed them carefully with lens cloth before peering into the microscope again.

"Gabe take a look at this," she said, backing away from the eyepiece. She cranked the magnification up another notch.

Gabe put his eye to the eyepiece and looked at the piece of bone. He ratcheted the magnification up and then backed it down a few stops.

"What in the hell made all those microscopic scratches on the bone? I've never heard of a parasite that attacks bone, at least not a parasite that is present in humans," Gabe said.

"Gabe, there would have had to have been hundreds of thousands of them, maybe even millions to do this extensive amount of damage," Tara said.

She walked around the bed a few times, stopping to lift the mattress up at each corner. Gabe knew something was bothering her from the perplexed look on her face.

"What is it, Tara?"

"There are no stains anywhere. The parasite must have survived long enough to devour the putrefaction sludge from these corpses and before they even began to decompose if that makes any sense. I've never heard of a parasite that cleans up after itself this well. There should be stains on the concrete from their bodily fluids even after all this time. There should at least be some stains on the mattress. Something is very wrong here. I think we are dealing with an organism unknown to modern science," she said.

With that revelation Paul started to head for the stairs at a brisk pace.

"Where are you going?"

"I'm not going to be hanging out down in a hole infested with flesh eating parasites," he said and disappeared up the stairs.

"He has a point. Maybe we should leave this for the authorities," Gabe said.

Tara's imagination had her skin crawling, so she adamantly agreed. They gathered up her gear and headed topside to meet up with Paul. On the walk back to the lighthouse Gabe couldn't shake the feeling that they were being watched.

~   ~   ~

"Hey, Tomas, have you seen Duke?" the grizzled foreman asked his underling.

"Not since he left on the tractor to take the portable generator back into the woods for some damned reason. Why, is there a problem?" Tomas replied.

"I just heard the Coast Guard on the scanner, there's a monster of a storm brewing out on the lake."

"How far out?"

"A couple of hours maybe more. They were talking like it was a doosie," Oleg, the foreman said.

"Do you want me to start packing up?" Bill, Duke's head carpenter chimed in, pointing up at the thunderheads looming on the horizon.

"Why don't you start getting the tools inside, cover up all the building supplies and make sure everything is unplugged while Tomas and I round up the rest of the crew and get them down to the boat. I'll send them on ahead of us, and we'll take the next one over," Oleg said.

"Sounds like a plan. You better leave Duke a note, so he knows what happened to us."

Tomas headed around to the back side of the lighthouse where the men were supposed to be working but he didn't see anyone, nor did he hear any sounds of tell-tale carpentry work. His anger ratcheted up a notch when he saw expensive power tools lying in the wet grass unattended. A flurry of motion in the hedgerow near the cliffs caught his attention and he wandered over to get a closer look. A few feet into the shrubbery he spied the soles of a pair of work boots jutting out from the greenery, toes pointed down.

Tomas was genuinely concerned that the workers in his charge had gotten drunk on their lunch break and passed out on the lawn where the homeowner might see them. He stopped in the yard and glanced around, hoping no one was outside to see the inebriated worker. A glint of metal in the sunlight caught his attention and his eyes walked up the lighthouse tower to see an old woman standing on the widow's walk. Her wrinkled hands, ruddy and adorned with turquoise rings on every finger gripped the railing as she leaned over to peer down. Tomas swore he saw her wave at him before she disappeared back into the lantern room.

"Crazy old bat," he said with a chuckle.

He kicked the bottom of the worker's boots who he believed belonged to the new kid from downstate. The moment his boot made contact a cloud of black dust rose in the air and the man simply disintegrated into ash. Dried leaves under the bushes began to flutter, softly at first, rising gradually until they reached a crescendo and exploded into disarray, revealing several miniature frogs scattered amongst the debris. Tomas was shocked, but curious as to what it was that he was seeing. These frogs were not ordinary looking frogs, but frogs with eight long, spindly legs like spiders and they were glowing an iridescent blue hue unlike anything he had ever seen.

Tomas dropped to his knees, cupped his hands, and trapped one of the amphibians under his palm. He raised his hand to his face, pulled his reading glasses from his pocket and started to examine the creature. He was startled to see it was also multi-eyed like a spider.

"What in the world are you? You look like some science fiction, creature feature movie mutation," he said to the little animal.

Without warning a tongue five times longer than the amphibian's entire body shot out and stuck to Tomas's glasses. He recoiled but then laughed at the image the tongue made plastered to the glass lens. The frog withdrew its tongue rapidly tugging the man's glasses off his face. Tomas looked down at his glasses which had now fallen to the ground and then back up to the amphibian. Before he could react, the tongue shot out again, this time connecting directly with his eyeball.

Tomas screamed in agony and staggered backwards cupping his face in his hands. The pain was excruciating, unlike anything he had ever experienced before. A spike of heat radiated inward toward his brain as his eyeball swelled until it burst. Ocular jelly oozed from between his fingers and Tomas withdrew his hand to look at it with his good eye. The tongue shot out like a bolt from a crossbow right into the man's open eye socket.

Tomas backpedaled and tripped over the dead worker's boots, landing on his back in the wet grass. The last thing he saw was an army of eight-legged frogs hopscotching toward him from out of the thicket. He could feel his brain swelling, pressing against the inside of his cranium. In a last minute of desperation, he managed to eke out a scream before his brain exploded from the pressure while a dozen tiny frogs invaded the cavity to dine on his fragmented gray matter.

"Tomas, what happened," Bill called out as he ran around the corner of the lighthouse, alerted by the man's screams.

Bill stopped dead in his tracks, captivated by the scene in front of him. A skeleton protruded from the hedges while his foreman lay prone on his back covered in hundreds of tiny frogs. Eight-legged frogs. One of the frogs noticed him and began to emit a radiant blue light. Bill didn't need any more encouragement than that to run.

As he ran toward the cliff's edge his brain was scrambling to formulate an escape plan. Each time he stole a glance behind him the frogs were even closer to him. He saw the yellow caution tape on the stairwell flapping in the breeze, so he made a mad dash for what he hoped would be safety.

Bill broke through the caution tape like Steve Prefontaine crossing the finish line. He trotted down the rickety staircase until he reached the final intact platform, but he was still at least a hundred feet above the rocks below. Homicidal frogs hell bent on his destruction began raining down on him from the cliffs above. The first sticky tongue landed on his cheek, the second went straight up his nostril. Bill didn't wait for a third and launched himself off the platform like Micki King going for gold. The frogs launched themselves into a miniature amphibian kamikaze attack down onto Bill's plummeting body. They attacked more voraciously than a starved wolf on a fresh kill. Although it felt like a lifetime, less than three seconds later Bill's arid corpse hit the boulders in an explosion of bones, blue amphibians, and ebony dust. His desiccated remains scattered across the water's surface before sinking beneath the cold depths of Lake Superior.

~   ~   ~

"Come on, squirt, quit messing with those moths and keep up with me," Travis stopped and called to his sister who had dropped back nearly fifty yards.

Travis was not too keen on taking his sister fishing, and in all honesty, he was not too keen on going fishing himself. Especially not deep into the forest. Even though he possessed a map and marked the trail in ways that would be nearly impossible to tamper with he still kept a wary eye out for the asshole neighbors. He stopped and rolled over an old, dead stump to harvest some bait and was startled when something darted off into the underbrush.

"You got scared," Amanda giggled, standing over her brother.

"It just startled me is all."

"What was it?"

"I'm not sure. It moved too fast to see. Maybe it was a girl-eating snake."

"Cool! I wanna see a snake."

"I was just kidding squirt; it wasn't a snake."

"Then what was it?"

"I don't know. I told you; it moved too fast."

"Then how do you know it wasn't a snake?" she asked.

"You know, I liked you a whole lot better before you could talk," Travis said and continued walking.

"And I liked you a whole lot better when I didn't understand what you were saying," she said, jamming her hands on her hips with a scowl etched across her face.

Travis set his tackle box down, opened it up and went to work setting up Amanda's fishing pole. He cast it out a few times to loosen the filament on the spool and added some more weight so she could cast further. He put a huge baseball sized red and white bobber on her line, baited the hook with an earthworm and gave her the Zebco. Her first cast hit the beach and bounced into the water. Her second cast nearly hooked him so he wisely helped her with her third cast before he lost an eye, finally casting the line out as far as it would reach.

Travis set up his pole, a brand spanking new Shimano, with a steel leader and a red and white Daredevil spoon on the end. He cast high and long, the lure making a small *ploop* sound like a diver entering the water on a perfect ten dive. He felt the resistance of the water against the lure as he reeled his line back in and anticipated a strike from a monster pike, but no strike ever came. Not on that cast or the next twenty or so. He changed to his trusty Rapala which resembled an injured perch but that lure also netted the same negative results. Amanda seemed content to just watch her bobber floating motionless on the surface of the lake, so he reeled in his line and set his pole down. He found it odd that not even the small, thieving fish managed to steal the bait from her sedentary hook.

After taking off his shoes and socks, Travis waded out into the icy water which seemed to be a little too cold for that time of year. He walked around the perimeter until his sister was just a little speck before he decided he better head back to her. Something wasn't right, but he decided to keep it to himself in case he was overreacting. But there were no signs of life whatsoever in the lake. Not even the tiniest of minnows sucking at the air bubbles on his toes. Hell, he would have settled for an empty crayfish shell. But there was nothing indicating anything ever lived in that water.

As he approached Amanda there was a loud rustling echoing from the tree line where he had just left. He saw a look of fear on his sister's face, so he hurried over to her.

"What was that?" she asked.

"I don't know squirt."

"Was that a bear?" Her voice trembled.

"I don't think there are any bears on this island. Maybe it was a deer. Let's move into the trees a little," he said and gathered up their things.

Suddenly the moths inside of the jar began to glow brighter than ever before. From the other end of the lake the sound intensified, and the children could see dead leaves moving on the ground even from that distance. The leaves stirred slowly at first but then quickly evolved into a flurry of motion. The sound continued to build into a crescendo and soon surrounded them.

"I'm scared Travis."

"There's nothing to be afraid of, it's just the wind."

Dead, dry leaves were being tossed into the air as whatever was in the forest was now moving toward them at an accelerated pace. Travis knew it wasn't the wind, but it wasn't a bear nor a deer. He was frightened as well, but he had to stay strong for his little sister. The crest of the small hillock which led to the beach began to glow the same blue hue as the moths in the jar. In turn the moths glowed even brighter, so bright in fact, the children were forced to shield their eyes. Travis found himself wishing his father was there. He would have taken his sister and run through the woods but whatever was stirring up the forest was blocking their return path and he wasn't taking the chance on them getting lost again.

"What are those?" Amanda pointed toward the small ridge which erupted into a flurry of chaotic motion.

"I don't have a clue."

Dozens upon dozens of tiny lizards swarmed over the hill like the armies of Hannibal descending the Alps. The air was electrified with an ultramarine haze spanning upwards at least ten feet. What Travis now realized were hundreds, if not thousands of miniscule reptilian creatures swarmed the beach and into the waters of Echo Lake. The surface of the water boiled in anger at the invasion, spitting, sputtering, and popping blue hued water several feet into the air. Travis thought it looked like someone poured blue dye into a geyser. And then all fell calm and quiet. Much too quiet.

"We need to go, Travis. We need to go home right now!" Amanda said.

Travis nodded and gathered up their fishing gear and started walking as fast as he dared. Amanda's little legs were pumping overtime to keep up with him, but she suddenly stopped.

"What's wrong?"

"I think they're dead," she said.

"You think what is dead?"

"The moths. Look, they turned all black," she said, holding the Miracle Whip jar up to her brother.

Travis tapped the side of the jar with his finger and the moths disintegrated into a fine black powder. He didn't notice the two sets of eyes peering up at him from under the blades of grass in the jar, but Amanda did, and she smiled.

"Come on squirt. We need to get home and talk to mom and dad about this."

~   ~   ~

Mishipeshu finished her third pass around the island and settled into the waves of the frigid Lake Superior waters beneath the beacon on the cliffs. With a heavy heart she prepared herself for what she must do because she no longer had the option of saving humanity on the island, the organism would infect them all. For the sake of the many, the few must perish. As she drifted on the current, she allowed the last remaining scrap of her own humanity to transport her through her ancient memories.

Waagosh, so called because she was both cunning and playful, hid in the tall grasses watching through her curious, chestnut eyes as her two brothers portaged their canoe through the forest toward the banks of Lake Superior. Makoons, the eldest, was about to embark on a journey, his vision quest into manhood, during which he would travel across the great water to Michipicoten Island where he would fast until joined with his spirit guide to learn of what greatness awaited him in this life. Andeg, the younger of the two accompanied his older brother for moral support. Once his older brother's journey to the island was underway, Andeg would stay behind with a signal fire and food for when Makoons' quest was complete.

The boys had no idea their little sister was buzzing about like a pesky mosquito or else they would have sent her back to the village with a reddened behind. Waagosh hid in the tall reeds listening to the boys' nonsense about Makoons becoming a man and shedding his boyhood name. He would come back from the island ready to take his place with the other men. To her, it was a ridiculous rite of passage as everyone in the village knew the strongest and bravest amongst them were the women.

Waagosh quickly tired of their bravado and decided to have some fun at her brothers' expense. One of her talents she was quite adept at, and quite proud of, was the ability to mimic nearly every creature in the forest. Her mother told her it was her gift and one day she would do remarkable things because of her great love of all creatures great and small.

"Did you hear that?" Andeg asked.

"I did not hear anything," Makoons replied with a dismissive glance.

"There is a fawn bleating for its mother over there in the trees."

"So, let the mother handle the whelp's cries," Makoons said and went back to stirring the fire, watching as the embers floated into the air like fireflies.

Waagosh played her game with her brothers for nearly an hour before she hatched a plan that would allow her to accompany her older brother to Michipicoten Island where she would embark upon her own vision quest. Makoons had wished for a fox kit for as long as she could remember so she crawled through the grass until she found a suitable spot to dig a den in the sand. Once she had her trap laid out, she began to mimic the cry of a lost little fox.

"Did you hear that?" Makoons asked.

"It sounded like a fox," his brother replied.

"Come on, help me catch it."

"But you have to leave soon."

"You can watch it while I am gone."

As the boys crept through the tall, dew laden grass looking for their quarry, Waagosh crept down to their campsite and stowed herself away under the blankets in her brother's canoe.

"I told you it was nothing," Makoons said, plopping down in the sand in defeat.

Both boys lay back in the sand looking up at the stars and were soon dazzled by a meteor shower as streaks of lights zipped through the great expanse of night sky. The only sound was that of the lake gently lapping at the sands and cicadas far off in the trees. Occasionally, a lone seagull would squawk, but even most of those boisterous creatures were asleep.

Suddenly the air was charged with crackling light and there began a thunderous rumble in the sky above them. Every hair on the boys' body stood straight on end. The rumble began slowly at first, but then grew in intensity until a deafening boom reverberated across the night. The sky above them split wide open and a giant fireball raced through the night sky so bright it forced them to shield their eyes.

"What was that?" Andeg asked with unease in his voice.

"I don't know, little brother."

They watched as the meteorite streaked through the air trailing a tail of fire for miles as it descended toward the lake. A huge explosion shook the night as the space rock impacted Michipicoten Island sending a ball of fire spewing into the air.

"Did that hit Michipicoten?"

"I think so, Andeg."

"Should we go back and tell the others?"

Makoons thought about this for a moment before he said, "No, that was a thunderbird, a sign from Gitchee Manitou that it is time for me to go to Michipicoten."

"I'm scared, don't leave me here alone."

"Would you rather go with me?"

The younger brother gave a vigorous nod.

"It might be dangerous."

"It is safer with you than here by myself."

Waagosh curled up in the bottom of the canoe and tried not to make a single sound. She timed her breathing with the sploosh of her brother's paddle dipping into the water. Even though she could not see anything, she knew her brother was paddling harder and faster than ever before. As they neared the island Makoons set his paddle down and stood up to scout the shoreline.

"What do you see?" Andeg asked, tugging at his brother's pants leg.

"I'm not sure. There is something glowing in the forest just off the beach."

"Is the island on fire?"

"No, Andeg, the glow is not red and orange like a fire, but blue."

"Let's just turn around and go back. We need to get father and the others," Andeg said on the verge of tears.

Makoons almost agreed with his little brother, almost. There were several places in the deep water surrounding the island where a blue glow materialized from the lake's bottom. He had been to the island several times with his father and knew the lake was deep here, too deep for even his father to dive to the bottom. What could possibly be shining so brightly they would be able to see it on the surface? Whatever it was, it was too important to ignore.

"No little brother, this is our adventure," he said, and eased the canoe toward the shore.

Makoons steered the boat for the shallows until they were in knee deep water before jumping out of the canoe. He towed the craft up onto the sand so Andeg could get out without getting wet.

"What now, Makoons?"

"You wait here by the canoe, and I will scout ahead to see if it is safe. Once you hear me whistle you can follow me."

With that, Makoons disappeared up a small dune trail toward the forest on a mission to solve this mystery. Tangles of dune grasses wrapped around his ankles and dropped him to the cold sand several times, stoking his anger with each stumble. Within a few minutes his calves were burning so as soon as he could see the tree line through the darkness, he took off on a dead run hoping to find a hard pack trail.

At the edge of the forest, he stopped to catch his breath, and once he was no longer gasping for air, he noticed how quiet everything was. There were no night birds singing, no coyotes yipping or even crickets belting out romantic ballads. A chill ran up his spine and he nearly headed back for the canoe but the puzzling glow bathing the dense forest in a blue haze compelled him to push on despite his apprehension.

As he drew closer the light became more intense and a slight hum traveled through the night air. The light became too powerful for him to be able to look at it directly, so he took off his shirt and used it to shield his eyes. Makoons was close enough to see the light was coming from a large rock, but it wasn't just any rock. It took him a moment, but he realized what he was looking at was a metal soft enough his father was able to pound it out to make tools, pans to cook with, and jewelry. But the rock was hard to find and precious to his clan.

Makoons smiled. This was the discovery of a lifetime. But it was much too large to be able to take back to the canoe, let alone paddle the canoe with it inside. He needed to take a closer look to see if he could break it into smaller, more manageable pieces.

The boy watched with fascination as the glowing blue rock appeared to be spitting out tiny sapphire embers like fireflies floating up into the night sky. And just like the embers of a fire the little blue sparks got smaller and smaller until they just disappeared.

Andeg watched his older brother from the shadows, and he too was mesmerized by the pretty blue lights. While the scene before him was rather peaceful and serene, there was also something sinister in the air that scared him. It was the constant humming sound reverberating all around him, tingling his very skin.

Waagosh eyed both of her brothers from the shadows, but her attention was diverted by the glowing blue rock. While wonderous in appearance, she feared all was not as it seemed. She perceived a presence in the air surrounding her when she began to hear an odd humming noise. She listened intently to the sound and concentrated on the vibrations it made through the air. Every hair on her arm was standing straight up and down.

Makoons stood in the forest, bathed in the azure radiance of this strange, shiny rock, while being dazzled by the brilliant light display of the tiny cinders. The humming sound created waves of vibrations that tickled the bottom of his feet, and he laughed which caught the attention of the drifting sparks, and they began floating toward him instead of upward. He was uneasy at first, but as they swirled around him in an elegant elliptical pattern, he embraced his vision.

The crystalline orbs of light rose from the boy's feet and proceeded to move up his body in a double helix pattern until he was fully encased in thousands of cerulean spheres. Suddenly the pattern began to swell outward away from his body until they were rotating around him several feet away. The array of lights abruptly tightened until they slammed into Makoons with such force they nearly knocked him off his feet. Once again, the lights moved away from him and once again, they slammed into him with such intensity he cried out in pain. The third assault saw the orbs penetrate his flesh.

Makoons looked down at his arms to see hundreds of blue lights crawling up his forearms just under the skin. He reached down, took one of the lights between his index finger and his thumb and squeezed as hard as he could until the light exploded. The pain was so intense it caused his knees to buckle, and he dropped to the ground.

"Makoons," Andeg cried out and broke from his cover at the edge of the forest.

"Run, little brother, run," Makoons cried out, realizing that whatever this strange rock was, it was not a good thing.

At the sound of Andeg's cries more of the blue orbs exited the glowing rock, held their place in the air for a moment as if looking for something and then made a beeline for the boy. Seeing this, Andeg heeded his brother's warning and ran for the beach, his little legs pumping harder than ever before.

Every inch of Makoons' body was on fire, even his internal organs. His muscles tightened and cramped against the onslaught. When he opened his mouth to scream, thousands more of the lights streamed down his gullet until he choked. He tried to scream for Andeg to run but it was useless. Not a single sound was able to escape. He felt a tingling sensation coursing through his veins and within seconds he had disintegrated into a fine, black powder.

Waagosh was horrified by the scene unfolding in front of her. Something was attacking her older brother and now had turned attention to her other brother. She could not let that happen.

"Hey," she called out with her hands cupped around her mouth.

The orbs stopped moving for a moment but then continued their pursuit of the small child running away from them.

"I said, hey, come and get me. I'm a much tastier meal," Waagosh screamed while waving her arms and moving in the opposite direction, toward the glowing rock.

She tried to ignore the pile of soot on the ground at the base of the rock which were the last remnants of her brother Makoons. Although frightened because she was certain of her fate, she was also relieved because the lights had abandoned their pursuit of Andeg and were now focused on her.

The strand of iridescent lights repeated their pattern of surrounding the girl in a double helix. Waagosh braced herself as they floated outward away from her and knew they were about to launch an assault. Just as she had anticipated, the lights held for a moment, and then raced toward her at blinding speed. Her eyes were closed as tightly as she could close them, and she wondered why these minute creatures were toying with her once she felt no impact against her flesh. A strange sound reached her ears, and she slowly opened her eyes to see the lights were indeed trying to attack her but for some reason they were unable to penetrate the air surrounding her. Carefully she reached her hand out and pressed her palm facing out against the air to feel it was solid. There was some sort of barrier between her and the lights.

"You are safe child," a voice said.

She looked around her in all directions but did not see anyone standing near her. It was then she realized the voice came from inside her own head.

"Who are you?" she asked.

"That is of no consequence."

"How?" she asked.

"That is also of no consequence."

Waagosh was distracted by the lights bombarding the barrier surrounding her. They were like little blue fireflies, and she would consider them beautiful if not for the fact they just killed her brother and were trying to kill her as well. She turned around to see if any of the lights had trailed after Andeg and breathed a sigh of relief when she spotted none.

"The boy is safe, child. He made it to the canoe and is paddling for home," the voice said.

"How do you know this? And how did you know what I was thinking?"

"I know and see everything."

"So, you know about this mysterious rock?"

"Unfortunately, yes."

She thought long and hard about what the voice had said and wondered if what she was thinking could possibly be true. If it were true, she was not worthy.

"Oh yes, my child, you are more than worthy."

Waagosh gasped. Her voice quivered as she asked, "Are you Gitchee Manitou."

"I have many names, and yet, I have none. Call me whatever you wish to call me."

"That wasn't much of an answer," she said before she could curtail her sarcasm.

The voice let loose a rumbling belly laugh. "I suppose it wasn't, now, was it?"

"And why is your voice so loud? It hurts my ears, and it is scary," Waagosh asked with her eyes strained upward.

"Is this better," the voice replied in a soothing motherly tone.

"How did you do that? Is this some kind of trick?"

The voice was quiet for a moment while reflecting but then responded to the child. "I suppose in a manner of speaking it is a trick of sorts."

"You still never answered me. Are you Gitchee Manitou?" she asked much more defiantly than one should question their creator.

"If you mean by this name Gitchee Manitou that I am your creator then, yes, I am the creator of not just you, but of all things."

"Even the moon and the stars?"

"Yes, and more beyond that you cannot even see."

"Even them?" she asked, pointing at the blue lights still besieging the barrier surrounding her.

"Yes, little one, even them."

"Why would you create something that wanted to kill your other creations?"

"You speak a sound logic. When I created all things, I imbued each of them with their own freewill and then they chose their own paths to take. And while creation can be incredibly beautiful, it can have a very ugly side as well. For creation, for your planet to work, to thrive and to grow, sacrifices were necessary."

She thought long and hard about her next comments. "You mean like when father kills a deer for us to eat and then we thank the deer for sacrificing itself to feed us?"

"Exactly like that."

"Does that mean I am to be their sacrifice?" she asked, pointing to the agitated specks of light.

"Unfortunately, yes. But as I stated earlier, I have given you the free will to choose your destiny. Though I will admit, your choices are limited, and you will probably not like either option."

"I can guess one of my choices is to let them eat me."

"You would be correct."

"I don't think I would like that choice one single bit."

"Then here is your other option. While this rock as you call it, is my creation, it does not belong here, and yet, I cannot put it back where it came from."

"Why not?"

"There are certain rules I must abide by."

"Doesn't the rock have to follow rules too?" Waagosh asked.

"My, you are a smart one, aren't you? Think of it like this, when you are told you cannot have another piece of maple candy do you always do what you are told?"

Starting to comprehend the scope of this disembodied spirit's power Waagosh opted for an answer she was certain Gitchee Manitou was already aware of.

"I wait until no one is looking and then I sneak one into my pocket."

"So, you break the rules?"

She nodded.

"So did this rock. And it does not belong here."

"Where does it belong?"

"Somewhere so far away you cannot even see where it came from," the voice said.

"Why can't you send it back there if it broke the rules to come here?" she asked.

"I wish it were that simple, but there are rules that cannot be broken even by me, which brings us to your big decision."

"No, I will not be eaten by whatever that thing is."

"I was hoping you would say that, and in my heart, I knew you would."

"What do I have to do?"

"This rock contains organisms that, if allowed to, will destroy all life. Not just here on the island, not just in your village, but every creature on this planet until there is nothing left for it to eat, and then this place would become a barren wasteland. It will be up to you to ensure that does not happen."

"I am just a little girl, how am I going to stop anything? If it weren't for you, they would have already eaten me."

"You forget who I am child. What do you like most in this world?"

"I love my brother even though he can be bossy," she said, glancing over at the black soot swirling about in the wind.

"What makes you smile and laugh? Think hard."

Waagosh thought about what Gitchee Manitou had said and being young she really had not much experience to draw from, but then it dawned on her.

"Ah, yes, little one. I knew you would figure it out. Now, think about all your favorite animals. Really think hard about the ones you love the most."

Waagosh thought about all the cute little animals she loved to trap, pet, and then let go. But rabbits, mink and squirrels would not be ferocious enough to deal with this accursed rock. No, she would need to be as cunning and ruthless as a lynx, as fast as a deer, and because she would be on an island, she would need to possess the ability to swim great distances too. She felt her skin begin to tighten, and when she looked down at her arms they had changed and were now shimmering like metal. She saw that her arms were covered in copper scales and much, much longer than they had been just one short minute ago. It was then she noticed the barrier was down and instead of attacking her the lights retreated to the glowing rock.

Waagosh, the little girl, was gone and Mishipeshu was in her place. She investigated her new form and found it to her liking. She found a fold of skin on her belly that turned out to be a pouch and understood that was where the rock belonged for now. She tried to pick up the metallic rock, but it was much too heavy and vibrated against her claws which tickled her paw.

A quick strike of her claws and the rock was now four smaller rocks that were easier to manage. She slipped them into the pouch and looked around as if awaiting further instructions.

"I cannot tell you what to do with the rock," the voice said, once again booming.

"Rules?" she replied.

A thunderous laugh echoed across the island. "All I can tell you is that time will march on, and your world will change. Eventually, mankind will find this island, and you as well if you are not careful. To protect them from the rock, you must find a place to hide it where no man could ever find it."

"Where? This island is so small."

"Oh, I think you will figure that problem out for yourself. One last order of business to attend to."

"Dare I ask?"

"How much of yourself do you wish to retain?"

"I don't understand what that means."

"You are going to be alone for a very, very long time. How much of your humanity do you wish to hold on to?"

"Do you mean I won't remember anything?"

"Not if you don't want to."

"Can you make it so I only remember the good things?"

"Most certainly."

"Then I want to remember my family, even my older brother like he is now. I want to remember everything that made me smile, but also the things which made me sad, because those moments will serve to make me stronger."

And without any further formalities Waagosh found herself standing in the dense forest of Michipicoten Island, no longer herself, and completely alone. But for some reason, she didn't seem to mind.

Chapter Seventeen

"Mom, I'm not lying, and I'm not exaggerating, there were hundreds of them," Travis said.

"Thousands, probably millions," Amanda added, her eyes wide with excitement. "And look, we caught a couple of them."

Travis looked dumbfounded at his little sister. As far as he knew they hadn't caught any of the lizards so where did the two amphibians in the jar come from?

"Mandy, where did you get those?" he asked.

She shrugged.

"Mandy, tell mom where those came from? Mom, we didn't catch any, they were way on the other side of the lake from us."

"Amanda, answer your brother."

She looked down at her feet while fidgeting before answering. "I don't know where they came from. They were just there."

"Amanda, things do not just appear out of thin air," Tara said, becoming irritated with her daughter being less than forthcoming.

"These did."

"Mandy, did they crawl into the jar while we were watching the lake?" Travis asked, trying to defend his sister.

She shook her head. "No, the lid was on the jar."

"Amanda Rose, there is no way those lizards got into that jar with the lid on. Now what is going on? Why won't you tell the truth?"

"I am telling the truth," Amanda said and stormed out of the kitchen. She stopped, turned back and said, "When the moths died, the lizards were just there. And they are not lizards, they are amphibians because they like water."

"Amanda, come back here. Travis, what is she talking about?"

"I don't know mom. All I know is that those moths lit up super bright, too bright to even look at and then they just went dark. Kind of like when the filament burns out in a light bulb. I tapped the jar and they just crumbled into a fine, black dust. I never saw those salamanders. Maybe Mandy took the lid off at some point and they crawled into the jar and killed the moths."

Tara nodded. "Travis, please go after your sister."

"So, are you more upset that you think Amanda is lying to you, or that you have no idea what these little buggers are?" Gabe asked, turning the Miracle Whip jar around on the counter.

"I am upset because I don't think she is lying. What in the hell is going on here Gabe?" Did our children just witness a stampede of salamanders? And now that I say it out loud it sounds even more preposterous."

222

"Honey, it's okay to admit you don't know everything."

She stopped him with a look that screamed *this is where I put out the danger, thin ice sign.*

"I'm just saying, maybe these creatures are something you have never encountered. Look through all those highbrow books of yours, I'm sure you will find something in one of them that explains everything. And if you don't, you will be famous for discovering a new species. Just think, you might have a lizard named after you."

Gabe made a swift exit before his wife could take aim with her shoe. They had been back from the bunker for more than two hours and yet not one single word was uttered about what they found. Paul retreated up into the lantern room, clearly shaken by the events of the day. Gabe wandered down the path out to the cliffs while pondering his next move. On one hand, he knew he should contact the Coast Guard, but on the other, he wanted more facts, so he didn't come across as a scared little schoolboy. He decided to sleep on it and would decide what to do in the morning. Afterall, the bones were not going anywhere.

~   ~   ~

Hugh LaPierre stirred the fire in the firepit with a sturdy, charred limb a few times and set a windbreak of cardboard to route the smoke away from where he and his wife were sitting before collapsing into a well-weathered

Adirondack chair with a loud sigh while sporting a devious grin.

"Do you think that was completely necessary?" Beth LaPierre said, followed by a light swat across her husband's shoulder.

"They deserve everything they get for that little prank. Getting those children lost in the forest was a dangerous move. That little girl is even younger and smaller than Gregario."

"But blindfold them, wander them around in the forest and force them to camp by themselves at night, that seems a little cruel."

"No crueler than what they did to those children, who I might add are brand new to this island and have no clue as to the lay of the land. They could have wandered off a cliff in the darkness," Hugh said.

"I guess you're right. But you wouldn't even have known about it had Frederico not started feeling guilty about it and made you go check on them."

"True. But just because a man confesses to his crime does not make him any less guilty, nor does it absolve him of any punishment. Besides, that boy has camped out in those woods on his own for years now, he'll be fine."

The pair sat wordlessly in their chairs listening to the crackling of the fire and watching tiny embers drift up through the ebony sky toward the stars. Hugh looked over and in the dancing firelight saw a tear clinging to his wife's eye.

"Beth, honey, look over there before you get too upset," Hugh said, pointing off into the trees to where a flashlight glow lit up the forest. "The boys are only a couple hundred yards away. Frederico won't realize it until morning because of the windscreen around the fire and I turned the porchlights off."

"You are devious."

"You call it devious; I call it opportunistic. When was the last time we had the place to ourselves for a night?" he asked while reaching over to squeeze his wife's right butt cheek.

~   ~   ~

Frederico dropped his backpack to the ground and took a long drink from his canteen. He scanned the forest in a three-hundred-and-sixty-degree circle hoping to pick up on a recognizable landmark. He knew they walked a lot further than they actually travelled away from the house. His father made certain to twist and turn and zig zag them through the trees to disorient them. But he could smell the smoke from their fire on the breeze so the house shouldn't be more than a mile away.

He wanted to be angry but deep down, he knew he deserved it. Those kids were inexperienced and hadn't done anything to deserve being bullied. And his father was right, real harm could have come to them. He was angrier with himself for succumbing to his little brother's goading in the first place. Gregario was the first to take the trail markers and at the time it was funny. His father was also right, he was no longer a child, and it was time to put away childish things.

"Hey runt, it feels like there is a storm brewing, we better get the tent set up pronto."

"Is dad going to leave us out here if it storms?"

"Don't worry, the tent is waterproof. Remember when I went camping earlier in the spring and it rained for three days straight? I never got wet once in the tent."

"Rainproof is one thing, but tornado proof is another. That storm looks pretty dark," Gregario said.

"Are you scared, runt?"

"No, I am not scared," he said, trying to mask the fear in his voice.

"Listen, it's only one night and then dad won't be so pissed at us. Besides, there is no way that mom will let him make us stay out here any longer than that. In fact, I bet she is nagging him to come and get us right now," Frederico said.

The two boys finished putting up the tent and unrolled their sleeping bags. The older boy gave his younger sibling a root beer he managed to stash away in his backpack while using the camp stove to boil water for hot dogs.

"Can you eat two?" he asked his younger brother.

"Yeah, I think so."

"Good. Make sure to eat everything up though, we don't want to attract any animals with leftovers."

"You mean like bears?"

Frederico balked at the perfect opportunity to screw with his runt of a brother and opted for the high road instead.

"No, more like raccoons and possums."

Gregario shrugged in acceptance of his brother's response and went about the task of getting his bedroll set up perfectly. A scream echoed through the darkness startling both of the boys.

"What was that?"

"Just a fox."

"That didn't sound like a fox to me."

"Well, it was runt. Now finish your hot dog so we can bed down for the night. The faster we get to sleep, the faster morning will come, and we can go back home."

~ ~ ~

Beth shrugged off a chill in the air by donning her raggedy but lucky Green Bay Packers sweatshirt. She poured herself another glass of Mogen David Concord Grape and sat back down next to the fire. Hugh was angling the bottle cap from his Goebel's beer trying to capture enough light from the fire to be able to solve the rebus puzzle. He wasn't sure if he was getting drunk or if the puzzle was a particularly difficult one to solve. Either way, the brainteaser was completely over his head at the moment. He took his wife's cue and put the beer cap down in lieu of something much softer, warmer, and not as hard to solve.

Lightning flashed horizontally across the sky far off in the distance over the lake while the two of them groped each other like teenagers. Fireflies sparked all around them tearing Beth's attention away from their wanton activities.

"Did you see that?"

Hugh mumbled incoherently while nibbling on a morsel of his wife's flesh. Her first nudge was subtle as was the second mainly because she was enjoying herself, but the third was more of a slap.

"Stop for a minute," she said, putting her girls back into her sweatshirt.

"Why? Am I hurting you?"

She laughed. "Fat chance of that."

"Then why did you make me stop?"

"Watch these fireflies, they're strange looking. I've never seen anything like them."

The insects meandered about the LaPierre yard doing whatever it is that fireflies do while Hugh hoped his wife would quickly tire of nature's luminary display.

"Have you ever seen them light up such a beautiful blue color?" she asked.

"Never, and not once in all of my years have I seen a firefly glow so brightly. It almost hurts my eyes to look directly at them," Hugh said.

Seemingly hundreds of fireflies twinkled like Christmas lights in the trees surrounding their yard. Hugh felt a strange sense of apprehension when it appeared to him as though the insects were encircling them in a precise pattern like an army surrounding their adversary to flank them. His wife seemed to be enjoying the light show, so he allowed himself to relax as well.

Hugh was trying to rekindle Beth's flame with a well-placed finger or two when something swooshed past them, startling Beth so badly she dropped her wine glass to shatter on the ground.

"What in the hell was that?" she asked.

Before Hugh could answer several more unseen creatures zipped past them in the darkness.

"Damn, must be bats," he said, ducking from the latest onslaught. "We better get inside, these bats seem to be agitated about something."

They got up from their chairs and started for the house but stopped dead in their tracks. Ahead of them on the small path were thousands of fireflies gathered in a ball of pulsating blue luminosity. The bugs slowly tightened their ball, pulsating as they moved causing them to look like the beating of a big, blue heart.

Suddenly the air became thunderous with the beating of black, leathery wings. The ball of fireflies exploded into a blue fireball and the bats lost their sense of direction. They slammed into the picnic table, the chairs, trees and the LaPierre's themselves knocking them to the ground. Then suddenly, all was calm.

"What in the hell was that?" Hugh asked, still covering his eyes with his forearm.

"You need to go get the boys, now," Beth demanded.

"I don't think I can, look," he said, pointing to the trail leading away from their house out into the woods where the boys were camping.

Dozens of bats formed in masse blocking the trail. The creatures hovered like hummingbirds while fanning out until they were a huge wall of bats. The firefly's glow dimmed but was now increasing in intensity.

"Is that bat glowing back at them?" Beth asked.

One of the bats assumed the front position like geese flying in a V formation. The creature's eyes emitted the same crystalline blue as the fireflies as it stared down the glowing ball. Neither entity paid any attention to Hugh or Beth, they were too engrossed in their brewing war.

"Hugh, what in the world is going on?"

"I don't have a clue, honey. You just get ready to run for the house."

"What are you going to do?"

"I'm going to grab the broom and swat those fireflies out of your way so you can get into the house."

"Is that necessary? They're only fireflies, can't we just walk right passed them?" Beth asked and took a step toward the house.

At that moment, a column of the insects broke away from the rest of the ball and swarmed her like angry hornets. She backpedaled into her husband's arms and shrank back in fear. Spots of blood dotted the backs of her hands, her neck and any other place on her body with exposed flesh.

"Hugh?"

"Beth, honey, I don't know. I really don't know."

Astonished, the couple watched as the ball of light blinked several times garnering a response from the blue-eyed bat who also flashed back at them as if they were communicating. As if by design the ball of fireflies began to swirl as one large mass until the ball began to unravel into a stream of bugs flying in a single file line. Pulsating light moved from insect to insect in rhythmic motion until the string of fireflies strobed through the night air. Hugh held Beth's hand tightly as it trembled. He tried to speak but only managed to eke out a barely audible squeak.

The cloud of bats continued to hover ten feet in the air until unexpectedly they exploded into a frenzy of erratic flapping. As the fireflies disappeared into the gullets of the flittermice, they began to take on the insect's azure iridescence. Within minutes the feeding frenzy was over, and the bats resumed their hovering formation above the LaPierre's heads. Hugh was finally able to break his mystified trance.

"Run!" He screamed out and shoved his wife toward the house while he turned away from her and ran in the opposite direction in an effort to draw the creatures away.

The indigo creatures ignored Hugh's ploy and fell upon Beth with their entire mass knocking her to the ground. One of the bats spread its wings as wide as possible and dug its two claws into the sides of her face. As soon as she opened her mouth to scream the bat turned and shoved its tail end deep into her mouth to gag her. Hugh watched in horror as prismatic blue guano began spilling out of the corners of her mouth. Wide-eyed, Beth struggled to breathe through her nose, but the bat continued to pull itself tighter and tighter to her face by extending its claws and dragging her skin towards itself.

Hugh tried to make it over to his wife but was besieged by a dozen winged creatures sinking their vicious talons into his flesh. They attacked his ankles and knees by wrapping themselves around the joints until he couldn't move. Fighting against the onslaught of a dozen inch long talons tearing through his flesh he managed to force his way over to the firepit.

Without hesitation Hugh plunged his hand into the blazing campfire and pulled out a three-foot-long flaming tree limb. In one quick motion he flipped the searing hot branch over onto his wife. All at once the bats retreated away from the smoldering log and emitted a high-pitched screech that forced him to cover his ears.

Hugh's heart seized in his chest once he realized Beth was already dead. Glowing blue sap oozed from her every orifice, and her face was frozen in the shock of excruciating pain. The bats were thrown into disarray from his outburst but were now congregating together to regroup. Anger brewed inside of him, and he staggered toward the fire pit again.

Hugh looked down at his right hand, it was charred to the point of being useless. He wouldn't have been able to grip another log even if he wanted to. Time stood still as man and beast sized each other up while contemplating each other's next move. He continued to flex and work his right hand hoping to regain enough dexterity to fight, no longer out of self-preservation, but out of a need for vengeance.

As if reading his thoughts, the bats disbursed into the night sky and would have been invisible to him had it not been for their translucent blue eyes piercing through the darkness. Before he could react one of them maneuvered behind him and swooped down to cover his head with its wings. Using its miniature talons, the beast gripped his eyelids near his eye lashes and pulled them up as high as they would stretch. Slicing down from high above another of the bats flew by him in a flurry of leather wings and ripped both of his eyeballs open with its claws.

The colony beset upon Hugh in full force, knocking him to the ground. He flailed at them blindly, even managing to knock a few away and break the necks of several others but eventually their numbers overwhelmed him. One of the bats clung to his head and forced its needlelike tongue deep into his ear canal. Another latched onto his face and probed his nostril with its spindly appendage. Hugh's brain erupted into a fiery ball of stinging pain. He could feel the organ swelling against the inside of his skull until the pain was so intense, he vomited. Splayed out before him on the ground was a puddle of viscous, blue bile that wriggled alive in the moonlight. An inhuman scream echoed through the forest.

~ ~ ~

Gregario bolted upright in his tent. Panic set in when he found he could not move, and it felt as if there were a thousand hands holding him down.

"Freddy, I am stuck," he cried out. "Something has me."

"Shhhh. You're just tangled up in your sleeping bag," he said. He reached over and tugged on the zipper of his brother's sleeping bag to free him.

"What's going on? Why are you sitting here in the dark with the flashlight hidden under the covers?"

"Shhhh, I thought I heard something."

"What did you hear?" Gregario asked.

"Keep it down. I think there's something walking around out there."

"Is a wild animal trying to get us?"

"No, it's probably just dad trying to scare us."

A woman's scream shattered the silence causing both boys to jump.

"What was that? Was that a woman screaming?"

"Shhhh, no I don't think so."

"Yes, it was," he argued, his voice laced with fear.

The scream echoed through the forest again and this time it seemed closer to their encampment. The sound of dried leaves crunching underfoot betrayed the fact there was indeed someone or something walking through the forest near their tent. The steps were soft and deliberate as if whatever was out there was stalking them. Frederico began to slowly unzip the tent door one zipper tooth at a time while trying to breathe as softly as possible.

"Why is that woman screaming, Freddy?"

"It's not a woman, I told you."

"Then what is it? Don't try and tell me that it's a fox because I know what a fox sounds like."

A low, guttural growl rippled on the night air. Whatever was out there was standing right outside their tent. Gregario opened his mouth to say something, but his brother clamped his hand down hard enough to draw blood from jamming his teeth into his lips. The boy struggled with anger in his eyes but calmed down when his older brother raised a threatening fist. A couple of sharp snorts and the creature began to move on. After several minutes, another scream split the night further away from their location.

"I think it might be a lynx, but it has to be the biggest one ever seen from the sound of it," Frederico said.

"A lynx? There aren't any lynx around here. Maybe it's a bobcat."

"A bobcat doesn't make that screaming sound when they cry out. You stay put. I mean it."

Frederico finished unzipping the tent, tucked the flashlight into his shirt and made his way out into the night. He could hear the creature padding along ahead of him and then it stopped. The night became disconcertingly quiet, and his bladder threatened to betray him. He swore he could hear his own heart beating against his breastbone.

The creature didn't move, Frederico didn't move, nothing in the forest moved. A flash of light caught the teenager's attention and he turned towards it. There was a thick, blue haze hanging in the air, almost like smoke. And then he heard another scream, a scream he recognized as his mother's.

A sound erupted from within the trees, and he brought the flashlight beam up in time for it to flash across something metallic that was moving at a fast pace through the woods right toward the blue lights.

"Mom," Frederico screamed as he dashed through the woods towards where he thought the house to be.

Hugh's screams echoed through the forest driving the boy on. Low hanging branches slapped and slashed his face until streams of blood trailed down his face and around his neck. Behind him he heard his little brother screaming frantically and knew the poor kid was terrified, but he couldn't stop running. He needed to help his parents, they needed him.

A huge bolt of lightning flashed overhead illuminating the forest with such intensity it forced the teen to shield his eyes. Thunder roared across the island as if it were covered by an invisible dome. Frederico turned his eyes to the sky and was muddled by the fact there was not a cloud in the sky, instead it was a canvas completely filled with stars.

The lightning appeared to be moving through the forest toward his house, but that was impossible. Frederico was leaning against a tree trying to catch his breath when Gregario came up behind him.

"You left me!"

"Mom and dad are in trouble. I need to get to the house. Why don't you stay here and let me see what's going on first?"

"Why is there thunder and lightning?" the boy asked, ignoring his brother's comment.

"What do you mean? Obviously because a storm is coming."

"A storm without any clouds?"

"Don't argue with me, there's a storm coming and that is that."

"What is going on Freddy, you're scared, I mean really scared?"

"Runt, something strange is going on and you're damned right I'm scared. You stay put until I come back for you and that is an order," Frederico said and took off running down the path toward the house again following the chain of lightning flashes through the trees.

"An order?" Gregario called after his brother. He was too scared to follow him, and too scared to stay there by himself so he paced, and he cried.

When Frederico finally burst through the trees into the clearing near the fire pit everything was quiet. There was no thunder, no lightning, and no screams. He dropped to his knees, tears streaming down his face as his gaze fell upon his dead parents. His mother's lifeless body was charred with electrical burns and there was a halo of fine, black soot surrounding her. His father was on his knees, propped against the picnic table, his eyes vacant and hollow. The same fine, black soot marked the corners of the dead man's mouth and streams of it poured out his nostrils. Hugh's ankles and knees bore patches of the powder as well, but there was something odd about the pattern.

The teen looked at the top of the picnic table and saw more black patches. He touched the powder with his finger, and it seemed to tingle so he withdrew his hand immediately. He walked around the table several times trying to decipher the marks when recognition finally hit him. They were bats.

Why would bats have attacked his parents? And even more confusing, why did they turn to ash? Maybe it was the storm. It drove them mad due to electrical interference and then they were struck by lightning. It was the only explanation no matter how piss poor and unfathomable it was.

A strange reverberation began to emanate from within the forest. Frederico dropped to his haunches and held his breath. It took him several moments to realize what he was hearing was something sniffing, smelling the air. Whatever was out there in the shadows, it was looking for him.

Frederico looked over at his mother, lying on her back with milky white, dead eyes staring up into the night sky and something stirred within him. An anger began to boil deep down inside of him, burning away the shock and grief of seeing his dead parents. An anger that refused to be controlled for even one second longer.

"Come on you son of a bitch. I know you're out there, come and get me," he screamed.

He leaned the broom handle against the bench of the picnic table at an angle and snapped it with a sharp stomp of his foot. Frederico picked up the sharp broom handle and walked over to the porch where he began rubbing it back and forth across the concrete while keeping a watchful eye on the forest. He was inspecting the point on his rudimentary spear when the creature first emerged from the shadows.

Mishipeshu stood before the brave warrior who dared to challenge her. An emotion rippled through her and even though she was a creature of legend, a living, breathing myth, she understood the situation on a human level. She was feeling remorse for having to kill, but it was necessary. It was always necessary.

Frederico nearly dropped his spear when the eight-foot-tall cat exposed itself. At least he thought it was a cat, but it was much too large, stood much too tall with antlers like a deer. Water dripped from his copper tinted coat and fell to the ground in a pool at its feet. Its face was twisted in a snarl with foot long fangs dripping a gelatinous, blue fluid which the creature lapped away from its lips with a long, pink tongue that was forked like a snake's.

Mishipeshu sniffed at the air, this one was not infected. This one did not need to die, at least not this night. She slowly turned her elongated body back toward the lake.

"Wait. What are you?" Frederico finally gathered the nerve to speak.

"Freddy, what is that?" Gregario said, stepping out of the shadows into the clearing.

"Go back. Stay away runt."

Mishipeshu spun back around quickly and took two strides toward the little one. Frederico took one long stride and let the makeshift spear fly. It merely deflected harmlessly off the cat's metallic coat. The creature turned to look at him but then returned its attention to the little one. It sniffed the air one long breath and then turned to leave. This one did not need to die either.

Frederico stared into the creature's eyes and could not believe what he was seeing. Lightning, there was lightning, no, an entire storm churning within the beast's eyes. It was impossible, but he was in the presence of an ancient legend that should not exist, and yet, it did.

~   ~   ~

A heavy smell of ozone hung in the air and the clouds on the horizon were black and foreboding. They were angry cumulonimbus stretching across the entire sky. Gabe walked briskly back to the house to find Duke and warn him to batten down all the hatches. A complete walk around the entire lighthouse and he didn't see a soul, not even Duke or either of the other two foremen. Maybe they knew the storm was coming and escaped the island before the brunt of the bad weather made landfall. Though he found it rather odd they didn't cover their tools or any of the building supplies.

Darkness washed over the day like a spilled ink well. The winds began to howl, and Gabe was worried they might lose electricity, so he gassed up the spare generator in the cellar before checking to make sure all the flashlights were in working order. Next, he brought down a box of emergency candles. The work light was burning in the lantern room, Noona was nowhere to be found, the kids disappeared into their bedrooms, so Gabe grabbed the lighthouse keeper's journal and joined his wife in bed to read.

Tara was sitting straight up in bed with half a dozen reference books spread open across the comforter. Gabe managed to find an open spot and claimed the territory as his own. He learned his lesson long ago about not interrupting her, so he leaned back against the headboard and cracked open the lighthouse logbook.

"How long have I been up here?" she asked.

"I don't have a clue."

"Well, what time is it?"

"About quarter to seven I think."

"What? Why is it so dark outside?"

"There's a pretty nasty storm brewing out over the lake."

"How bad?"

"Bad enough that I prepared the storm cellar just in case. This isn't an area prone to tornados, but I'm sure this storm will bring some high winds either way. And honestly, I have never been up here on the cliffs when a storm blew through, so I have no idea what to expect."

"Don't you think these storms have been odd?"

"Odd in what way?"

"They seem to be sporadic, and they crop up in different parts of the island."

"I guess I haven't paid that much attention," Gabe admitted. "That's all part of life on an island I suppose."

"I just think it is odd," she said.

Tara lost interest in the conversation and went back to poring over her menagerie of reference books while Gabe continued reading the dry logbook.

"Is that interesting?" Tara asked, taking off her glasses and rubbing her eyes.

"About as attention grabbing as the US Tax Code."

"So, a nerd like you is being thoroughly entertained," she quipped.

"You say that like it's a bad thing," he said and started reading from the journal.

I was forced by the state to hire an assistant today. A Swede of all things. Bonni and I are quite capable of looking after this place on our own. I fear there are agents who feel I have grown too old for the job and are preparing to force me into retirement.

"You said that was just a logbook?"

"It is, that was just a loose piece of paper, folded up and tucked between the pages."

"That is so sad."

"What is?" Gabe asked.

"Having someone else decide you have grown too old to perform your duties. It must have been scary for him."

"Taking care of this place was no easy task, especially back then. He would have had to carry buckets of fuel up that spiral ladder to the lantern room at least once a day. That would have to be between seven and eight pounds a gallon so a five-gallon bucket would be forty pounds."

"Besides all the carpentry work, we saw firsthand how well he took care of the place," she said with a smile.

"Oh, you are rotten. He had been gone from this place over seventy-five years by the time we bought it. Did you find anything interesting in those exciting books of yours?"

"Not one single mention of glowing blue moths that somehow metamorphose into two-inch salamanders with a blood red stripe down their backs. And beady little eyes I might also add."

"What about parasites that devour human bones?" Gabe asked, not comfortable with the question once it was spoken aloud.

"I haven't gotten that far. I think I'm done for the night. I just want to lie here and listen to the rain."

"And the banshee winds," he said, reaching over to turn off the light. "It almost sounds like a woman screaming."

"Thank you for putting that thought into my head. I'm waking you up if I can't sleep," Tara said.

Up in the tower, Paul stood alone out on the widow's walk overlooking the lake watching the storm inch ever closer. It wouldn't be long now. He loved the onset of a storm, but not so much the storm itself. From as far back as he could remember he had a deathly fear of lightning and thunder, but he could not recall a specific incident. The ominous shades of gray dancing in the clouds left him in awe. There was a rare roll cloud forming in the storm near the reduced horizon that looked like a roll of dirty cotton candy spanning across the sky.

The first several drops of rain were copious and within seconds he was drenched. Paul came back inside the lantern room and closed the door. As he was changing into his pajamas and laying out his bedroll, he looked out of the window overlooking the forest. A strange blue haze hung in the air in the general vicinity of Echo Lake to the southwest. He was still pondering the origins of the radiance when he drifted off to sleep.

Chapter Eighteen

Mel pulled the short bus into the even shorter garage and covered the rear with a large blue tarp to keep the rain from getting in through the leaky windows. He looked up at the night sky and made a mental note to give the Coast Guard a call in the morning and ask them about these strange weather patterns around the island the last couple of days. He kicked off his mud encrusted boots in the breezeway by the front door and slipped into his worn-out moccasins. He learned many, many years ago that tracking mud across his wife's floors was a capital offense. Death by a thousand insults.

"There is a sandwich there by the television for you. The power went out twice and I was tired of monkeying with the generator, so I didn't cook dinner," his wife Ester called out from the kitchen.

"Well, it is back on now," Mel said and switched the television on.

"Don't sass me."

Mel shrugged and picked up the lightly toasted egg salad sandwich, toasted at the number three setting on the toaster. The sandwich was cut diagonally from corner to corner perfectly. Mel took a large bite and savored the morsel. Ester's egg salad was the best he ever tasted and although she would clobber him for it, he managed to learn her recipe. The first trick was to not hard boil the eggs so long they were firm, but to boil them just until the center yolk was still soft, spongy, and golden yellow. The next trick was two tablespoons of Miracle Whip and two tablespoons of mayonnaise followed by just a spit of yellow mustard. The final coup de grace was two taps of yellow curry powder, no more, no less. She would then lightly toast the bread and lightly butter the toast for a perfect egg salad sandwich. There was a dollop of mayo-whip clinging to the corners of his mouth as he switched on the television set and sat down in his favorite chair.

Archie Bunker's voice echoed across the RCA telling Edith to stifle it. Mel briefly thought about sending the retort his wife's way, but he learned a long, long time ago that was also a capital offense, so he kept his comments to himself.

Meathead was babbling on about some kumbaya bullshit, but the screen was black. Mel gave the set a few sharp whacks to the side, adjusted the tin foil on the rabbit ears and stepped back to admire his handiwork. The thirteen-inch screen was no longer black but filled with squiggly lines running from top to bottom and sweeping from the left side of the screen to the right.

"Damn storm has the antenna going wonky," he called out.

"By the way, the toilet is still gurgling, you need to speak with Duke and see if he can come by and take a look at it," she called back.

"All in the Family is one thing, but I don't want to watch the Streets of San Francisco all squiggly like this."

"I know he's pretty busy up at the lighthouse, but he can tend to us folks who kept him going in the lean times you know."

"I'm going to head up to the roof to check the antenna," Mel called back.

"For cripe's sake Mel, did you even hear a word I said?"

"Yes dear. Toilet's gurgling, you think something is stuck in it and you think Duke is a pretentious asshole."

"I did not say that."

"Tell you what, let me monkey with the antenna before the lightning gets here and then I'll take a look at the toilet."

"But I have to use the toilet right now," Ester said.

"There's nothing to worry about. The noise is just air being forced through the pipes because of the wind."

"Or a big sewer rat dead set on eating my bum."

"I'll be back in five or ten minutes," Mel said, ignoring her comment. Responding to her would only make things worse. "Ain't a rat big enough or hungry enough for that meal," he said under his breath, accompanied by the screen door slamming shut behind him.

"Any longer than ten minutes and you better bring the mop and bucket back in with you," Ester called after him. She swiped the other half of his sandwich and sat down to watch a squiggly Edith. "And I heard that," she said over her left shoulder with her mouth full of egg salad dropping a few morsels onto the front of her nightgown which she picked off and plopped into her mouth one by one.

The grandfather clock by the fireplace mocked her with every passing of the minute hand. It seemed to move slower and tick much more loudly than normal. Before long, her bladder began to keep rhythm and became quite obstreperous about being made to wait. Edith was running after Gloria when Esther's bladder finally decided enough was enough.

Ester hurried into the bathroom, lifted her nightgown, and sat down on the commode. Having spooked herself trying to light a fire under her husband's butt she found herself having difficulties even though she was experiencing the pain of a full bladder that had been denied relief for far too long. She started reading the old vintage newspaper articles on the bathroom wallpaper as she did on occasion when things didn't go as smoothly as planned.

She tapped her feet and sang an old ditty all the while cursing Mel for his stubbornness. Ester felt a slight tickle against her thigh and jerked in response. At first, she thought she might have gotten all twisted up down there and peed down her leg a little by accident. She reached down to feel her leg and it was dry as a bone. That was when something tickled the back of her hand and she gasped.

"Esther, it's just a spider. Quit overreacting," she laughed at her own skittishness.

Something moved the front of her nightgown that was pulled across her lap. At first, she thought it might be from the drafty room, but then it moved again. Every fiber of her being told her to just pack up and run but her curiosity got the better of her. She lifted the hem of her nightgown and cautiously peered into the toilet.

The toilet bowl was empty, but the water was green. Why on earth would the water be green? Suddenly the hole in the bottom of the commode began to bubble and a blue glow grew in intensity with each passing second. The toilet burped one large burp as a large, blue snake's head appeared from the hole. Poor Esther was mesmerized and unable to move as the snake coiled itself inside the toilet bowl. Without warning the creature launched itself straight up inside her.

Ripped from her trance, Esther grabbed the snake's body with both hands. When she tried to pull it out, the animal buried its fangs into her tender flesh. She instinctively released her grip and grabbed for her stomach, during which time the snake advanced. She grabbed the snake in a death grip and once more it buried its fangs into her. The two of them danced that tango until Esther finally ran out of snake to grab onto.

The creature bit her mercilessly until there was no fight left in her. Her belly swelled to the point she thought it would burst and then it began to squirm as if there was a nest of angry vipers inside of her. There was a subtle popping noise and Esther looked down to see the surface of the water was covered in a fine black powder as if someone had shaken a pepper shaker over the bowl. She could feel whatever was inside of her careening through her body wriggling, biting, and eating her alive.

After ten minutes spent fighting with the antenna Mel finally got it to break free and turn west toward Marquette. He stood up and gathered his tools before starting down the roof to where the ladder was propped up. Something by the LaPierre's place caught his attention. An eerie blue haze hung over their homestead but from that distance Mel couldn't see the cause of the oddly colored fog. Maybe the pompous prick bought himself some fancy new outdoor light or something.

The first bolt of lightning caused him to jump a little, while the second one startled him even more. The lightning didn't come from the sky, it emanated from the ground. Mel suddenly had a bad feeling that Hugh screwed up the electrical system on the island and that was why they lost power during the day. He was on the top rung of the ladder on his way down to go give LaPierre a piece of his mind when he saw something moving through the trees toward the house. It was too far away to see what it was, but it was big. Huge in fact.

Mel's first impression was that it was a bear, but the only bear large enough to make that much ruckus would be a grizzly and there weren't any grizzlies for hundreds if not thousands of miles. A scream split the night and he bounded down the ladder thinking it was Esther, but it hadn't sounded human. Before running into the house, he turned back toward the forest. If it wasn't the damndest thing, there were little lightning storms marching through the forest toward him.

"Esther honey, we have to go, now!" Mel said once he was in the breezeway. He didn't bother to take his boots off before walking into the house proper. "Esther?" he called out again when there was no response from his wife.

A soft moan followed by his name carried through the house. Mel headed for the bathroom hoping his wife wouldn't start in on him for tracking mud before he had a chance to explain what was happening. They didn't have the time for arguments. He put his ear to the bathroom door and rapped lightly with his knuckle. When Esther did not respond he slowly opened the door.

An audible gasp escaped his lips when he saw his wife sitting on the commode with her nightgown pulled up over her distended stomach which was now the size of a blue-ribbon pumpkin. He glanced down at the black water in the bowl and then back at her.

"Are you sick?"

Tears flowed down her waxen cheeks. It was all she could do to shake her head slowly from side to side. For a moment Mel forgot all about the danger lurking outside. He cautiously extended his index finger and poked it into her spongy flesh. The finger buried beyond the first, almost to the second knuckle and he quickly removed it. Even more shocking was the fact then when he poked her again, he noticed a flurry of activity that seemed to gravitate toward his fingertip like tiny blue ants under the surface of her skin.

Another scream penetrated the house, whatever that creature was, it was now in their yard.

"Esther, we have to go. We have to get out of here," Mel said.

"I can't move. You go without me."

"I'm not leaving you here. Tell you what, I will sneak out the back door, run for the bus and pick you up in the back yard. But you must get moving. Just like you are, no need to pack."

"Mel, you're scaring me."

"And with very good reason, Esther. There is something very wrong here."

The house exploded in a brilliant white light and Mel knew it was due to lightning strikes outside in the yard. He knew, but he sure as hell didn't understand how it was possible.

"Mel, something is happening," Esther screamed.

He ran back into the bathroom to see her spread eagle on the commode with her protruding stomach extending sideways until it rested against the bathroom wall. He stared at her with disbelief scribbled all over his face.

"It feels like all of my innards are moving to one side. Like my insides are trying to escape my body. I'm scared Mel, I'm so, so scared," Esther said.

Mel stood there thunderstruck, not knowing what to say or do.

"You get out of here, leave me," she said.

"I'm not going to leave you, not in a million years."

Mel went out to the kitchen to grab him an egg salad sandwich and her some water. While running the tap he found the nerve to look out of the window at the creature standing in his yard. He could not believe what he was seeing, it just was not possible. Mishipeshu turned to look at the man and sniffed at the air. Several moments elapsed as man and beast scrutinized one another before the monstrous cat let loose a scream that sounded like a woman in the clutches of death.

The sky surrounding the house darkened to the point the inkiness bled into the house. Blackness oozed down the walls, threatening to choke the air from anyone inside the house. Static electricity crackled in every corner of the room and what little hair Mel had left was standing completely on end.

"Mel," Esther screamed. "Something is happening."

As soon as he entered the bathroom his stomach churned. His wife's stomach had grown to impossible proportions and a putrid stench permeated the tiny cubicle.

"Esther?" he said, just as her stomach erupted into a geyser of electric blue sap.

Mel was transfixed by the look of horror on his dead wife's face. Viscous fluid oozed down from the ceiling in long strands that moved as if they were alive. And then he realized, they were indeed filled with living organisms. Organisms that immediately sought out another host and turned their attention towards him.

The creature outside bellowed and the house shook from a clap of thunder that seemed to emanate from the very walls themselves. The crackling of static electricity in the air continued to swell in intensity until the entire house was bathed in a brilliant, blue glow which seemed to agitate the aquamarine goo.

Mel was in a state of shock as the slime puddles oozed and seeped together, melding into a larger pool of writhing organisms which turned their attentions toward him. He backpedaled out of the bathroom and into the living room where the incandescence from static electricity intensified into a blinding aura of energy. The behemoth in the yard stared back at him from just beyond the porch through the breezeway door.

All at once Mel felt something strange, something powerful growing inside of him. It was as if thunder was rumbling from the depths of his own bowels. Suddenly he was wracked with a pain that dropped him to his knees. He managed to utter, *our father, who art in heaven*, before a ball of St. Elmo's fire shot from the belly of the beast, into the house and exploded with such ferocity that it leveled the domicile, destroying everything inside.

Chapter Nineteen

"Coast Guard calling Grand Island Station, Grand Island station come in."

After a long silence followed by a loud squelch a single word was transmitted. "Aniin."

"Come again."

The word aniin was repeated.

"Who is this?"

"Noona."

"Noona? What is Noona? I do not understand," the voice on the radio crackled.

"I am Noona. What you want?"

"Is this the Grand Island Light Station?"

"No, this is Noona."

"And where is Noona?"

She thought long and hard, searching for the English word. "Noona is in the kitchen."

Gabe stumbled into the kitchen headed for the coffee pot when a hand mic was thrust at him. Noona shuffled through the kitchen to the door. She slipped outside with her long, flowing robe trailing after her.

"Isn't it still raining?" He called after her.

She simply shrugged and kept walking with her plate of food.

"This is Grand Island Light Station."

"Gabe, is that you?"

"Yes, Bill, it's me."

"Did we have a bad connection? Who was that?"

"It is a long story. How can we help you, Bill?"

"I'm just calling to see how you folks weathered the storm."

"I'm just getting up and around. I'll take a look around and see if any of the equipment was damaged."

"No need for that. It's automated and I can see it is working just fine from here. Although I wish I could say the same for our equipment here. Our boat took a beating. That's what I was calling you for. You folks are on your own for at least a day or two. Not much is going to move from the harbor, the crane barge collapsed and is blocking the channel."

"We have enough stores to weather at least two weeks so we will be fine."

"Fair warning, another storm is coming and will probably make landfall before dark. Strangest thing though, I have never seen such isolated storms as these have been. No one is being hit outside of Munising, not even Christmas or Au Train."

"So, it isn't just my wife's crazy ramblings, these storms have been isolated. Great, now I am going to have to put up with her smugness for a day or two," Gabe said with a laugh. "Like I said, we have plenty of supplies and more than enough gas for at least two weeks."

"Sounds great. I will send a boat out first chance we get."

"No rush. Hey, have you seen Duke or his crew?"

"No, but it was chaos in the marina yesterday preparing for the storm so they could have easily been missed."

"I can imagine. On second thought, we will need to see you out here on the island when things settle down a bit for you though," Gabe said.

"Is there something wrong?"

"Nothing that can't keep a day or two."

"Nothing medical I assume," the Coast Guard officer said.

"Nothing that can't wait. Besides, we have a small dinghy here if we absolutely need to get to the mainland."

"Okay. I will give you a call in the morning to check again."

"Thanks Bill," Gabe said and clipped the hand mic back onto the receiver.

He poured a cup of coffee and looked out of the screen door at the light, summer rain drifting down. Noona was on to something, so he joined her outside. They both stood in the yard near the cliffs staring out at the lake. It was raining harder than Gabe first thought and he was soaked within minutes. But he was damned if he was going to let a little old lady endure something he couldn't.

"What is it you are looking for when you stand out here?" Gabe asked.

"I look for that which most men do not see," she replied.

"And what exactly is that?"

"The truth about all things."

"That's a bit vague, isn't it?"

"But it's the truth and that you did not see."

Gabe decided drinking his coffee in silence was the more prudent and much less exasperating avenue to take. He watched the old woman as her eyes scanned the horizon slowly from left to right and then back again never staying in one place.

"What do you make of these storms?" Gabe asked.

"Storms happen, it is all part of nature's plan."

"Yes, I understand that, but these storms seem to be odd."

"Odd in what way?" she turned to him and asked.

"Look over there," Gabe said, pointing across the water at Sand Point. "There is a definite line of demarcation. The storms are only affecting the island and the immediate area."

"That is no great mystery."

"How so?"

"Because that which makes storms happen is only present here on the island and not over there, or over there, or over there," Noona said while pointing to all points on the horizon causing Gabe to return to his now cold coffee in silence.

While looking out at the calm lake it dawned on him, their boat was not in the harbor, it was docked on the eastern side of the island below the cliffs.

"Travis," he called up the stairs.

"Yeah, dad, what's up?" he said, rubbing his eyes as he trotted down the stairs missing a step with each stride.

"Grab your raingear, we need to check on the boat."

It took a minute for what his dad said to register, but when it did, he felt a slight sense of panic. The storm had been rough the night before and after what he witnessed at Echo Lake, he was not in the mood to be stranded on the island.

The narrow trail down the cliff to the water's edge was sloshy and slick sending them both down onto their backsides more than once. They were forced to stop frequently to clear the path from downed limbs and other debris. To make matters worse, it began to rain even harder, and visibility dropped to nil. Gabe felt like turning back for the house, but he could hear the waves crashing against the cliffs, so they pressed on.

"Dad, where is the boat? Hell, where is the dock?"

"Watch your mouth. You know your mother would not approve."

"Okay, where in the H E double hockey sticks is the dock?"

"You don't have to be a wise ass all the time," Gabe said, regretting it the minute it passed his lips. "Don't even say it."

They continued down the beach toward where the dock sat the previous day only to find it was no longer there. They spent the next half an hour combing up and down the beach looking for any sign of their boat. The visibility was so poor they could barely see the lake standing on the beach.

"Over here dad," Travis called out. "The dock is underwater. It appears as though one of the legs are bent."

Gabe went over to where his son was standing and inspected the dock for himself. He climbed up onto the platform, his shoes completely underwater, and peered down the beach to the south. There were no signs of the boat, so he eased himself down the rickety platform to the cleat. He pulled a piece of rope from out of the murky depths and found it was no longer attached to anything, not even a sunken boat. They were stranded on the island. He didn't like what he saw when he studied the piece of rope, so he untied the remnant and put it into his pocket before he and Travis made their way back to the lighthouse.

Something was nagging Gabe on the way back up the hill, just as he jumped from the dock to the beach, he noticed another piece of rope on the other side. It too was tied to the cleat, but it was not a full length of rope. He was certain Duke tied his boat up to that side of the dock and now it was gone as well. He feared it didn't leave under its own power.

"Are you up for a little hike?" Gabe asked.

"In the rain?" Travis protested.

"It's letting up. It's only sprinkling now."

"Where do you want to go? And please tell me this is not one of those father, son bonding moments or God forbid, *the talk*."

"I want you to show me where you saw those lizards go into the lake."

"Salamanders."

"What?"

"According to Amanda they are salamanders, not lizards."

"You spend too much time with your sister."

"How are we going to get there? I don't know the way from here."

"We just have to follow the creek. I am sure it leads to the lake."

"But dad, there's no trail. We'll have to bushwhack it the entire way."

"Are your shoes wet?" Gabe asked.

"Yeah, why do you ask?"

"Well so are mine so we simply walk through the creek to the lake. It is only a couple of miles from here, maybe the sun will be out by then and we can go swimming," he said, nudging his son with his elbow.

"I don't care if it was two hundred degrees outside, I am not swimming in that lake."

Chapter Twenty

Travis and Gabe were soaked to the core and near exhaustion by the time they got to the lake. It was a much more difficult undertaking than Gabe imagined, but they persevered. Droplets of rain dotted the surface of the lake with centrical circles as far as the eye could see.

"Where were you and Mandy standing?"

"Over there about a quarter of a mile," Travis said, extending his arm to indicate the far shore.

There was not much shoreline to speak of and the water was waist deep, so they bushwhacked the short distance to the beach where Amanda and Travis had been fishing.

"We were right about here," Travis said.

"And where did the lizards, excuse me, salamanders enter the lake?"

Travis pointed toward the northern shore, so they started to walk around the lake, but then Travis stopped.

"What is it?" Gabe asked.

"This beach wasn't black yesterday. It was normal yellow sand."

"Maybe the storm kicked up sediment from the bottom of the lake," Gabe said, stooping down to scoop up a handful of the black sand.

"No, dad, it's not that this is black silt or debris, the sand itself is black," he said, holding a palm filled with sand up to his nose. "And smell it?"

"It smells burned. Maybe a lightning strike," Gabe speculated. "Do you have something to carry some of this in?"

"My pocket," he replied and scooped three large handfuls of the black sand into his back pocket.

They continued around the lake until they reached the point where Travis thought the creatures entered the water. Gabe was worried during their hike to the lake that the rains washed away all evidence and he was correct in his assumption. There was nothing odd about the lake other than the black sand. The sky was growing more ominous by the minute and Gabe did not want to be stuck out in the forest during a storm.

"Let's hustle up back home. I want to stop and check on the tractor and the generator on the way. Which trail leads to that old bunker?"

Travis turned to point toward the northern trail when the lake made an odd sound behind him. Almost like it had belched. Both Gabe and Travis were buckled by a stench unlike anything they had ever experienced. A blue haze settled in over their shoulders and they slowly turned around to look at the lake to find it glowing from beneath the depths.

"Dad, I don't like this. We need to leave."

"But what is that?"

"I don't know, and quite frankly I don't give a shit," Travis said, on the verge of tears.

"It must be some kind of a gas bubble. Maybe there is a fissure under the lake. That could be where those moths and salamanders came from."

"I don't care if they came from outer space, I don't want to be near whatever is in that spooky water."

"Travis, this could be an important discovery."

The water began to roil, and the surface of the water began pushing upward into a dome. A few inches at first but then the dome rose more than a foot off the water's surface. While Travis opted for discretion and moved ten feet away, his father was enraptured by the spectacle. The rain began pelting the earth with hard slapping rain drops but Gabe didn't even notice. He was too captivated by the scene unfolding in front of him. This was something utterly amazing to witness.

A scream split the air tearing Gabe from his trance.

"What in the hell was that?" Travis asked, pivoting from side to side unsure of where the sound emanated from.

A second, much louder guttural screech echoed even closer to them. Whatever it was, it was moving fast. At that moment, the dome bubble exploded, and a translucent blue fish leapt from the depths, grabbing Gabe in its gaping maw. It dragged him kicking and screaming toward the water. Travis was transfixed, but only for a moment. He grabbed a dead tree limb from the ground and started to attack the creature disrupting its assault on his father while Gabe scooted up the sand on his backside in retreat.

"What in the hell kind of fish was that?" Travis asked.

"That was no fish, it had my legs gripped in hands of some sort."

"But it had a tail like a fish."

Suddenly the water erupted, and the beast leapt from the depths once more. This time it bit down on Gabe's arm, breaking the bone at his wrist. The animal shook its head like a dog trying to separate the man from his appendage. Travis beat on the head of the creature with the tree limb, but it swung its beefy arm in a wide, sweeping arc and knocked him backwards. Its teeth were centered over Gabe's throat and the man was struggling with every bastion of strength remaining to keep the creature's teeth from finding his flesh, but his strength was waning.

"Travis, run," he managed to call out.

"I am not leaving you."

"Run for the bunker. Lock yourself in," Gabe said through labored breaths.

Gabe stared back into the human-like eyes of the creature and was imbued with a level of fear so intense it caused him to shudder. The gnashing teeth were a conglomeration of teeth, fish, bat, and human. The strength the creature possessed was anything but human. Gabe knew he had but mere seconds left before the beast would be able to sink its teeth into the tender flesh of his throat. Travis crumpled to the ground with the wind knocked out of him but struggled to his feet while fumbling around for the broken tree limb.

The beast wrenched its hand free of Gabe's grip and began squeezing his throat. When he weakened the creature grabbed his arm with both hands and snapped it like a twig. Gabe recoiled in pain, exposing his neck. Haunting blue eyes stared down at him and he swore the grotesque being smiled back at him.

"Damn, it, Travis, run!"

Travis wiped the tears from his eyes and started for the forest but then turned around. He was not about to run away like a little coward. He turned back for the fight and started running back for the beach. Another scream ripped at the air behind him, and he felt himself being flung to the side. Travis looked up in time to see an enormous cat-like creature soaring through the air. Just as the water beast was about to rip open his father's throat the cat hit it full force and they both plunged into the depths of Echo Lake. Travis scrambled to his feet and ran to his father's aid. The two of them ran for the bunker in fear for their lives.

"You run ahead, get the tractor started, and we will take it to the house."

"But dad."

"Do not argue with me on this one Travis. I'll be right behind you," Gabe said, leaning against a tree to catch his breath.

Although every fiber of his being told him to stay and fight, Travis obeyed his father's wishes and ran for the tractor. His father was right, he was the faster of the two and he also knew the tractor better than his father. It was cantankerous and required a delicate touch to get it started, especially in this wet weather.

Dark clouds swarmed overhead, and the forest fell into the shade of night. Travis ran through the forest, fighting the urge to look back with every step. He stopped to catch his breath and realized something was shadowing him, hidden within the ebon timberland. He could hear his father's labored breathing coming from behind him and took off running again. He could barely make out the shape of the tractor on the trail ahead of him and picked up his pace, fighting against the thundering pain in his sides. Something swooped out of the trees and knocked him to the ground only to disappear into the treetops.

Once he got his bearings again Travis saw the tractor radiated the same blue glow above it as the moths, salamanders and whatever the hell attacked his father. He laid still and flat on his stomach on the ground looking for the cause of the indigo light. Gabe came limping up after him.

"I told you to get to the tractor," he said between breaths.

"There is something up there. Something came down out of the trees and knocked me down."

"Was it a bird of some kind?"

"I don't think so."

"I can't believe I am going to ask this, but was it the same blue shade of the moths?"

"I can't really say because I never even saw it. In fact, I think it was trying to warn me away," Travis said, nodding at the glow over the tractor.

Two distinctly different animalistic cries rose above the din of the driving rain. The father and son hunkered behind the largest oak they could find.

"I sure am regretting letting you watch those Saturday afternoon movies with Sir Graves Ghastly, especially the Creature from the Black Lagoon," Gabe said, trying in vain to add a little levity to their situation.

After a long pause Travis asked, "What was that thing in the lake dad?"

"I have no idea. Some sort of mutant fish I would imagine."

"But it had arms, like a man. But also claws like a beast," he said, pointing at three long scratches on his father's arm.

"The tail was a fish's tail."

"I read this book not too long ago, it was about mermaids, except they were men, so I guess mermen."

"Travis that was fiction."

"I know, but it really did look like a cross between a man and a fish," Travis argued.

"A little far-fetched don't you think?" Gabe said, more annoyed from pain than anything his son said.

"Not any more far-fetched than moths that glow and then turn into lizards."

"Salamanders."

The blue haze moved away from the tractor giving them their opportunity to escape. Travis helped his father navigate from tree to tree until they made it to the vehicle. The engine was shredded.

"These mermen of yours, could they walk on land?"

"For short amounts of time and distances, yes. They grew short legs when they were out of the water."

"Fantastic! Just what I wanted to hear. It's getting dark, and I don't think we are going to be able to make it back to the house, at least not in my condition. I saw medical supplies down in the bunker. It's time for you to earn your merit badge in first aid," Gabe said as he struggled to keep from passing out.

Travis checked the generator and found it was still operational, so once he managed to get the hatch to the bunker lifted, he filled the tank and fired it up. He hurried to get his father into the stairwell and down to the first landing before returning to the surface to move the cords from the generator and thread them in through the opening. He saw something reflecting fifty yards into the woods, so he ran over to see what it was. It was Duke's corpse; he could tell by the ring on the man's pencil thin finger.

The young man gasped at the sight of the once brawny man, now emaciated and barely more than a skeleton. But that was impossible. Even if something happened and Duke died out there, he would not be decayed already. Hellish sounds resounded through the trees and Travis knew he didn't have the time to try and figure out what happened to Duke, nor did he have time to be frightened. He ran for the bunker entrance, dropped the lid, and barred the door behind him.

Gabe slid down the steps on his butt one by one until the two of them were down in the bunker.

"Dad, where is the first aid kit?"

"It was in that other room, attached to the wall," he said while pointing toward the sleeping chamber.

Travis made his way down the short, narrow passageway and into the chamber where the bed was and immediately stopped in his tracks when confronted with the bones. The first thought to flash in his head was that whoever these people had been, they must have died down here hiding from whatever that thing was lurking on the surface. His second thought was that he read way too many horror novels.

~ ~ ~

"Mandy, darling, do you know where your father and brother took off to?" Tara asked.

She buttered the backsides of two pieces of bread, tossed one in a cast iron skillet butter side down, put a generous slice of Velveeta on top and then the other slice of buttered bread, butter side up, on top of that before covering the pan with a lid.

Amanda sat at the kitchen table pouting with her hands tucked under the tabletop.

"Amanda Rose, did you hear me ask you a question?"

The child spun around so that her back was to her mother and wiped her tears.

"Young lady, are you listening to me?" Tara asked as she stormed across the kitchen to face her daughter. "Why are you crying?"

She noticed the Miracle Whip jar was lying over on its side on the floor and there were two black stains that resembled a Rorschach test on the floor on either side.

"Did you spill something on the floor?"

Amanda shook her head. Paul was just coming down out of the lantern room and overheard their conversation.

"Then what are those stains?"

Amanda shrugged.

"I am going to send you to your room if you do not tell me what you spilled all over the floor? Is that some of Mr. Rainbird's paint?"

Amanda shook her head and sniffled.

"That's not paint, it's a dry powder. And my goodness, it smells terrible," Paul said, stooping to get a closer look.

"It's my salamanders," Amanda said, looking up to face her mother.

"Your salamanders? What happened to them."

"I stomped on them," she said, a look of angry defiance spreading across her face.

"Why on earth would you do something like that?" her mother asked.

"Because one of them bit me."

"That is no reason to kill a living creature, Amanda," Paul said.

"Yes, it is. And the other one was trying to bite me too."

"Let me see where it bit you honey."

Reluctantly Amanda pulled her towel wrapped hand from under the table, a towel which was soaked in the child's blood. Tara sucked in her breath. There was a lot more blood on the towel than would have resulted from a small amphibian bite.

"My finger hurts, mommy," Amanda finally broke down into tears.

Tara began to slowly unwrap the towel from around her daughter's hand while Paul grabbed the first aid kit from the closet. Amanda's hand was clenched into a tiny fist, and she refused to open it. Even with her hand closed Paul could see that the child's knuckle was three times larger than normal.

"Are you ready honey? Look at Mr. Rainbird and not at your hand?"

Amanda nodded. "Mr. Paul, were those things Pukwatchamacallits?"

"No, I'm not sure what those things were. They are a species of salamanders I have never seen or heard of."

Tara gasped when she saw the near inch long gash on Amanda's middle finger penetrating almost to the bone. The edges of the wound were jagged and torn, as if her finger had been bitten. She had assumed her daughter cut her finger and was making up stories, but the child was surely bitten.

The soft sound of shuffling drifted in from the other room and within seconds Noona appeared in the kitchen. She was dressed in a child's one-piece pajama with plastic soled footies that swooshed along the floor as she glided into the room. Her already pudgy cheek was bulging so much so that it would have been the envy of any Detroit Tiger. She masticated whatever was in her mouth until she reached the table where everyone was sitting. In a surprisingly quick motion she grabbed Amanda's hand, turned it palm up and brought it up to her face. She spat a gooey, tarlike substance with more accuracy than the Outlaw Josie Wales right onto the girl's finger while spreading the wound apart.

"Hey," Amanda protested and tried to jerk her hand free.

"What in the hell was that?" Tara objected and started to wipe her daughter's finger off, but Noona stopped her.

The two of them struggled for control of the little girl's finger, but Noona was much stronger than she appeared and won the battle.

"Mom, it feels better," Amanda said.

Noona let go and Tara started looking over her daughter's damaged phalange. The swelling had already gone down more than halfway, and the bleeding stopped.

"What was that you spit on her finger?" Tara asked.

The little old lady shrugged. "Noona don't know. Secret even to Noona."

"How could it be a secret; you were chewing it in your mouth."

"Noona get medicine from elders, not know what is in it."

"What was that creature that bit my daughter."

Again, she shrugged. "Noona, doesn't know."

"Then how did you know what to do to help?"

"Medicine helps everything."

Paul sighed deeply and rose to his feet. "Auntie Noona, you can cut the tourist trap charade. Tara, she speaks English better than you or I."

Noona shrugged and shuffled out of the room the same way she shuffled in.

"Wait, Noona, do you know where my husband and son ran off to?"

"He talked to the man on the radio, from the Coast Guard. And then he went outside. He said something about checking on the boat," Noona said.

Noona disappeared to wherever it was she managed to vanish to while Tara cleaned Amanda up. The grilled cheese in the skillet was cold and a little burned but Paul was hungry, so he claimed it as his own. He scraped the burned side into the trash with a butter knife, cleaned the pan with a paper towel and started making two more grilled cheese sandwiches.

Amanda was no longer crying but she was staring at her finger as if she accidentally stuck it into the dog's mess while cleaning it up. She held her hand as far away from her face as possible.

"Paul, please don't take offense, but do any of your legends, myths, stories say anything about glowing moths and salamanders that attack children?"

"No offense taken. But in our defense, pukwudgies are no different than the sprites of Iceland or the Leprechauns of Ireland. What does strike me as peculiar is that these stories, while idiosyncratic, are also remarkably similar to one another. This leads me to the belief that maybe there is some validity to these tales of little gremlins who pester humans."

"But nothing about the oddities we have witnessed as of late?"

"No, no man-eating salamanders," Noona called out from somewhere in the house.

Tara and Amanda ate their grilled cheese sandwiches in silence. Paul rummaged around in the hall closet until he found a suitable raincoat that would fit him and started for the door.

"Where are you going?" Tara asked.

"I thought I would walk down to the docks and see if Travis and Gabe are down there."

"That would have been hours ago. They would either be back here, or they headed out to Echo Lake."

"I guess you are right it is starting to get late. They probably should be back by now," Paul said.

"Maybe they got caught in the rain and were forced to take shelter," Tara said.

Tara bobbed her head toward Amanda and shot Paul a cross look which he immediately understood and kept his next comment to himself. After a long, drawn-out argument it was decided, not mutually, that Amanda would stay at the lighthouse with Noona while Paul and her mother went to fetch the others.

"How do you plan on getting to the lake?" Paul asked, following behind Tara as she walked out past the tool shed."

"We're going to take this," she said and pulled a tarp away revealing a Frankenstein's monster of a 1961 powder blue and white Chevrolet Apache Suburban that had been chopped down into an open-air dune buggy.

"Is there a road?"

"There is a trail and that is good enough for me right about now."

Paul watched her go through all the motions of pulling out the choke, rolling it over a few times without success before she finally popped the hood. Tara rummaged around in the rear compartment and came back around to the engine with a war whoop. He was an artist, not a mechanic so he had no idea what she was up to.

"What is that?"

"Ether."

"Are you going to knock it out?"

"No, a squirt of this in the carburetor should get her up and running just fine. She will be purring like a kitten in no time."

"Why didn't Gabe just take this beast instead of walking down to the pier?"

"Because of what I am doing right now. Gabe might be one of the smartest men I have ever known, until it comes to a combustion engine that is," she said with a smile and went back to the driver's side to turn the key.

The Apache groaned and rolled over a few times before emitting a loud bang and shooting a ball of fire from the carburetor. Twice more and Tara had the engine running. Paul thought it sounded more like a wild hog with indigestion than it did a purring kitten.

The rain was coming down a bit harder now and Paul was miserable. He tried to make the best of it, attempting to convince himself that this was all just one big adventure, but in his heart of hearts he knew better.

There were several trails criss-crossing the area and every time Tara stopped to read her hand-drawn map Paul swore the car was going to stall and leave them stranded in the middle of nowhere. Not to mention, every time she stopped it also made it seem as though there was more rain hitting them than when they were moving which held a modicum of truth because each stop was in a clearing and not inside the limited safety of the canopy of trees.

"I had a chance to look over those bones last night," Tara said as she looked up from the map and put the Apache into first gear.

"You took the bones from the bunker?"

"Just one small bone from each of the skeletons."

"Why would you do such a thing?"

"I'm a scientist, it's what I do," she said with a wink.

"But you don't know anything about them. Aside from pissing off the authorities, they very well could be contaminated, diseased or worse."

"I wish that were the case, at least then I would have some tangible explanation," she said. She stopped the truck and turned in her seat with a squeak to face him. "Something chewed their flesh to the bone and into the bones themselves. What on earth could do something like that?"

"There was a wolf down there with them."

"Paul, the markings were on the wolf's bones too. No, something ate them. Some kind of parasite, but nothing like anything I have ever seen. Nothing like anyone has ever seen. And those casts you made, there is no animal known to man that could make those tracks. Now, parasites devouring humans to the bone, I could wrap my head around that. A presumed extinct animal making an appearance or a newly discovered species, I could wrap my head around that as well. But the two of them together, in one remote, barely inhabited place, I can't fathom that. And I do not believe in coincidences."

"There has to be a plausible explanation. Try not to speculate until all the facts are in," Paul said, wanting to end the conversation as abruptly as possible as it was invoking a depth of fear within him he hadn't felt since the tunnels of Nam.

The next two miles of the drive were spent in silence except for the rain slapping metallic against the hood of the Apache. Tara caught a glimpse of a small clearing in the trees and the reflection off the water of Echo Lake and put the vehicle in reverse. She put the Suburban in neutral, found a couple broken limbs and chocked the tires before walking through the open area down to the lake.

"You're not going to turn it off?"

"I want to keep our escape options open," she said, causing her cohort to stop abruptly. "Paul, I was kidding. You saw what a pain in the ass it is to get started."

The narrow path was flanked by jack pines on either side but widened out as they approached the lake. The black sand caught Tara's attention as soon as they broke free of the forest. She bent down and scooped up a handful. She looked up at Paul who simply shrugged back at her. She put a handful of sand into a baggie and slipped it into her jacket pocket.

Paul walked down the beach ahead of her, making sure he stayed high to the grass line so as to not obscure any trail the others may have left. He came across a sneaker print in the sand and stopped. He squatted down to get a better look. It was between a size nine and ten shoe print.

"What did you find?" Tara asked, coming up from behind him while following in his footsteps.

"What size shoe does Travis wear?"

"I'm not sure. Gabe usually gives him money to go to the mall and buy his own. Nine and a half I think."

"I was afraid of that."

"Why, what's the matter?"

"I think these are his prints. And those prints down there look like they were made by someone's knees."

"You think Gabe was down there on his knees?"

"It appears someone was. And then Travis took off running with Gabe limping after him."

"So, you think it was Gabe on his knees?"

"I can only speculate, and you know what assuming does."

"Let's brave being speculative asses for a moment. Why would Gabe have been on his knees?"

"That's the thing, there are no other footprints in the sand. It appears he was alone on the beach. There's a strange pattern in the sand leading to the water. I've never seen anything like it so I can't say what made the tracks."

"It looks like Travis was running for the bunker. Can you tell if something was chasing him?"

"Not that I can see."

An unrecognizable sound reverberated through the forest on the other side of the lake catching their attention. Two figures emerged from the ebon timberland, two blond headed boys on Schwinn bicycles riding as if their lives depended on it. Boughs were ripped from trunks and tossed through the air in every direction causing huge trees to sway back and forth.

The children spotted Tara and Paul on the other side of the lake and veered into the sand toward them. A bluish miasma crested a small hill near the lake, whatever was chasing them was moving fast. A colorful smear of motion leapt from the trees into the lake with a large splash. Paul and Tara were both yelling at the top of their lungs for the kids to ride faster while poised to make a run for the Apache as soon as the children made it across the lake.

Tara's heart sank. A wake headed across the lake straight for the children. The sand was loose and the smaller of the two went down. His older brother jumped off his bike and ran back for his sibling. He picked the smaller lad up and shoved him down the beach as Paul and Tara took off running down the sand toward ill-fated brothers.

Frederico realized there was no way his little brother was going to outrun the creature in the water, so he doubled back. The older boy ran about twenty yards in the opposite direction and stopped. He began yelling, waving his arms frantically and throwing whatever he could find into the water. Tara watched in horror as the creature's wake changed course and headed straight for the defiant teenager.

Paul was able to make it to the smaller boy and tucked him under his arm as he ran back toward Tara who stood stupefied at the scene unfolding across the beach. She didn't even know what she was witnessing. The boy turned and looked at her with a look of rebelliousness. The very next moment an enormous fish, with the head of a man and long arms with saber like claws leapt from the water at the teenager. The boy rolled out of the way and skewered the creature with a limb he concealed behind his back. Lamentably the beast was able to make a wide, arcing sweep with its sinewy, blue appendage, slashing the boy's abdomen wide open with ease. Tara could see the teen's intestines being dragged across the beach as the creature slid back into the murky depths with Frederico's upper half leaving the teen's twitching legs behind on the beach.

Paul covered the younger sibling's eyes as he ran toward Tara who started toward him to help but he waved her off, so she headed up the trail toward the Apache. Her mind was numb from the horror she had just witnessed as she tried to make sense of it all. There was no making sense of any of it. A large splash emanated from the lake behind her, but instead of turning around she put her faith in Paul and ran as hard as she could for the truck.

She moved the logs from under the tires, opened the back door on the driver's side and jumped into the driver's seat. Paul and the young boy were less than a minute behind her. She didn't even wait for the door to close before slamming the vehicle into first and jamming the pedal to the floor. She looked for a place to turn around, but the two-track narrowed too much. She checked the rear view and felt relieved to see nothing was behind her. She stopped to catch her breath and gather her thoughts.

"What's your name?"

The boy just sat there staring into vacant space.

"We need to get you back home to your folks and tell them what happened," Tara said, reaching over the seat to caress him.

The lad recoiled and started to cry.

"Paul, you said you knew who this boy is, do you know where his parents live? We have to take him home."

"If I recall the LaPierre's live on the western side of the island. Let me see your map," he said.

Tara handed him the crude map. While Paul pored over the map, she tried to comfort the boy who was having none of it and she couldn't blame him one bit. What they just witnessed terrified her, so she could only imagine the range of emotion the poor child was experiencing.

"Here, follow this two-track and take the left fork ahead about a quarter of a mile."

Tara put the Apache in gear and started down the path. The boy cried out like a wounded animal, and she stopped driving.

"We can't go back there. We can never go back there," the boy said.

"Back where, honey?"

"Home."

"Why can't we go to your home?"

"They're all dead."

"Who is all dead?" Paul asked, but Tara already knew and nearly vomited from the gravity of the revelation and what it could possibly mean for her own family.

"All of them," he finished and slunk down in the seat, defeated.

"We have to get to Travis and Gabe and then get off this damned island," Tara said, her voice quivering.

"This road dead ends into a tee, take the right fork, which should lead us close to the bunker. Although, this thing won't make it through the woods so we will have to hoof it for about a quarter of a mile through the forest," Paul said.

"Do you think 'dead end' is a wise choice of idioms right now?"

Chapter Twenty-One

"Dad, where did these bones come from?"

"I wish I could tell you son, but I have no idea."

"You need to lie down, but you sure as hell can't do it on that bed. I need to find something for you to sit in."

"Your mother will skin you alive if she hears you talking like that."

"It's not her skinning me alive that I'm worried about," Travis said and began to reconnoiter the bunker.

He saw there were two more short passageways off the living quarters and mentally flipped a coin for which path to take next. He took the hallway to the left which led him thankfully to what appeared to be a small kitchen with a panty and not a nursery for flesh eating blue monsters. He found a couple of blankets and two small pillows that were less than desirable in a deteriorated old trunk. He made his way back to the main room and made a bed on the floor for his wounded father.

"How are you feeling dad?"

"I'm okay I think," Gabe tried to stand up but fell back down onto his haunches.

"Damn, you're bleeding," Travis said, seeing the large wet spot on his dad's shirt for the first time.

"That's nothing, it's just a scratch." Gabe smiled weakly and closed his eyes.

Travis used the pair of scissors in the first aid kit and cut open his father's shirt. He slowly peeled it away, so that he could inspect the wound, but at the same time trying to avoid seeing just how bad it was. An audible gasp escaped his lips.

"How bad is it?" his father asked through thick, sticky lips.

Travis didn't reply. The gash was deep and bleeding profusely. He was certain he was able to see one of his father's ribs.

"Is there any alcohol in that kit?"

Travis rummaged around in the steel box and pulled out a glass decanter. "Yes, I think so."

"Take the stopper out and smell it. You know what alcohol smells like."

"Whoa," Travis said and swooned almost dropping the glass bottle.

"What's wrong son?"

"I don't know, I just got dizzy all of the sudden."

Gabe gave a weak chuckle. "I forgot just how old this medical kit is. I'll bet that was ether. Is there another bottle?"

"Yes," he said and opened the decanter, giving it an apprehensive sniff. "Okay, this one is alcohol, what am I supposed to do with it?"

"Is there a needle and thread in that kit?"

"What? Dad, I am not sewing you up. We need to get you to a doctor."

Gabe sighed. "Son, I'm afraid that is presently not an option. The coast guard boat was damaged in the storm, and I already told them I would speak with them tomorrow, so we are on our own, at least until then."

"But if I can get back to the house I can radio for help."

"And I will have bled to death by the time you got back."

"Listen, Travis, I'm too damned weak to be giving you the it's time be a man speech."

Travis ignored his father and turned his attention to the first aid kit. He was reading through the comprehensive instruction book trying to find a chapter on sewing up wounds caused by radiant blue mermen with six-inch razor-sharp claws. As his run of luck would have it, the first aid kit was from a time nearer to the Neolithic period before crazy glue and butterfly stitches.

The needle in the kit looked more like the needles his Uncle Tom used to reupholster furniture in his shop and the suture thread was not much thinner than the thread he used either. He soaked the needle in alcohol and since there were no gloves, he poured a generous portion into his palm and vigorously rubbed his hands together. With trembling hands, he thread the needle through his father's skin like he and his friends would do in school threading their fingers together to gross out the girls.

"No, son, you have to go deeper, deep into the meat. I'm kidding of course," he said after seeing the look in his son's eyes. "Use those small pliers and pull up one side of the wound, you should be able to see where the muscle and the skin meet. That is how deep the needle has to go."

Travis nodded and took the curved needle between his fingers and after a brief hesitation he used the pliers and saw what his father was talking about. He gently slid the needle through the epidermis down into the dermis and out the other side. He then did the same thing to the other side of the wound. When he tried to tie the knot like the manual showed he kept screwing it up and dropped the needle.

"Nothing fancy Travis. In one side and out the other back and forth. It doesn't have to be pretty, just effective," his father said with a fading smile.

The teen went back to suturing the gash in his father's abdomen and even though his efforts stopped the heavy bleeding on the outside he wondered what was going on inside. He recalled an episode of Marcus Welby M.D. where a patient nearly died from internal bleeding but was saved by the good doctor at the very last minute. But that had been in a hospital, with an exceptionally good doctor, not in a bunker with a pimple faced teenager as the attending physician.

Gabe passed out during the deficient procedure eliciting a sense of loneliness within Travis he never felt before in his life, and tears flowed down his cheeks. He sat by his father's side staring at his blood encrusted hands for more than fifteen minutes before the normal boredom of a hormone riddled teenager took hold. He decided to explore the passageway not already taken, the one to the right.

It was another short, dark corridor eerily illuminated by his flashlight beam. The light cast shadows along the walls that resembled creatures lurking in the darkness all around him.

"You're watching way too much Twilight Zone, Trav," he said aloud to himself just to hear something other than the utter silence. "There is a fifth dimension, beyond that which is known to man." His voice resounded off the concrete walls and made him even more uncomfortable, so he shut up.

The hallway ended after six long strides and opened into a room similar to the pantry room. On one wall of the room there were numerous lumps covered by tattered canvas tarps. He shined the flashlight, and something sparkled through the tatters. While panning the flashlight two odd looking suits hanging from hooks caught his attention. He knew from the many books he read about underwater exploration that those were diving suits. Ancient diving suits.

Up against the third wall was a large trunk. He tried to unlock it but even though it was nearly one hundred years old, it was still sturdy as the day it was put there. He went back to the main room and found a crowbar hanging on the wall from a hook. He returned to the trunk and began prying at the latch. It was tiresome work so every five minutes or so he took a break and checked on his father.

On one of the return trips a thought occurred to him. Why on earth were there diving suits in a bunker with no access to water and was at least a mile from the nearest inland lake and at least three miles from Lake

Superior in any direction? He walked the walls and didn't see any moisture whatsoever and shrugged off his curiosity as nothing more than just that. After nearly an hour he was finally able to open the trunk.

Once the lid was cracked it revealed a treasure trove of old maps, journals, and scribblings on antiquated paper. Travis grabbed one of the innocuous looking journals and went back to sit with his father. Because nothing good ever happened in the first few pages of a book he flipped toward the center and began to read.

I never liked that Swede, and I trusted him even less. The state thrust him upon me no doubt by the urgings of the consortium who, in my humble opinion, were up to less than legal activities on my island. Within that first week I spied that Swede cavorting with some of the consortium workers. I was certain he was feeding them information on my doings at the lighthouse.

But after finding his body mutilated the way I did, I am not so sure of my suspicions was scribbled in the margin.

Travis checked on his father, dabbed a wet cloth around the injured man's lips and flipped to another random page closer to the front of the journal.

Bonni and I argued today. I caught her snooping near the consortium's property. I tried to warn her away, but she was determined to find out exactly what it was they were up to. I am not sure I can trust her here alone on the island when I go into town. Maybe having the Swede here will not be all bad.

Travis flipped closer to the end of the small journal.

I still tremble at thought of those damned moths. They seemed to be instilled with significant intelligence, communicating with one another of one single mind and common goal which seemed to be my elimination. No, that is incorrect, elimination of all mankind, I was just the one who was currently in their way.

Travis closed the journal and put it down, it had gotten too difficult to read with teary eyes. The gravity of their situation had not managed to establish a foothold in his brain until he read the words. Someone else's words. The bone's words.

Chapter Twenty-Two

The small entourage couldn't see or hear anything following them, and yet they felt shadowed just the same. Paul's head was on a swivel and his heart threatened to break free from his chest. Tara did her best to comfort the little boy, but he regressed into a near catatonic state. A canopy of darkness hung over them like an itchy wool blanket.

"Are you sure this is the way, Paul?"

"No, not really. But right now, it's our only option considering what's behind us," he replied.

The boy said nothing.

The path narrowed to the point that overgrown shrubbery brushed against them as they hurried toward the bunker. Occasionally, a sharp, broken limb would catch Tara's arm invading her thoughts with sharpened claws. Lightning flashed overhead, glinting off the chrome accents around the lawn tractor headlights alerting her they were close to the bunker, so she picked up the pace.

Travis was lost within the secrets of the journal when a loud banging from above startled him. It found them. He prayed the bunker door would hold, and then he thought about the bones. The hatch must have held for them all those years ago.

"Gabe, are you and Travis down there?"

Paul impatiently banged on the door before giving anyone inside a chance to reply, earning a disapproving glance from Tara.

"Travis, honey, if you are down there, please let us in," she called out again.

Minutes passed and she felt their plan suddenly turned into a dead end. Defeated, she started back out on the trail, a trail she hoped led back home.

"Where are you going?"

"We can't stay here."

"But someone is down there. The door is barred and that can only be done from the inside," Paul said, banging ferociously on the door with a small log he salvaged from the forest floor.

"If there is anyone down there your approach is to scare them into opening the door?" she asked. She cupped her hands against the door and called out once more. "Travis?"

A minute later the first bar slid open with a grinding metallic sound. "Mom, is that you?"

"Yes, honey, it's us."

Travis slid the second bar open and shoved open the hatch while climbing up the last few steps. As soon as the hatch was open Paul shoved little Gregorio through the opening and dashed through the doorway. Tara followed closely behind, not hiding her disgust with the man's cowardly behavior.

"Mom, dad is badly injured," Travis said through choked back tears.

"Okay, son, but right now, we need to get inside and lock the door."

"You come on down and close the door, I need to go fill the generator or we will be down there in the dark," Travis said.

"No, Travis, it's much too dangerous. Paul, I need you to go fill the generator," she called down the stairs.

"No way in hell am I going out there. I would rather sit down here in the dark."

"Mom, I have to. You're going to need lights to look after dad."

She nodded and slid down a few steps. Travis paused long enough to shine a flashlight beam out into the growing darkness. No eyes lit up from the shadows as he panned the light, so he felt it was as good a time as any. Tara vehemently refused to close the door after him so rather than waste any more time arguing with her, he made a dash for the generator.

Travis turned the engine off and let it cool for a minute before opening the gas cap. He reached for the gasoline can and started to pour the fuel into the tank. Once it was filled, he reached for the pull start. The damned thing didn't start on the first pull, or even the second.

A loud noise echoed through the forest. Something was headed toward him and by the sound of it, it was moving fast. He jerked at the rope over and over as his mother yelled at him to forget it. The generator fired up, the bunker opening exploded with light, and Travis took off on a dead run. Whatever was behind him was closing fast. He jumped down into the bunker opening and Tara started closing the hatch.

"Wait," he called out. "It's Zappa."

A filthy, shaggy golden retriever bounded into the bunker doorway with something fast on its heels. Tara slammed the door shut and Travis barred the hatch. Within seconds there was a loud hammering against the steel portal. The mother and son duo quickly retreated into the bowels of the bunker to meet up with the others. Gregorio was fixated on a bloody patch on his knee he received when Paul Rainbird shoved him down the stairs. Tara went to help him while averting her eyes from the man to contain her anger.

"Mom, I'll take care of the kid, you need to look at dad," Travis said. "He's in pretty bad shape."

Tara nodded wordlessly and went to her husband's side while her son looked after the child's injured knee. Travis wanted to punch the brat in the nose, but for some reason, he wanted to punch Rainbird even more. What had he done that was so bad for him to be surrounded by cowards and jackasses? Was this all some sort of karmic retribution?

He applied a generous amount of Mercurochrome and took a perverse sort of pleasure in how much discomfort it caused the miscreant. Which in turn made him wonder if his mother needed to use the stuff on him so often.

"Oh my God, Travis, what happened to your father?"

"Some kind of a fish with arms and claws attacked us."

Tara stared back at him, tears seeping from the edges of her eyes.

"Mom, I'm not lying."

"Travis, I know you're not lying."

"Then why are you crying?"

"Because I'm not crazy or seeing things that aren't real and that scares me. And what scares me even more is that your little sister is out there, with that creature, or possibly creatures all by herself."

Tears escaped Travis' eyes as well.

~   ~   ~

Noona watched the sun disappear beyond the trees on the western side of the island while she heated up some leftover macaroni and cheese and boiled some hot dogs.

"Eat, dear, it will make you big and strong," Noona said, sliding a plate in front of the child.

Amanda picked at her plate while looking at her rapidly healing finger which perplexed her, but not as much as neither of her parents nor her brother being home. It was one thing to leave her in the company of a complete, awkwardly strange acquaintance during the day, but it would be unheard of for them to leave her alone at night.

She studied the little old woman as she glided around the kitchen while mindlessly slipping macaroni noodles onto her fork tines. Although she seemed like a sweet, little old lady, there was something about the woman's eyes that Amanda didn't like. She tried not to show she was frightened, but she knew it was apparent. But at least she wasn't crying.

"Noona," she said, pushing a hard macaroni coated with fake cheese sauce around on her plate.

"Yes child?"

"Are those pukthingamajigs going to get my mom and dad?"

"Why no child, of course not. Bagwajinini are mischievous, but they are not altogether harmful."

"What are bagwajees?"

"Bagwajinini, that is the real name for the puckwatchamathingies Paul calls them." She smiled a wide, friendly smile.

"But they are friendly, right?"

"Friendly enough. Why all the questions child?"

"My family is out there in the dark, all alone without me and they are probably scared," she said, a break in her voice revealed her own fear.

"Let me make you some hot chocolate," Noona said and shuffled to the cupboard to pull down two large mugs.

She scrounged around in the bottom cupboard for a saucepan, but the miniature marshmallows were in the upper cupboard and were too high for her to reach so she climbed up on the counter just like Amanda did when she needed something her parents tried to hide. Noona poured some milk into the saucepan and set it on the stove to heat. Then, using a cheese grater, she shaved some Hershey's chocolate bars into the warming milk. She dropped two pats of butter into the mixture.

"Was that butter?"

"Yes child, it is Noona's secret ingredient. You cannot tell anyone," she said with a wink and went about the task of slowly stirring the mixture with a wooden spoon while bringing it nearly to a boil being careful not to scald the milk.

Soon the room hung heavy with the sweet aroma of warm sugar. Noona began to sing a little song as she stirred the chocolate concoction. It was a melodic, enchanting tune and soon Amanda found herself humming along.

"What is that you are singing, Miss Noona?"

"Noona, just Noona, no Miss Noona."

"My mother says I should call everyone Mister or Miss when I use their name if they are older than me."

Noona cackled, "I guess that will be fine then, Noona is definitely older than you are."

"What is the song about?"

"Praise and thanks."

"Thanks to who?"

"Whom. It is praise to whom."

"Great, now you sound like mother," Amanda said, suddenly feeling gut punched.

"It is a silly child's song praising the mythical beast Mishipeshu."

"You mean the fishy cat Mister Paul was painting?"

Noona went back to stirring and singing with her back to the child. She tasted the brew and added just a pinch more sugar and a touch of cinnamon.

"Yes, but Mister Paul does not believe so he does not honor Mishipeshu the way he should. He draws it more like a child's cartoon than the majestic creature it truly is."

"Is Mishipeshu a mean creature?"

"She can be. But only because she is very protective."

"What is she protective of?"

"She protects the copper beneath the great lake we call Anishinaabewi-gichigami."

"What is copper?"

"It is a metal that men use to make tools with. The wiring in this house is made from copper. But that is just ordinary copper found in rock under the earth. Mishipeshu's copper is much more special. It is pure and was given as a gift from the gods to be admired for its beauty. It should never leave the bottom of the lake."

"Mishipeshu sure looks mean in the pictures Mister Paul has," Amanda said.

"Not mean, angry. When Mishipeshu gets angry she is dangerous, so it is best to leave her and her copper alone. But men do not listen, and men die," she said in a tone that startled Amanda.

Noona let her stern expression slide away and ladled two large mugs of steaming hot chocolate. She dipped her long, leathered fingers into a plastic bag and plucked out a half dozen tiny marshmallows and dropped them into the child's mug. The old woman sat down at the table with the child and loudly sipped at her mug of decadence without a care in the world. Amanda sat across from her bobbing the marshmallows down into the liquid with her fingertip, careful not to use the finger that had been bitten.

"Noona, is Mishipeshu angry with me? Is that why my family is in trouble?"

"No, Mishipeshu is not angry with you and your family is not in trouble, they are simply taking shelter from the storm. They will be back here before you know it. Now finish your hot chocolate and then get your pajamas on."

Amanda nodded, finished the last drink from her mug and disappeared into her bedroom to get ready for bed while Noona cleaned up the kitchen. She couldn't escape the extreme weight pressing down upon her chest. The child was doing her best to contain her tears, to stay brave and strong like her brother taught her to be.

Once she was in her pajamas Amanda stole away to the lantern room of the lighthouse. She began to carefully go through the stacks of photos Paul had taken of cave paintings and local artwork depicting Mishipeshu. Without realizing it, she had been reciting Noona's song while studying the photos. She almost forgot what brought her to the lighthouse cupola in the first place.

Amanda undogged the door and walked out onto the widow's walk shivering against the wet winds. She circled around until she was on the western side overlooking the forest while observing an ominous blue glow spreading across the forest floor like flood water. She sang a song to the water panther and cried. And then she prayed.

"Goodnight mommy, goodnight daddy and goodnight Travis," she said through heaving sobs and reached an outstretched hand to the heavens with her fingers splayed as wide as she could stretch them.

The ultramarine glow in the woodland seemed to pulsate and she jerked her hand back which resulted in the glow diminishing in intensity. Amanda repeated her gesture with the same results. She looked down and saw it was her injured hand with the bitten finger she was holding up, so she switched hands. She held her undamaged hand up to the forest and nothing changed. Once more she offered her wounded finger and once again the forest emitted a dazzling luminosity. In her innocent, untarnished mind she convinced herself that it was Mishipeshu letting her know she was watching over her family. She would go rescue them in the morning.

~   ~   ~

Tara finished splinting and bandaging Gabe's broken forearm and wrist. She dabbed sweat from her forehead and leaned back against the cool concrete wall with a deep sigh. Travis was sitting on the top step intently listening to the hatch.

"Well?" Rainbird asked in a tone that conveyed he was the one in charge and sent Travis to scout their situation. Travis knew better.

"I can hear breathing. Whatever is up there must be lying on the hatch."

Travis looked at the hair on his forearm, it was standing straight up on end. He knew enough about science to know that storms created static electricity in the air, but in all the storms he encountered, never had the air been charged with this intense amount of electrical disruption. These were not your ordinary, everyday, run of the mill storms. Maybe whatever was causing this electricity was also causing the wildlife on the island to go berserk.

"I want to go home," Gregorio cried.

"Shut up, kid, we all want to go home," Rainbird snapped.

Tara started to rouse but Travis put a firm hand on her shoulder.

"Listen, Mister Paul, that young boy just lost his brother and for all we know his parents as well. He is just as scared if not more than any one of us so cut him some slack. If you can't say anything nice, don't say anything thing at all. Come on, Greg, let's see if we can't find some food in this place," Travis said, hiding his trembling hands in his pockets.

In another time and place Tara would have chewed her son's ass out for speaking to an adult in that tone, but at that very moment, she could not have been prouder of him. Gregorio followed the self-appointed leader to the pantry where they scrounged for food and figured out how to work a little device called a pocket stove. Following the directions, he poured some alcohol from a glass bottle onto a piece of gauze in a metal tin. He set the tin on the stand and then lit the gauze. He was impressed that something made in the eighteen hundred's worked perfectly fine a hundred years later.

"Hey mom, how would you like some hundred-year-old water?"

"I think I'll pass. But that does raise another concern. We won't last very long down here without water, your father especially."

Travis nodded even though she couldn't see him and capped the flame on the pocket stove. While there were plenty of food stores, he feared they were far too old to be of any use to them. He gathered another handful of materials from the trunk and went out to sit next to his mother.

"What is that stuff?"

"It's maps of the island, diagrams, charts all sorts of other stuff. There are a lot of notes that sound like they were written by the lighthouse keeper after he locked them all down here. Listen to this," Travis started to read from the notes.

We received some visitors from the Keweenaw Peninsula on the island today. The state bureaucrat told me they were rich mining folk who were building a hunting retreat. Their plan is to stock the island with wildlife and exotic game which they then plan to hunt. When I questioned the man, worried they might be talking about lions, tigers and the such he laughed and assured me they would be elk, caribou and gazelles not normally found in these woods. They erected a fence on the first day and I have not been able to see what they are up to. I doubt I will be able to dissuade Bonni for very long, she is a very curious beast that one.

"Your father never told me about there being elk or caribou on the island."

"The keeper jotted down something here in the margins about thinking the creatures ate the animals on the island before going after the men at the consortium."

"What creatures? Is he talking about the things we saw? How could they have been on this island for a hundred years without anyone seeing them?"

"There are a bunch of drawings here, and the word Mishipeshu with question marks after it," Travis said, handing his mother the loose piece of parchment.

"Mishipeshu? Isn't that one of the panels you are painting in the lighthouse cupola?" Tara looked over at Paul and asked.

"Yes, but Mishipeshu is nothing more than a myth, a legend to frighten children and fools," Paul replied.

"It seemed pretty real to me," Tara snapped back.

"Do you think that's what the creature was who ate my brother?" Gregorio asked, breaking his silence for the first time since taking shelter.

"No kid, Mishipeshu is a legendary creature made up of all sorts of animals. It is part lynx, part deer, part fish, part snake and whatever else the elders wanted to add to scare the village children with. Whatever that thing is out there, it is certainly not Mishipeshu. Mainly because Mishipeshu doesn't exist."

"Like I said, it seemed pretty real to me," Tara said. "And to him."

"It is too real. Me and Frederico saw a big cat in the forest, but it didn't hurt us," Gregario argued.

Tara slid across the floor to where the boy was trembling and tried to comfort him. In the last hour she learned the kind of human being Paul Rainbird really was, the type she abhorred. She was not sure why, but she was getting a vibe that he was up so something or at the very least, the man at least knew more than he was letting on.

"Paul, I was reading through your literature and somewhere I read that Mishipeshu's main purpose for existence was to protect the copper in Lake Superior," Travis commented rather harshly, drawing a stiff look from his mother.

"And is there a point to your train of thought?" Paul replied.

"It says here that this hunting consortium was anything but. What they were really doing was mining for copper. They believed there was a vein of pure copper on the bottom of the lake. Seems to me that would have pissed Mishipeshu off don't you think, Mister Paul?" he asked contemptuously.

"Travis, watch your mouth."

"Sorry mom. Listen to this."

I didn't like those consortium folks when they arrived here in seventy-one. That Rainbird fellow had a mouth on him and a set of eyes which told a man he was up to no good. I knew he was lying about setting up a hunting camp. I suspect this compound of theirs has nothing to do with hunting.

"What Rainbird fellow was he talking about?" Tara asked, turning her attention to Paul.

Paul laughed. "Rainbird is a pretty common name around here, even more so a hundred years ago."

"If it isn't your water panther, what are those creatures out there? Gabe didn't slash his own stomach open. There is something out there that requires some explaining," Tara said.

Again, Rainbird laughed. "Why are you asking me? You are the scientist here. You tell me what you think it is we saw?"

Tara ignored the man and checked on her husband before sidling up to her son to read over his shoulder.

Bonni and I discussed our predicament for hours until she finally fell asleep. What she believes chills me to the bone because I tend to agree with her no matter how horrific. She feels this organism cannot be killed; it can only be contained. When I pressed her to elaborate, she uttered only one word before succumbing to her fatigue, Mishipeshu.

Travis closed the journal and was scanning through the loose papers tossing them quickly aside if nothing specific caught his attention.

"Wait, go back to that one," Tara said.

Travis picked up the cast aside sheet of parchment and handed it to his mother.

"This mentions blister copper."

"What's that?"

"It is the purest form of copper as a result of refining the ore. According to these notes they hit a motherlode vein of one hundred percent pure copper."

Travis began rifling through the papers again, this time looking for anything annotated Cu. There were three more sheets of parchment that mentioned the copper, so he handed those to his mother as well.

"What is ultramarine?" he asked.

"It's a pigment of blue, a very vivid deep blue."

His voice wavered. "You mean like the same colors the moths were when they glowed?"

"Yes, I imagine so. Why?"

"I'm not sure. It just says *we blew the ultramarine*."

Tara reached her hand out, so Travis passed her the documents he had been perusing and went to see if he could find any potable water. She read through the papers, understanding a lot more than her son due to her familiarity with scientific terminology. It seemed this consortium was a collection of wealthy mine owners who dreamed of being even more prosperous after finding a vein of the purest copper ever recorded. Their main impediment, it was on the bottom of Lake Superior beneath layers of bedrock.

According to their scientist's notes they discovered an ultramarine-colored vein of rock. Thinking it was covering the copper, they dynamited the rock. This created a fissure that released superheated water into Lake Superior which was harmful in and of itself, but it released something else as well. Tara set the pages down and looked up at her son.

"Now that you have read what the miners found, let me show you something," Travis said, taking his apprehensive mother by the hand.

Travis led her back to the room where the diving suits were kept. He walked over to a large square cube covered by a tarpaulin and slowly rolled the tarp back to expose a pile of glistening orange-brown metal ingots. But there was something very odd about these ingots. They were surrounded by a substance emitting a dark blue hue in their reflections as if imbued into the metal itself.

"Not that I have seen a lot of copper ingots, very few in fact, but I have never seen anything that looked like these," Tara said.

"Listen," Travis said, picking up the twenty-pound ingot and holding it up to his mother's ear.

"It hums. Why on earth would it hum?"

"You're the scientist."

"Hypothetically, if this was in one of your sci-fi stories, why would this metal be humming? How could an inanimate object emit sound?" Tara asked, perplexed by the bizarre circumstances.

"Hypothetically? The sound would be a form of communication. And the only way an inanimate object could communicate would be one of two answers, it was not truly inanimate, or it was mechanical in some way or another. I can't see this ingot having a robotic brain or any other form of mechanical mechanism imbedded inside."

"So, then you think it's alive in some way?"

"I didn't say that. I said hypothetically. And even that would be fiction," he said while reaching his hand out to grab another ingot.

"What are you doing?"

"Testing a fictional theory."

Travis set the first ingot on the floor of the bunker against the wall furthest from the stack of ingots. He took the second ingot and walked the fifteen feet across the small chamber to the other end and set that ingot down as well. He returned to the center of the room with his mother to watch the outcome. At first, it all seemed for naught. Then suddenly, the ingot in the far corner emitted a soft glow. The ingot in the opposite corner responded in kind. Shocking them both, the stack of ingots then responded with a much stronger pulse of light and an audible hum. As if drawn by magnets the two ingots began to slide across the concrete floor toward the stack of ingots. Filaments of ultramarine light reached out between the three metallic entities to connect them together.

A loud clamor resounded throughout the bunker sending little Gregario scampering for the safety of Tara and Travis. The hatch above boomed again as something tried to gain access. There was a long, chilling silence before the lights started to flicker, fade, and then go out completely.

"What the hell," Paul cried out.

"The generator must have run out of gas," Travis said.

"We need to fill it," Paul said, clearly meaning Travis needed to go topside and fill the generator.

"No one is leaving this bunker. We have oil lamps and flashlights, we will be fine," Tara said, tugging both children out of the chamber filled with glowing copper ingots.

Chapter Twenty-Three

Amanda waited until half past midnight to embark upon her mission to rescue her family. She packed her bookbag with the first aid kit from the closet, a Ziploc baggie of Milk Bone dog biscuits just in case she found Zappa, a few snacks, and some jars of water in case her family was thirsty. She stopped at the hall closet for the two emergency flashlights and the funny hat with the light on the front her dad would wear when searching for earthworms at night. It didn't fit her, so she wedged a dish towel between her head and the headband to snug it up. As a last thought she took the flare gun attached to the wall near the front door. Her brother showed her how to use it even though he knew it was against their parents' wishes.

The storm stopped dumping rain by the buckets full, but the wind screamed like banshees as it swirled amongst the treetops. Shadows cast by scraggly tree limbs danced along the path stretching out like long goblin fingers. Now she understood Dorothy's fright when traveling through the haunted forest. She prayed she would not run into any flying blue monkeys. Amanda was old enough and bright enough to understand the Wizard of Oz was only make believe while what was happening to her family was a reality which only served to scare her even more. She was so frightened she felt like crying, but she pushed on. Step by step, tree by tree, and shadow by shadow.

The wind murmured in the pines and Amanda could swear she heard people talking, no, it was more like they were singing. Nervously she swung the flashlight from side to side illuminating boogeymen behind every tree. She wiped her tears and trudged down the path, stalwart against all odds, yet ready to run in the blink of an eye.

She paused long enough to reach into her backpack for Brutus, a stuffed animal of unknown origins, but he was ferociously courageous and bore many battle scars to prove it. She hugged her fiber filled friend and wiped her tears with his ears before putting him back away. It was not time for him to fight yet.

Amanda tried to imagine she was simply in a Scooby Doo cartoon and when the monster was revealed it would just be a greedy man from town trying to steal money. But greedy men were just as scary as monsters, and sometimes they hurt people too. The trail narrowed which squeezed the darkness in around her and chilled the poor child to the bone, but she persisted and pushed on despite the hardships. She was determined to save her family.

~   ~   ~

Travis slowly regained consciousness. His mind was treading water in a sea of confusion, and the room was pitch black which disoriented him even more. There was a thickness about him that was hard to put his finger on. He smacked and licked his lips trying to get some moisture back into his mouth. For some reason, his mouth was dry, sticky and there was a lingering sweetness on his tongue. A dim glow from a flashlight illuminated mere inches of the floor in front of him. Travis scooted across the floor and grabbed the light.

The batteries were so weak he could barely even see his own toes. He inched over to where he imagined his mother was and saw she was sleeping. The boy was sleeping as well with a long strand of drool reaching down to the floor. Both were lying in odd positions as if they collapsed to the floor. Zappa managed to crawl into a corner, but the poor dog was out like a light.

As the fog in his brain receded certain details began to emerge. There was a glow emanating from beyond the spur tunnel and there was an odd, muffled metallic sound. Travis banged the flashlight against the palm of his hand which resulted in one single brilliant flash of light before reverting to the dull yellow glow. It was enough for him to see that his father was no longer on the bedroll.

Travis started moving toward the other glowing room when it dawned on him, he had not seen Paul Rainbird in that brief flash of light either. He eased himself down the short tunnel wanting to keep the element of surprise in his court. Paul was acting strangely and was not to be trusted as far as the teen was concerned. His family came first, no matter what.

"It's nothing personal, Gabe, you're just the bigger threat at the moment. And of course, you're in the way."

Travis heard Paul's voice echoing off the concrete walls. Then he heard his father moan and say something, but it was too muffled for him to make out what he said.

"We are just about where we need to be and then this will be all over. Well, all over for you anyway," Paul said with a certain amount of enjoyment in his voice.

Travis remained in the shadows inching ever closer to the two men. Paul was moving from side to side which also swung the flashlight beam back and forth as well making it almost impossible to piece together the scene in its entirety. The teen's heart sank when he noticed there was a familiar object around his father's waist. Paul had fastened a diver's weight belt around the crippled man. Travis knew his father didn't have the strength to swim, but swim where? There was no water.

"I'm really sorry it had to come to this, but once your son found the bunker my hands were tied. Can you believe it? That kid of yours must be a lucky charm or something. I've been searching for this place for six months and the very first week on the island your kid stumbles on it by accident."

Gabe found the strength to speak. "Why?"

"Why what? Why am I doing this? Why did I rekindle our friendship and trust just to betray you? Power, Gabe, good old-fashioned power."

"What are you talking about?"

311

"You saw that thing out there. You saw what it can do. Now just imagine being able to harness that power and control that beast. And from what I have read in my great grandfather's journals we have only witnessed a miniscule part of what it can do. But alas, all things must eat."

"You killed them, didn't you?" Gabe asked.

"Killed who Gabe?"

"Your platoon. It was you who betrayed them wasn't it."

"Whatever gave you that idea? I am deeply hurt that you would think I was capable of something as callous as murdering my own men," Paul said, unable to hide his smirk.

"I truly hoped I had been mistaken or that Gonzalez was out of it because of the morphine and the loss of blood. Probably both," Gabe said.

"What did Nicolas tell you?"

"He said it was his fault the men were killed."

"There you have it. Nicky killed the platoon, not me. You even said so yourself."

"He said it was his fault for not stopping you. What did you do Paul?"

"Gonzalez and I had a little deal going with some of the VC in a village south of our location. They supplied us with drugs, we in turn sold those to our platoon and in return we promised to bypass their little village when out on patrol."

"You are beneath contempt. Keeping your own men stoned while fighting a war. How could you betray people who considered you their friend, their leader? So, what happened, why did you assault the village if you had an agreement?"

"The louie."

"The louie?"

"Don't you remember, we got that fresh boot lieutenant in right around Christmas time. His daddy was some high-ranking pencil pusher at the pentagon. This kid was gung-ho to the hilt and wanted feathers for his cap to prove something to his old man. God, I hated that little bastard," Paul said.

"You hated him enough to kill him?"

"I didn't kill him, the VC killed him."

"Your platoon was ambushed and the only way for that to have happened was if the enemy had been forewarned," Gabe said while trying to get up.

Paul put a boot against the man's wounded arm to hold him in place.

"Gonzalez warned the VC about the assault on the village."

"You're a lying bastard, Paul. I knew I should have never trusted you."

"You're a little late to that party, Doc. If you cooperate, maybe I won't feed your family to this monster right along with you," Paul taunted.

Travis sank back into the shadows and leaned against the cold, concrete walls while listening to them talk. Did this lunatic really intend on feeding his father to that creature, whatever the hell it was?

"Ah, finally," Paul said and pulled on the handle of a trap door in the floor of the bunker that was obscured by the pallet of copper ingots. "Nothing personal, but like I was saying, everything must eat. Long ago, being atop the food chain, homo sapiens lost sight of the fact that all animals are driven by two equally important forces, all things need to eat, and all things are food for something else. Such is the vicious cycle of life," Paul said as he got to his feet and began dragging Gabe toward the open hatch.

The portal revealed a deep hole bored through the solid rock, so deep in fact it dropped down into an underwater cave which led into Lake Superior. Travis left his concealment and stepped into the open chamber with a stone look of defiance etched on his face.

"What in the hell do you think you are doing?" Travis yelled, his voice echoing off the hardened walls.

Paul looked up and shot a dismissive glance the boy's way. "This does not concern you child. You will have your turn soon enough."

Paul dragged Gabe closer to the hatch while Gabe fruitlessly struggled against the assault.

"I said stop," Travis said, moving completely into the room and squaring himself up against the demented man. He relaxed his stance and bobbed up and down lightly on the balls of his feet.

"Ladies and gentlemen let me introduce the incomparable Mr. Bruce Lee," Paul said, mimicking the roar of the crowd.

Without hesitation Travis launched himself planting a left foot squarely on the right side of Paul's jaw which dropped him to the floor. The man shook his head and wiped a trickle of blood from his mouth before sliding up the wall to regain his footing.

"That was a little Billy Jack for you," Travis said, bobbing back and forth on his feet.

"Damn, kid, I didn't think you had it in you. But now you have a choice to make."

"And just what choice might that be? Because in my mind I only have one choice and it is to kick your ass," Travis said, resuming an attack posture.

"You have to make the very important choice of whether you leave a psychotic killer here with your mother, or saving your dear old dad," Paul said as he dropped to his knees and shoved the weighted Gabe through the hatch in the floor. There was a long silence followed by a splash echoing up from the bottom of the portal.

Without thinking Travis grabbed one of the diving helmets from the wall and jumped into the hatch after his father. Without the suit attached the helmet would only hold a few small breaths of air and that was only if he could keep the air from burping out during the descent. He chased after his father like a skydiver chasing after someone whose parachute didn't open. Gabe hit bottom first in less than twenty feet of water, his eyes bulged, and his cheeks were expanded to maximum capacity.

Travis caught up to his father in the icy depths in less than two seconds. Gabe was vehemently shaking his head while pointing to the surface. He knew there was no way Travis would be able to get him to the surface and he didn't want his son to die in a hopeless attempt to save him.

Suddenly something streaked passed them as quick as a lightning flash. Travis could see streams in the water from the current trailing behind it, but he couldn't see what had created the currents. He prayed it was a boat and started to fumble with the weight belt strapped around his father's waist. Gabe shook his head in protest and pointed to the north of them. Something was coming at them fast from out of the depths.

A large fish came into view swimming straight for them. At first Travis thought it resembled a shark, but this was no ordinary fish. The tail rotated from horizontal to the vertical position giving the creature incredible speed and control of movement. It circled them with blinding speed while keeping its distance. It was close enough to them that Travis could make out shades of blue shimmering off the beast's skin.

As if taunting them, it stopped twenty feet away from them and hovered in the chilly water, letting them get a good look at it before it attacked. Travis was staggered by the beast's appearance. The creature was a fish from the middle portion of his body to the tail, but the chest and arms were that of a humanoid. Images of a poster of mermaids and dolphins hanging on his sister's wall flashed through his mind. But this was no comely cartoon. The four fingers on each of its hands were tipped with razor sharp dagger-like talons and the beast's biceps bulged with sinew. Travis thought, if Aquaman had an evil counterpart, this creature would be it.

The creature inched forward like a goldfish kissing the glass of its bowl. Flaps of skin extended away from the sides of its neck and fluttered in the current of the water. There were rows of needle like spines rimming the undulating appendages which were bowed inward indicating their purpose was to grip anything dumb enough to get within the creature's range. Travis gasped when he could finally make out the face and saw that it was an amalgam of every deep sea fish he studied in his marine biology class. The gaping maw that served as its mouth glistened with rows of razor-sharp shark-like teeth and yet there were long protruding needle-like fangs of the vampire fish gnashing at the water in a macabre display of malevolence.

If its face had not been so horrifying, the body would have been almost comical. There were stubby legs on the creature's hind quarters just above where the tail began. They resembled the short, squat legs of a reptile but dangled uselessly in the water reminding him of his sister's cloth dolls with the hard rubber legs.

Travis managed to unbuckle the lead weights from around his father's waist and dropped them onto the lake bottom. He took a deep breath, indicated to his father to exhale, and then rebreathed the air into his father's lungs. It was not the best-case scenario, but it would have to suffice. He took the last lungful of air from the diving helmet and ditched it to the bottom of the lake floor as well.

As soon as he started their frantic ascent, he felt a stirring in the water and noticed the sea creature was gone. Flashes of blue swirled around them like a drawing from his sister's Spin Art set. They managed to make it nearly ten feet up when the creature stopped and faced them. Travis swore the thing smiled at him through rows of jagged, pointed teeth before launching itself straight at them.

Gabe struggled to hold his breath until he saw the demon fish heading straight for him. He looked up at Travis and mouthed *I love you* before exhaling all his breath. He held steady long enough to give his son a warm, loving smile before inhaling as hard as he could. Immediately, every fiber of his body was wracked with an unfathomable amount of pain. As he was convulsing in the water the creature shot across above him and flicked out a phalange as easily as flicking a pea off the kitchen table and laid Gabe's stomach wide open. The man's intestines burst forth from the wound, propelled by the remaining gas bubble in his stomach cavity. The pristine waters of Lake Superior were stained with the remnants of Gabe Roster.

Tears streamed down Travis' face as he watched his father's limp body hang suspended in the cold water for several seconds before it began to sink. Gitchigami never gives up her dead. He felt a woosh of water current rush by him and knew the creature was circling him. It flashed toward his father's corpse, grasping the dead man's intestine in its ferocious grasp before jerking it toward the surface. It let Gabe's body go and spun around with the nimble grace of a figure skater on ice to face Travis. It gnashed its scraggly teeth in warning as it prepared to unleash its fury on the boy.

Travis poised himself for a dying attack on the beast once it committed to the assault. He knew it was a futile move at best, but he was not going to leave this earth whimpering. Something just beyond the blue glow of the water surrounding the man-fish caught his attention. The water was shimmering, moving in and out of focus as if warmer water were mixing with the chill of Lake Superior. From out of nowhere something slammed into the creature sending it careening out of control through the water. Before he realized what happened Travis was on the surface gulping at fresh air. Whatever dragged him to the surface had disappeared back into the icy depths. Could it have been Mishipeshu he thought just before he blacked out?

Chapter Twenty-Four

Every snapped twig and every shadow that danced across her path caused Amanda to startle. She fought back her tears, wiped her running nose on her pajama sleeve and forged ahead down the dark path. She tried singing songs to comfort herself, but she only knew a few and it was making her throat sore anyway, so she stopped after a few. There were only so many times a girl could sing Frère Jacques before she tired of it, especially when she didn't even know what the song meant.

She stopped near a large tree and put her back against it like her brother taught her during their games of *war* in the backyard back at their house on the mainland. Amanda took several sips of water and ate two soda crackers to help settle her stomach before pulling Brutus from the backpack for a much-needed hug.

With her tummy feeling better she set out on the path once more. She plodded at the ground with a long limb she managed to forage. It made a good walking stick, and it might do some damage to a pinata if one were to attack her, but that was the extent of its power. Still, it made her feel better, so she brandished it as if it were King Arthur's Excalibur.

The batteries in the headlamp were starting to run low and the beam was growing dimmer by the minute. The child, sensing the trouble she was in, picked up the pace until she was winded and needed to rest. This was truly a foolish thing she had done, and she was bound to get into a heap of trouble. But somehow, she knew her parents were the least of her troubles.

It was not long before the gravity of her situation was thrust upon her. Another ten minutes down the trail and the headlamp batteries gave out plunging her into complete and total darkness. She found another large tree, put her back against it and slid down to the ground.

Amanda began to cry. Not because she was scared so much as because she failed her family.

"Why do you cry child?" a voice echoed from the darkness.

"Noona? Where did you come from?"

"I have been here all along child."

"I didn't see you."

"Because I did not want to be seen."

"And I didn't hear you either," Amanda said.

"Because I did not wish you to hear me. This is your trial, not mine."

"What do you mean my trial?"

"It is your test."

"Who is testing me?"

"Why, you are testing yourself brave little one. And others are testing you as well."

Amanda was not sure if she was more frightened without Noona there, or if she was more terrified of the odd old woman than she realized. She was not very old, or worldly, but she was smart enough to know that there was something very wrong about this woman.

"What others? Who else is testing me?"

"No one you need to concern yourself with child."

"How can they test me if they can't see me?"

"Oh, child," she said with a cackle. "They can see you just fine."

~   ~   ~

Paul shoved Tara and the boy through the woods back toward Echo Lake. He wore an angry red badge under his right eye thanks to Travis and a knee that was swelling up with each painful step courtesy of the Grasshopper's mother. As he rubbed at the imprint the little shit's teeth left in his forearm, a tinge of guilt passed over him as he thought about how hard he punched the child in the mouth, but it was a small tinge and it passed rather quickly.

Events were progressing much faster than Paul anticipated, and he was not ready. He needed Noona to be there when he confronted the beast, only she knew how to communicate with it. That was if the old hag was to be believed.

Tara's head was swimming with confused, jumbled thought. What in the hell was Paul up to and why did he only bring her and the child? Had he done something to her husband and son? She was still groggy from the effects of the ether Paul dosed her with back in the bunker but the longer she was in the fresh air, the less cloudy her thoughts were.

Gregario stumbled over a protruding root, tripped, and fell. Paul snatched the boy back to his feet by his hair. Tears streamed down the boy's face, but he was too frightened to protest.

"Paul, what are you doing? He's just a child," Tara said.

"You shut up or I will give you some of the same. Now get moving," he said, shoving her in the back with his palm.

"What in the hell are you up to?"

"Nothing that needs to concern you."

There was a long silence and then Paul's laughter broke the silence.

"Now that I think about it, I guess it does concern you after all."

Tara held her many questions hoping to ease the man's wrath on the child. Paul drove them forward through the dense forest toward the shores of Echo Lake. Whenever she tried to separate herself from the child in hopes he could run off, Paul would round them up back together. Along the way he picked up a sturdy limb and used it to poke his captives in their backs, every so often giving the boy a sharp whack on the top of his head when he slowed down.

"Paul, if you do that again I will beat you with that stick. I have only been cooperating with you for the boy's sake, but if you continue to harm him, we are going to come to blows. I see my son gave you a good thrashing, who do you think taught him how to kick like that?" Tara said, stopping in her tracks on the trail.

"Get your ass moving. And it's your turn to carry the bag," he said, dropping a bag filled with several of the copper ingots at her feet.

"I am not going anywhere until you tell me just what it is you are up to? This metal cannot be more valuable than human life."

"Oh, but my dear, it is. It's not just metal; it's power, and power is everything."

"Paul, have you gone completely insane? What kind of power are you referring to?" Tara asked, trying to engage the man in conversation until she figured out just what in the hell was going on and what she might possibly do to escape this madman and get back to her family.

"Did you see the creature that killed the other towhead? Imagine being able to harness and control a creature such as that."

"Are you trying to tell me that those copper ingots have something to do with that fish?"

"They have everything to do with it, and that was no fish."

"Then what was it?"

Paul shrugged, "I'm not sure if it even has a name."

"So, this is not the Mishipeshu Noona spoke of?"

"On the contrary, it is a mortal enemy of the legendary beast, if Mishipeshu even exists. I have my doubts, but Noona insists she is real, so I have to believe her until proven otherwise."

"Doesn't the legend say Mishipeshu protects the copper in the lake?"

"That's what the legend says, but what it really protects is humanity from the copper. It's not protecting copper per se, it's protecting mankind from this," Paul said as he opened the bag and pulled out an ingot. Careful not to contact the metal with his skin, he drew his knife and lightly scraped it across the surface causing the ingot to glow an iridescent blue.

"That's the same color as the moth Amanda found. Are you trying to tell me that those moths, those salamanders, that fish-creature and this metal are somehow related to one another? That is a preposterous notion," Tara argued.

"According to my grandfather's notes the creature is the end result of a long and arduous transformation process."

"Wait, what do you mean by your grandfather's notes?"

While she kept Paul talking Tara continued to surveil her surroundings hoping to find a weapon or some other way to surprise the man in a blitz attack. On the rare occasion he would avert his eyes she tried to send signals to the young boy. She hoped Gregario understood she wanted him to run the first chance he got.

"My great grandmother was the lighthouse keeper's wife. After her disappearance, along with the keeper, my grandfather was allowed to come to the island to gather her belongings. It was in her diary that he read about what the consortium had really been up to. Now, enough of the history lesson, we need to keep moving."

"Just give me a few more minutes to catch my breath. Exactly what was this consortium up to?" she asked, still trying to buy herself some time.

"Dear granny was able to steal some documents from the hunting camp, papers not down in that bunker with the things your son found. She was trying to gather evidence of what they were truly up to, but they must have caught her snooping around and kidnapped her. But not before she was able to squirrel away a few documents in the lighthouse cupola. I found them when I first arrived to set up my workshop."

"What does that have to do with anything going on here, right now?"

"You asked, so let me finish. This consortium, as granny called them, was supposed to be a hunting club of sorts providing exotic prey for the filthy rich from every corner of the globe. Strange saying don't you think? Every corner of the globe? But I digress, according to her notes the hunting camp was only a cover for a mining operation they were conducting on the bottom of the lake which was highly illegal."

"Am I to assume they were mining for copper?"

"Yes, the purest of pure. They hit the mother lode of precious metal at the time. Sure, gold would have been much more profitable, but copper prices hit all-time highs because of the Civil War. These already wealthy mine owners were poised to become multi-millionaires, hell, even billionaires."

"I still fail to see what any of that has to do with our current situation," Tara said, hoping to keep him talking.

326

"You're the one who wanted to rest. If you would rather proceed to the lake, we can do that."

"Continue," she said, tired of the loathsome man and his babbling.

"Being a scientist, I'm sure you are aware that the Keweenaw Peninsula is actually a large lava flow, in fact one of the largest in the world."

"Yes, I am aware of that."

"And you are also aware of the idiom that Lake Superior never gives up her dead."

"Yes, I'm aware of that as well. The water is so cold it retards bacterial growth thus gases are not built up in the corpse and therefore the corpse does not float to the surface."

"Very good."

"I am still not sure where you are going with this."

"Here's where I am going. Somehow these miners managed to break through a very thin layer of the earth's crust, this in turn allowed super-heated water to flow into the lake. This water came into contact with a very large chunk of what they thought was copper ore but in fact was an egg of sorts."

"An egg? From what kind of animal?"

"I just said egg because it was the first simile that came to mind. Neither I nor they knew where this thing originated. When they first encountered it, they thought it was just a mother lode chunk of pure copper. In their haste to get the copper smelted down into ingots they could transport off the island they failed to take notice of the strange blue glow of the metal."

"Are you trying to make me believe that a hunk of metal pulled from the bottom of Lake Superior resulted in that creature who is stalking us?"

"That creature is not stalking us, it is stalking you."

"Why on earth would it be stalking me?"

Tara's stomach roiled with nervous apprehension. Somehow, she knew what his answer was going to be.

"Once this organism claimed the lives of several of their crew mates there began a squabble over what to do with the ore they mined. One argument was to dump it back into the lake from whence it came, those few men were on the losing side of the argument. These rich mine owners knew they had discovered something unique which also meant it was probably valuable and needed to be studied further. They sent word to Europe, Switzerland I believe, to summon a world renown scientist who was an early researcher of genetics."

"Are you saying someone created this creature in a lab?"

"Not intentionally. Hans, the scientist, was merely trying to classify these organisms. Remember, at that time these were just microscopic creatures, not moths, salamanders or the creature we saw."

"Paul, what you are saying is completely insane. Everything happened so fast I'm not sure what it was I even saw."

"What you saw was the metamorphosis of a miniscule single cell, into a glowing moth that communicated with one another, to man eating salamanders and eventually into a mermaid for lack of a better term. I might add, with numerous unknown links in between."

"If that is true, then how do you plan to control it? If that is your plan," Tara said, her fears increasing the more he talked. With each sentence spoken it was painfully obvious the man had gone completely insane.

"I plan to proceed much differently than those aristocrats and scientists did. They had no plan, no outcome in mind, and no direction to speak of. They allowed those organisms to breed with whatever they came into contact with. They were in essence throwing spaghetti at the wall to see what would stick. If I adhere to a strict regimen, I will be able to create whatever I wish to create. But Noona insists we need to get them off this island and away from Mishipeshu first."

"What do you mean by breed?"

"I watched these creatures, and while they do eat their prey, they somehow manage to impart their DNA into their host as well. They are also able to extract DNA from the source in the process. They then perish themselves with this DNA going on to live in the new host."

"So, they are like you, parasites?"

"Precisely. And you can dispense with the vitriol, it is so unbecoming of you."

A peculiar shriek split the silence of the forest. It was not the cry of prey, but rather an arrogant warning from a superior species. Like a cougar perched high atop a cliff at the very instant before it pounced to tear the throat out of its next meal.

"What in the hell was that?" Tara asked.

"That, I am afraid was the demise of your husband and son. And will soon be the death of us if we don't get this show on the road."

"I'm not going anywhere until you tell me exactly what in the hell is going on, Paul."

He spun around on the balls of his feet and punched Gregario in the temple, dropping him to the sand. Paul reached down and grabbed the dazed child by the hair and dragged him down to the lake. The poor child was too dazed to even put up a struggle.

"You seem to think you have a voice in these matters. Well, you do not," he said before plunging a knife into the boy's side.

The boy's eyes went wide with horror as he looked down at the gaping wound in his side. Before he could say a word, Paul grabbed him by the shoulders of his jacket and flung him out as far as he could into the depths of Echo Lake. The boy struggled in a panic for a minute before realizing the water was shallow enough to stand up. His relief was short lived as a crimson stain spread around him and he realized he was not alone in the water.

"Paul, you rotten bastard," Tara said and started for the water.

"I wouldn't do that if I were you."

"Fuck you, Paul."

Tara was nearly knee deep in the water when she felt a current swoosh around her legs. She felt as though she were being circled by something in the water.

"You just stay still, honey, I'm coming to get you," she said to the child who stood panic stricken in waist deep water.

The surface of the water began to roil as if there was a large school of fish in the middle of a feeding frenzy. The turbulence swirled around the child and then suddenly stopped. Tara was sure it was the calm before the storm. Her scientific mind calculated the possibilities and settled on the fact that somehow a shark had been let loose in these waters and even more astounding, it somehow not only survived, but thrived in fresh, ice-cold water.

"Run," she yelled to Gregario, but not only was her warning too late, it was pointless as well. The child would never be able to outrun an attacking shark.

The surface of Echo Lake exploded into a geyser of blood as the shark burst from the water's surface with the top portion of the severed child hanging from its teeth. Tara backpedaled and shook her head to clear the fog. That was no shark. For all intents and purposes, that was a merman.

Tara followed a trail of bloody bubbles with her eyes as they circled the lake in front of her. Pieces of Gregario floated to the surface and trailed behind the current left in the wake of the creature. She got the impression the animal was making a victory lap around the lake to gloat. And then the bubbles stopped along with the current. She felt an eeriness wash over her when she realized the creature was lurking just below the surface with its eyes trained on her.

"What in the hell does it want?" she cried out.

"First it feeds, and then it breeds," Paul said.

"My God, you are insane if you think I am going to breed with that monstrosity."

Paul laughed long and hard as he backed away from the lake's edge.

"It doesn't plan to breed with you," he said and gave a head bob across the lake where Noona and Amanda were emerging from the forest.

"Absolutely not!" Tara said and lunged for the man.

Paul lashed out with the tree limb, but she managed to catch it under her arm and jerked it away from him. Without losing her momentum she spun completely around and planted the branch across the side of the lunatic's head. She dropped the weapon and headed for the water but thought better of it when she saw a swirl of bubbles on the surface. There was no way she would be able to outswim that beast. She took off running down the beach toward the other side of the lake.

As Tara passed him, Paul lunged out and caught her ankle causing her to stumble. Despite her best efforts to stay upright she lost her footing and ended up sprawled out face first in the wet sand. She was dazed from her head smacking the hard sand and fought to shake off the cobwebs as Paul lumbered toward her with the tree limb. Tara feigned injury until he was within striking distance. She leapt to her feet and planted a roundhouse kick squarely in his breadbasket dropping the man to his knees, and then she was off and running again.

"Is that my mommy?"

"Hush child," Noona responded. She cupped her hands around her mouth and called out something in a language Amanda didn't understand.

The terrified child screamed out to her mother, but Noona clamped her hand even tighter over her mouth. A fin broke the surface of the water and made two large, swooping circles before heading straight for Tara who was more than halfway around the lake in a desperate attempt to make it to her daughter. Tara was winded and sore, but she kept on running as fast as her legs would take her.

"I'm coming, Mandy, baby," she called out.

At the precise moment relief began to peck away at her brain Tara was knocked to the ground, her breath stolen by the force of the blow. It took several moments for her to be able to roll over onto her back and ready herself to fight the bastard. She lashed out with a defensive kick that was easily deflected by the creature hovering over her.

The fight was immediately taken out of Tara once she was face to face with the menacing beast. While emitting a beautiful translucent blue, it was anything but appealing to the eye. Both of its long, hairless arms dangled toward the ground with razor sharp nails extending from each of the fingers. Tears flowed from her eyes when she realized there were human entrails wrapped around two of the talons along with shreds of her husband's sweatshirt. It snarled through multiple rows of jagged teeth showing scraps of torn flesh and a piece of black t-shirt with a rainbow prism her son Travis had been wearing.

Anger and maternal instinct overpowered her fear and Tara attacked the animal with a fury it was unaccustomed to. It backed away on its tiny hind legs using its broad tail to propel itself back into the water. It wasn't much taller than she, so she was able to land punch after quick punch to its face. She felt bones crush under one of her blows that connected squarely with the creature's broad nose. The strike staggered the beast and instilled in her a sense of confidence that betrayed her.

Tara was moving in close enough to be able to roundhouse kick the monster in the stomach with the hope of following with a blow to the temple. The creature finally had enough of her defiance and flicked its long, sharp fingernails outward, catching her wrist and severing her hand from her body. While she was dazed from the blow and transfixed on her damaged arm the creature skewered her through her arms and legs with all four talons and pinned her to the sand.

"Damn, that must have hurt," Paul sneered and said, "Kill her."

The creature looked at him and then back to her before lifting its free hand high above its head. Tara gagged as putrid saliva smelling of rotten flesh and decaying fish dripped from the beast's mouth down onto her face. She turned her head to the side and smiled through crooked, bloody lips as the creature's claws started on their downward arc.

"What in the fuck are you smiling about?" Paul asked.

Mishipeshu's feline scream split the air and she closed the expanse between herself and the merman. Without much more than an afterthought the legendary creature swiped out with its front and rear paws as it lunged, catching Paul square in the chest with all four paws while tearing outward and shredding the man's flesh in one quick motion. Paul lay in the blood-soaked sand, frothy black blood oozing from the numerous gashes across his chest. He died without so much as a whimper.

The cat leapt through the air again, and the two creatures collided with such force the impact rocked the ground. As they rolled across the earth Mishipeshu's spines dug into the earth sending a plume of sand high into the air. Tara watched in fascination as fish-like iridescent scales floated down through the dust, flitting, and fluttering on the wind like prismatic snowflakes. The sun reflected off their surface and they shimmered with an ethereal glow.

Somehow the merman broke free of the cat creature's grasp and leapt for the water. Mishipeshu followed the beast into the depths with a screech so loud it forced Tara to cover her ears. She eased herself up onto her elbows long enough to see the water percolating into an angry, red boil.

Beneath the surface of the lake each of the creatures were landing blows against each other. Mishipeshu was in control of the battle, its fangs securely gripped around the merman's neck. The merman spun his tail from the vertical to the horizontal position and punched it up into the feline's gullet breaking the bond between them. The fish-man swooped through the water with the grace, speed, and agility of a peregrine falcon, ending up behind the water panther before she could react. The beast enjoyed one more lopsided advantage; it didn't need to breach the surface to breathe.

Tara watched the surface of the water, unsure of which creature she should be rooting for as she was certain neither of them were a true ally. After several minutes of unnerving silence Mishipeshu surfaced and paddled slowly to shore. A tinge of pity washed over her as she watched the defeated creature drag its battered, bleeding body up onto the sand. Its chest heaved with heavy panting, and then it heaved no more.

The merman surfaced and slowly made its way to shore. Tara almost laughed at the way the creature walked on its short, stubby legs but then she remembered her son's flesh hanging from its teeth and any levity she may have felt quickly disappeared. She struggled to get to her feet, but the beast backhanded her to the ground before she could even manage to get to her knees. Blood poured from the deep gashes across her neck and Tara collapsed into the soft sand.

Chapter Twenty-Five

Travis ran until there was nothing left. He willed his legs to move and his lungs to breathe but his body would not cooperate. He was exhausted. He rubbed the area where the creature had bitten him, luckily, he sucked in his gut at precisely the right moment and there was not much damage other than a torn shirt. He used a scavenged tree limb he fashioned into a spear to lean against while resting.

He could see the bizarre old woman guiding his sister up the trail. He wasn't sure what she was up to, but with the events of the past twenty-four hours he was certain it wasn't anything that would work out well for Mandy. The woman was related to Paul Rainbird and in Travis' book that made her an enemy, and it was up to her to prove otherwise. He yelled after them, but he was still so winded that his sister did not hear him.

The child sobbed at the image of her mother's lifeless body lying on the sand. Noona cupped her hands around her mouth and called out to the creature, her voice echoing across the surface of the water. The creature limped over to the bag Paul dropped, the bag with the copper ingots, took the bag in its teeth and plunged back into Echo Lake.

Once on the other side of the lake the merman dragged himself from the depths and dropped the heavy bag at Noona's feet. Travis leaned against a tree, trying to capture his breath. Tears streamed down his face as he helplessly watched his mother courageously battle the monster until she finally collapsed. He just didn't have the energy left to make it to his mother. Travis didn't make it to the lake in time to join the battle, he could only suffer witnessing the aftermath. Both his mother and the creature who saved him from the merman lay motionless on the beach. He could not save his mother, but he sure as hell was going to save his sister. He shook off thoughts of failure and focused on the one person he might be able to save, his sister Amanda.

He watched in horror as the merman limped over to his where his sister and Noona stood on the shore. The woman sneered at him and turned the child to face the beast. Travis fought against his pain and exhaustion and began to run toward them as fast as he could possibly go. The creature stood before the petrified, sobbing child and sniffed at the air. Suddenly, two large flaps of skin spread away from its body at the neck like Dumbo's gargantuan ears and wrapped around her in a macabre cocoon.

"Get away from my sister!" Travis screamed and let the spear fly.

While crude and rudimentary, the spear was also effective. It struck the monster in the back of the head causing it to relinquish its grasp on Amanda. It turned its face to the heavens and let loose an eerie cry before exploding into a cloud of fine black dust.

Travis clutched his sister and pulled her close to him but there was something wrong. She was cold and distant. Her tears stopped, and she didn't even seem to notice he was there. He released his hug and dropped down to his knees to look her in the eyes. Her eyes were a translucent blue hue. The little girl he knew just a few hours ago was no longer there.

"What in the hell did you do to her?" he screamed at the old woman.

Noona looked at Travis with a sinister grin painted on her face. She pulled a knife from her waistband and handed it to Amanda.

"Child," was all Noona said but it was enough impetus to cause Amanda to thrust the knife under her brother's ribcage and into his heart.

Travis dropped to the ground while Noona and his sister simply walked away without ever looking back.

Chapter Twenty-Six

The Coast Guard vessel pulled away from the dock at Grand Island and out into the open waters of Lake Superior. It was a beautiful day with a sharp, blue sky contrasted by puffy white cotton candy clouds. The chug of the outboard engines droned on as the boat picked up speed, accompanied by the hiss of water kissing the hull.

Amanda sat on a small bench affixed to the deck of the boat in the open air with her knees tucked up to her chest. A drab wool Navy blanket was draped over her lap, but she felt nothing. Absolutely nothing.

"Poor kid, I hear her whole family was killed except for her grandmother over there," the young coast guard seaman commented to her shipmate.

"A mass murderer on Grand Island of all places," the crewmate responded.

"I heard it was a wild animal attack."

The two of them stood and saluted a passing vessel flying command colors. The officers onboard saluted back with solemn faces and continued their journey to the island.

"Hello there sweetie, would you like some hot chocolate?" Petty Officer Myra Davis asked, sliding into the bench seat next to the near catatonic girl.

She tried several times to hand the mug to the girl, but the child didn't respond. Myra nodded to her crewmate, Seaman Marissa Miller and handed her the steaming mug which she set on the boat's console.

"Your name is Amanda, right?" Myra asked.

Amanda slowly turned her head toward the woman at the sound of her name. The sound was familiar to her, but she didn't know why. She glared at her for several minutes while trying to compute the information. When nothing triggered a memory, she slowly returned her gaze toward the distant shore.

"Oh my, you have the most beautiful blue eyes. They seem to glow."

Suddenly the boat lurched to a stop and the engines fell to idle speed. They bobbed up and down in the water for several minutes.

"Miller, what in the hell is going on up there?" Lieutenant Josh Morris called from the bow.

"Sir, you need to come and see this. I've never seen anything like this before," Miller said.

The vessel's commanding officer grumbled, tossed his logbook on a small bench, and made his way to the cabin.

"What in the hell," he said.

"What do you make of it skipper?"

The coast guard officer reached into a side pocket of the boat's cabin and pulled out a set of binoculars. He scanned the horizon back and forth for several minutes before dropping the binoculars down to his chest.

"Davis, get on the radio and contact the command vessel please. Tell them we have a storm front moving this way."

"Yes sir," Davis responded and keyed the radio.

Seaman Miller was transfixed by what she saw. While she never witnessed a roll cloud in person, she studied them in school because she was fascinated by meteorology. But this was something far different than any storm or cloud she ever read about. Instead of being linear along the horizon it was curling up on the ends creating a horseshoe shape is if trying to box them in. Lightning flashed across the span of the cloud formation from left to right.

"Sir, all I can get is static."

"I hope they see what is heading straight for them," the lieutenant said.

Amanda began singing softly to herself which drew the attention of the others. She was singing in a language that sounded like gibberish, but it was having a negative effect on the old woman causing her to become agitated. In a quick motion the child swept the blanket away from her lap and dozens of electric blue moths fluttered about. She stood up and went to the rail of the boat and chanted her song out to the open water.

"Sir, what in the hell is happening?" Seaman Miller asked as she pointed toward the horizon.

The storm changed course straight for the small craft. Thunder began as a low growl but grew in intensity as the storm moved closer to them.

"Davis, try that radio again. I think we need to send a mayday," Lieutenant Morris yelled over the din of the storm.

Petty Officer Davis reached for the hand mic but was transfixed by something she saw hovering at the bow of the boat.

"Sir? What is that?" she asked, pointing to a glowing blue orb hovering over the surface of the water.

"That's called St. Elmo's fire. Normally it's harmless, but I don't want to take any chances with what has been going on so put that hand mic back on the cradle and turn the radio off."

Once Davis complied with her lieutenant's order the ball of static electricity moved away from the boat and hovered further out over the water as if it were waiting for something.

"Sir, what is it doing?" Seaman Miller asked.

"Don't ask me, I haven't a clue," he responded.

Amanda began chanting louder and louder until she was screaming out at the open water. The storm picked up speed and intensity.

"Stop it child. You stop it this very instance," Noona demanded.

"You be quiet. You killed my family," the girl screamed in such a thunderous voice it shook the small boat.

Her eyes quickly changed from an angry red back to a luminescent blue and a smile spread across her face. She reached into her backpack and pulled out her stuffed animal.

"You look like a nice lady. I'm sure Brutus will like living with you," Amanda said and handed Petty Officer Davis her beloved confidant and went back to chanting at the wind.

Lightning flashed all around them as the storm continued to circle the dwarfed vessel. Amanda elevated her song to rise above the deafening tempest.

"Sit down child, you will kill us all," Noona screamed while tugging at the girl's shirt.

"Don't touch me," Amanda yelled and lashed out with her tiny fists.

Seaman Miller grabbed her by her wrists to put a stop to the child's onslaught. "Honey, your grandmother is right, you need to sit down before you fall overboard. She's only trying to help you."

"No, she is not my grandmother, and she is trying to kill you. She wants to kill everybody."

"Young lady, you're understandably scared and have been greatly traumatized but that is no reason to be so vicious toward your grandmother," the lieutenant said while putting a firm hand on the child's shoulder.

"I said, she's not my grandmother. And please, keep your hands off me," Amanda said. She pulled the flare gun from her backpack and pointed it at the coast guard officer who quickly put his hands up and backed away.

"Be careful with that sweetie, you might hurt yourself," Petty Officer Davis said.

Being a mother herself she sensed the child's inner turmoil and pain. There was definitely more to this story than what was on the surface.

"She wants to kill everybody," Amanda said, her tone no longer thunderous but soft and defeated. Tears streamed down her cheeks.

"Give me the flare gun please, before you hurt yourself," the lieutenant said.

She thrust the gun at him angrily. "I know how to use this, my brother Travis taught me, before she made me kill him."

"Child, you stop this foolishness right now," Noona said while forcefully grabbing Amanda by her arms.

Amanda ignored the old woman and once again started her song. Incensed, Noona slapped her across the face hard enough to leave a red handprint. The child simply turned her head to the crone and smiled.

"I know what I have to do now, but I can't do it," she said and pointed the flare gun at Noona. "I suggest you remove your hands from my body. Don't you know that it is wrong to touch a child when they don't want to be touched."

The squall seemed to intensify with the child's anger. Lightning flashed all around their boat threatening to electrocute them all.

Davis dropped to one knee and in a motherly tone she said, "honey."

"Amanda. My name is Amanda, or Mandy if you are not mad at me."

"Mandy it is. What did you mean, you know what you have to do now?"

"She put something inside of me. Something really, really bad," the child said through clenched teeth.

"What did she put inside of you?" the lieutenant asked, suddenly quite suspicious of the elderly woman.

Lieutenant Morris and Seaman Miller whispered back and forth between each other that they needed to contact the authorities when they made it back to shore because this looked like a case of molestation.

Amanda shrugged. "I don't know. It has something to do with the moths, the salamanders, and the fish that killed my mommy."

"See, the child is traumatized. She doesn't even know what she is saying," Noona said.

"Yes, I do. I know exactly what I am saying. You and that mean Mr. Paul took something that does not belong to you, and I have to give it back. But I can't," she said and started to cry.

"What can't you give back, Mandy?" the lieutenant asked.

Amanda pointed to the canvas bag on the floor of the boat between Noona's feet.

"What's in the bag?" the lieutenant asked, stepping slowly forward.

"Stop!" Amanda called out and swung the flare gun in his direction. "Do not open that bag unless you want to die a horrible death."

"Can't you see the child is distraught and talking nonsense," Noona said.

The lieutenant took another step forward but was stopped in his tracks by a lightning strike so close to the boat that it sprayed them with water.

"What's in the bag, Mandy?" Davis asked.

"Something very bad and we need to give it back. But it's too heavy for me to lift."

"Who do we need to give it back to?" Seaman Miller asked.

"Her," Amanda said and pointed toward the heart of the storm.

"Holy Mother of God," Seaman Miller said and backed up until her back was against the cabin wall.

Mishipeshu bobbed in the lake in front of them, lightning spewing off in all directions. The cat's eyes were slanted into razor thin slits and a snarl wrinkled its nose. She let loose a shriek that sounded more like a human woman than it did an animal. Amanda turned and sang to the creature which seemed to placate the beast for the moment.

"That thing is going to kill us," Miller said.

"Not if she gets what is hers," Amanda said.

"The bag?" the lieutenant asked.

Amanda nodded.

The storm seemed to abate slightly as the lieutenant started for the duffel bag.

"No, I will not let you," Noona screamed out and slashed at the lieutenant with her knife slicing the man deeply across his stomach.

The blade dug deep into the man's flesh causing him to stagger back against the boat's cabin. Blood poured from the gash and the lieutenant was stupefied by the speed of the old woman's vicious attack.

"Miller, get us moving, now!" Davis called out.

Seaman Miller stepped into the cabin and forced the throttle levers to full speed. The boat lurched forward but a bolt of lightning two feet in front of the bow forced Miller to throttle back down to idle.

"She will kill you all," Amanda said.

"But the lieutenant needs a doctor ASAP," Miller argued.

"Then we give that monster whatever the hell she wants," Davis said and started for the bag.

Noona lashed out with the knife once more, barely missing the petty officer. "I will kill you all if you touch my belongings."

"I am so tired of your bullshit," Amanda said as she raised the flare gun and fired.

The cartridge hit Noona square in the chest and staggered her back against the rail of the boat. Miller didn't hesitate, she kicked the knife from the old woman's hand and then kicked her over the side of the rail. Mishipeshu let loose a banshee shriek and charged the old woman. She grabbed her in her gaping maw, held her for several moments before diving beneath the depths.

"Miller, now is our chance, throttle up," the lieutenant said.

Before she could react, the beast breached the surface of the water in front of them. Sunlight broke free of the clouds to the north of them and shone down in an unbroken fan of beams that sparkled off the cat's coppery coat while the beast let loose a low, guttural growl.

The seamen heard a noise and turned to see Amanda struggling to drag the duffle bag across the deck. Davis and Miller quickly went to her aid and within a minute lifted the bag onto the rail of the boat.

"Are you sure about this?"

"Positive," Amanda replied.

Davis nodded and shoved the bag overboard. As the bag sank into the depths of Gitchi-Gami the storm lessened until the waves were calm and the only lightning was isolated around the beast itself, but neither the storm nor the creature moved out of their way.

"What else does it want?" Miller asked.

Amanda felt a churning within her. An internal struggle that was not being waged by herself. The parasite within her was fighting to be free.

"Me," Amanda replied.

"What do you mean you?" Davis asked and stepped toward the child.

"Stop. That mean old woman put the same thing inside of me that was in the bags. I won't let it hurt anyone else."

"Hurt anyone else? How can it do that?"

"Stay back. Whatever is inside of me is evil. It only exists to kill. I have to die and kill these things with me," she said and stepped up onto the rail of the boat.

"What are you doing?" Davis asked.

"Take care of Brutus for me," Amanda said with a smile and plunged into the icy waters of Lake Superior.

Mishipeshu watched with interest. The little girl was the bravest human she ever encountered. She could not let her perish after such great sacrifices. The beast gently plucked the child from the waves with her mouth and began the long journey back to her home, their home on Michipicoten Island.

Epilogue

Bob and Gertie Harrison sat in their fourteen-foot Starcraft bobbing up and down in the near waveless bay. Bob was busy changing lures on their fishing poles so they could get back to trolling, which meant Bob could get back to drinking his beer. The couple just rounded Sand Point and were headed out toward the eastern side of Grand Island where it was rumored the lakers were running hot.

Nearly a week had passed since the coast guard and all sorts of other folks cleared off the island and life was starting to get back to normal. Gertie tried to relate the gossip to Bob but he wanted none of it. Monsters, murderers, evil spirits, he could not give two shits.

"Bob, what is that?" Gertie asked, pointing to an object bobbing in the water ahead of them.

"What is what, dear," Bob droned predictably.

"Over there in the water. Is that someone swimming?"

"I don't give a rat's ass if it is, Gertie, I want to fish."

"Quit your bellyaching and go check it out. Someone might be in trouble."

"Or someone might be a frigging idiot which is the better bet."

"Bob," Gertie said.

He pulled the rip cord on the Johnson fifty horse three times before she started. His biggest regret was after tuning up the motor it was no longer loud enough to drown out his wife's nagging.

"It's a dog," Gertie shouted gleefully. "Get closer, the poor thing needs our help."

The golden retriever nearly capsized the boat climbing over the side. Once he was inside the small vessel Gertie started toweling the dog off which was shivering from the cold.

"That's that I suppose," Bob grumbled.

"What's what?"

"Fishing trip is over. The poor dog needs to warm up inside."

"Bob, admit it, you are really a pushover. Which is precisely why I married you."

"I don't really give two shits," he said and turned the boat back toward Munising harbor.

"Would you look at his eyes?"

"What's wrong with his eyes?"

"They are the most beautiful shade of blue I have ever seen. I have never seen anything like it in all my years. He's got a tag too. It says his name is Zappa."

"Huh, strange name for a strange dog I suppose," Bob grumbled and opened another beer.

www.ingramcontent.com/pod-product-compliance
Lightning Source LLC
Chambersburg PA
CBHW072118250626
47159CB00007B/2488